I0646028

THE PERFECT MRS. CLAUS

BARBARA MATTESON

5 PRINCE PUBLISHING

Copyright © 2022 by Barbara Matteson, THE PERFECT MRS. CLAUS

All rights reserved.

This is a fictional work. The names, characters, incidents, and locations are solely the concepts and products of the author's imagination, or are used to create a fictitious story and should not be construed as real. No part of this book may be reproduced in any form or by any electronic or mechanical means, including information storage and retrieval systems, without written permission from the author, except for the use of brief quotations in a book review.

Published by 5 PRINCE PUBLISHING & BOOKS, LLC

PO Box 865, Arvada, CO 80001

www.5PrinceBooks.com

ISBN digital: 978-1-63112-289-7

ISBN print: 978-1-63112-292-7

Cover Credit: Marianne Nowicki

10-28

For CGM , DGM and Sabrmoho

THE PERFECT MRS. CLAUS

CHAPTER 1

WINDBLOWN SILVERY STRANDS OF HAIR BLINDED SAVANNAH BRADY. The blustery October breeze propelled her through the brass, revolving doors and into Howardson's Emporium, Boston's only family-owned department store, a haven of tradition and value.

Like a witch at her cauldron beckoning the unsuspecting victim, the store's Halloween sale promised to lure all of the local office folks en masse into its retail clutches, as the bell in the store's clocktower tolled the lunch hour.

Savannah laughed at her silly analogy, brushing the flyaway hair from her eyes. She was happy to be a Howardson's Halloween victim, and along with her fellow prey, she joined the lunch time throngs and excitedly entered the main foyer of Howardson's. Savannah quickly met her fate as she was immediately assailed by dangling skeletal limbs hanging from the ceiling with bright orange 75% off decals stuck to bursting eyeball sockets and exposed bony elbows and kneecaps. Halloween was still a week away, but the merchandise was marked so low because the store was shipping out the muted autumnal tones of Halloween and ushering in the bright lights of Christmas. As Macy's

Thanksgiving Parade-sized inflated haunted houses fell flopping down upon the hardwood floors, majestic evergreen trees were erected like skyscrapers. Howardson employees teetered on twenty-foot ladders stringing multi-colored sets of lights. Garland and ribbons the color of frosty ice and diamonds were threaded through the life-like branches of the Christmas trees.

Because of her strict budget, Savannah wasn't purchasing anything; she loved to browse a good sale. She rounded the corner of one of the many discount aisles, she came upon a huge jack-o'-lantern on sale for five dollars. It was very festive, with its big black triangle eyes and mouth forming into a happy grin. It would look adorable in her front bay window, but right now she was not going to part even with five dollars, as that meant five dollars less in her Christmas stash of cash that was enabling Savannah to have the Christmas-movie Christmas she had been dreaming about since earlier in the year. All traditional Christmas plans were dashed when Patrick, her son, relocated to Switzerland for work. Savannah's husband of three decades had died of a brain aneurysm two years before, so now, without her husband and son with her, the thought of spending both Christmas Eve and Christmas Day alone was unbearable.

Savannah knew the only solution was to *not* be at home. She had seen a beautifully photographed flyer in her office kitchen that promised a storybook Christmas experience at The Blue Spruce Inn, located in the heart of the White Mountains in New Hampshire. A storybook Christmas was exactly what Savannah needed this year.

Our Christmas package includes a festively decorated room with trees adorned with antique ornaments and sparkling fairy lights. Sleep in the comfort of a queen-sized bed wrapped in Egyptian cotton flannel sheets topped with a hand-sewn quilt. A Christmas Eve supper will be served with mulled wine and fresh cider from our friendly local vineyards and orchards, and the evening concludes with hot cocoa and cookies before a roaring fire as one of Santa's elves reads The Night Before Christmas.

Awaken to a traditional Christmas brunch and open presents under the blue spruce Christmas tree on the grounds of the Inn. But it doesn't end there. Join us for a sleigh ride through the charming town of Brightmore, where Victorian carolers will serenade you along the snowy trails, or stroll along the frosty grounds with the Inn's specially trained golden retrievers who will guide you through our very own winter wonderland. A traditional turkey dinner will be served, followed by a viewing of the 1948 classic It's a Wonderful Life. *Your enchanted Christmas awaits at The Blue Spruce Inn.*

Savannah was now one payment away from her Blue Spruce Inn Christmas, and the bright orange pumpkin would not be taking up residence in her bay window this Halloween.

"You'll go home with someone else. I'm sure of it." She gave the jack-o'-lantern an affectionate tap and a wink and silently congratulated herself.

To paraphrase one of my favorite patriots, five dollars saved is five dollars earned towards my enchanted Christmas, she thought with a smile as she wandered from the Halloween aisle.

Savannah decided to take the escalator to the second floor for more sale perusing. She spied an elfin-like woman at the top of the escalator. Her slicked-back shiny black hair was pulled into a tight bun, and she had the shimmery thin complexion of an older woman. Her heavily mascaraed lashes, framed by cat-eye shaped glasses, made her blue eyes pop like Fourth of July firecrackers. Her movements were graceful as a ballerina's as she tied a beautiful red velvet scarf around the thick shaggy neck of a stuffed brown moose. Howardson's annual Christmas display was officially under construction, and the moose seemed like the ultimate Christmas present. The woman looked at Savannah, gave her a salute, and danced behind a huge silver aluminum tree.

The holiday spirit wrapped around Savannah like the Blue Spruce Inn quilt promised, and she decided to walk through what would become the legendary Howardson's Christmas display. Each year the store presented a different theme, and memories of visiting with her son, flooded her mind.

She recalled when Patrick was eight, and Howardson's featured a Superhero Christmas that included all of Patrick's favorites dressed in holiday costumes—Spiderman wearing a huge Santa hat, Wonder Woman with her lasso of thick green velvet, and Patrick's favorite, the Hulk, wearing a way-too-small red vest and large black Santa boots. She still had the picture from that Christmas with Patrick and his Superheroes and pulled out her phone to send herself an email to remind her to dig it out when she got home. *I'll scan it to him*, Savannah thought, adding that into her email so she wouldn't forget.

Savannah then approached what would be the formal entrance to the Christmas display and read the placard in front of a giant snowman that announced:

Howardson's Emporium Annual Christmas Extravaganza
The Enchanted Land of Claus
Official Opening
Saturday, November 16 at Noon
Holiday cookies and beverages will be served
Experience Howardson's Christmas Magic Come to Life as we
promise our customers the most magical season in Howardson's
history!

Under the new management of
Mr. Matthew Buck, Creative Director of Special Events and
Miss Fern Rhodes, Special Events Costume Designer

Two oversized, colorful lollipops stood on each side of the snowman, the welcoming sentinels to this *Enchanted Land of Claus*. Savannah then glanced at her watch.

Darn, I only have fifteen more minutes, she thought as she continued to be mesmerized by the employees dressed in red vests with name tags declaring them *Enchanted Land of Claus* staff. As busy as they were shuffling trees, stuffed life-size reindeer and foxes, Savannah thought they looked happy being a part of such a cherished Christmas tradition. Howardson's Emporium was a dying breed—privately owned and not a big box store where everything was made to break. No, Howardson's carried the best of the best; English Spode tea sets, Irish crystal decanters, along with linen tablecloths and shiny silver napkin holders. When a special gift was needed, the perfect present was always found at Howardson's.

"Oh, excuse me, Ma'am." One of the red-vested elves bumped into Savannah while pushing an extraordinarily large green chair.

"Hey, Leo, watch where ya goin'," said an older man on the other side of the chair. He, as well, was in a red vest with a name tag that said FRED, *The Enchanted Land of Claus* Workshop Elder.

"I know, again, I'm so sorry, Ma'am." Savannah saw his name tag said LEO, *The Enchanted Land of Claus* Workshop Apprentice.

"No worries, Leo," she smiled. "I probably shouldn't be here anyway."

She saw the young man's face redden at the mention of his name, and he turned to Fred and shouted, "C'mon Fred, a little more push!" He turned and smiled at Savannah, who gave him the thumbs up. The chair was a small mountain of bright green velvet, which had to be the throne upon which Santa would sit and listen to endless children's Christmas wishes. Savannah remembered the last time Patrick sat upon Santa's knee. He was ten and at the age where the reality of Santa was becoming blurred and constantly questioned.

Please, just one more time, Patrick, she remembered thinking as she watched her little boy under the spell of that wonderment that only happens when a child is sitting upon the lap of Santa. It is as if they cannot believe they have come face to face with the great guardian of the North Pole, caretaker of elves and reindeer, especially Rudolph, and toy maker extraordinaire. Santa was the rock star of every child's fantasy, and it was time to meet him face to face once again. Whatever doubt Patrick had earlier in the day about the reality of Santa Claus quickly vanished, and he excitedly rambled to patient St. Nick about video games and basketball shoes.

Thank you. Savannah silently gave thanks as her happy son hopped from Santa's knee bounding toward her, grabbing her hand and leading her to the cocoa stand to discuss what Santa would be leaving for her well-behaved child under their Christmas tree. As a mother, there was nothing more important to Savannah, than to make sure Patrick believed in the magic of Christmas.

Savannah strolled through the store, mentally wandering further down her own Christmas memory lane, to one of her own visits with Santa at Howardson's over forty years before. Through the years, it became a family legend. As it occurred, it was not funny at all, but utterly embarrassing to a well-behaved girl eagerly waiting for her annual visit with Santa Claus.

Nine-year-old Savannah was spending the weekend at her Uncle Guy and Aunt Louise's house the week before Christmas. Uncle Guy and Aunt Louise lived a couple of towns over from Savannah's family. They had six children, all much older than Savannah except for her youngest cousins Terri and Ricky, who were always referred to by her aunt and uncle as their "precious little surprises." Savannah had no idea what they meant by that, as it was always accompanied by lots of loud laughing and hugging, with Aunt Louise turning a deep shade of Christmas red with her saying "Oh, Guy, knock that off," and hitting him on the shoulder.

They were a boisterous family, nothing at all like the quiet of Savannah's house where it was just Savannah, her mother, and father. Even with the three older cousins gone and on their own, three were still at home: Colleen who was 17 and pretty much paid no attention to her two younger siblings: Terri, six months younger than Savannah; and Ricky, six, whom they lovingly referred to as the Tiny Terror. Ricky was thin and wiry and as fast as a gazelle running from a predator. He was always getting into trouble like climbing on top of the roof when his parents were out to dinner or running around the neighborhood in just his underwear. As long as Ricky was the center of attention, and his antics certainly made him so, he was happy. Savannah overheard her aunt talking to her uncle one day about Ricky's exploits, and she chalked it up to being the youngest of six and that was "how he gets all of our attention—by acting out and doing kooky things—and it works. You have to admit to that, Guy."

Work it did, and Aunt Louise and Uncle Guy thought he was adorable and never punished him for his shenanigans.

"I don't know why we are even bringing Ricky," Terri had complained on the day Uncle Guy was taking little Savannah, Terri and Ricky to see Santa, and the three children were dressed in their holiday finery. Savannah wore her favorite red and black plaid dress and shiny black patent leather shoes with red tights. Terri was dressed similarly but with green tights and red leather Mary Janes. Even Ricky was dressed for the occasion with a clean pair of slacks, and a white Oxford shirt with a festive red and green striped tie.

"Okay kids, picture time!" Uncle Guy meticulously took his camera from the bright yellow box and attached the flash bulb to the top. He had Savannah stand on the left side of the tree, with Terri on the right, and smack dab in the middle of them both he sat down Ricky.

"Okay kids, on the count of three, everyone smile and say *Christmas tree!* Ready? One, two…"

"Christmas tree!" shouted Ricky, as Terri gave him a smack on his shoulder. Savannah watched as her little cousin grinned up at his sister like a possessed Halloween ghoul, showing a mouthful of gums.

The flash bulb exploded as Uncle Guy clicked the shutter, and the brightness would leave the subjects of the photo seeing the dazzling flash for hours.

Uncle Guy looked at his watch.

"No time for another one. Maybe later. We have to hit the road!"

They all piled into the back of Uncle Guy's beloved green and brown Chevrolet station wagon, with Ricky again sitting in the middle of the two girls, his non-stop fidgeting seriously irritating Terri.

"If you can't sit still in the car, how in the world are you going to sit on Santa's lap?"

Terri was beyond agitated with her little brother in the tight space in the rear of the station wagon. Ricky's little fists were in constant motion, punching his sister on the arm. When Terri swatted him away, he turned his attention to Savannah.

"Savannah," he said, jabbing her in the arm like a boxer,"I'm glad you're here. You're a lot nicer to me than she is."

Ricky turned to his sister and stuck out his blue-coated tongue.

"You need to stop chewing that blue bubble gum," Terri bossily said. "Pretty soon the dye is going to start moving from your tongue to your face."

"Dad!" shrieked Ricky, "Terri says I'm going to die before I see Santa!"

"Kids, cut it out," was all Uncle Guy could muster as he steered the car into the already crowded parking lot at Howardson's.

"Boy, we just got lucky!" Uncle Guy exclaimed to the three clamoring children in the back of the station wagon. As he was pulling into the packed lot, a car pulled out of a spot, and Uncle

Guy expertly maneuvered the station wagon into what seemed like the only empty space.

"C'mon, kids," he commanded as the three hopped out of the wagon and they made their way into Howardson's. Savannah felt her heart beat quicker with every step that took her closer to Howardson's, and to Santa.

"Wow!" exclaimed Ricky, upon entering Santa's workshop. It was located on the first floor, behind the large silver and black escalators.

SANTA'S CANDY LAND
Loved By Kids Of All Ages!

In the center of the sentences were two candy canes tied together with sprigs of holly and berries.

"That's such a pretty sign," Savannah said, turning to Terri, who was on her tiptoes trying to peer over the heads of what seemed like hundreds of people in front of them.

"Well, kids, the line is long, but lots to see," said Uncle Guy, as they inched down the path of red velvet, leading to the ultimate destination of Santa's throne. The path leading to Santa was cordoned off by thick ropes of green velvet, and on the other side of those ropes were scenes of Christmas from various periods throughout the years. Savannah and Terri became enthralled with the life-like mannequins of boys and girls dressed in Victorian garb. The first scene was of a boy looking skyward, dressed in a gray woolen coat. He was standing in front of a storefront which had the words 'Howardson's Apothecary' frosted across the window. The windowsill was adorned with cut glass bottles containing green and blue liquid, with wooden stoppers plugged in the bottles' top openings. The boy had a rectangular wooden basket strung over his neck with the words *Apples 5 cents* painted on the front of the basket. It was lined with hay with several bright red apples nestled carefully inside. Cottony mounds of snow covered the boy's worn leather boots, but Savannah didn't think the boy looked cold at all—he had a friendly smile, and she felt as if he was offering the apples just to her.

"I can't see, I can't see!" Ricky shouted, as he started to push between Savannah and Terri.

"Stop your shoving, Ricky!" scolded Terri, as she grabbed on to the back of her brother's jacket.

"Dad!" screamed Terri, desperately trying to hold onto her squirming brother.

Savannah saw that Terri was losing her grip and she managed to grab the cuff of his coat, but he was too fast. Ricky, who was as smart as he was quick, crouched down like a panther ready to pounce and easily escaped the grips of Terri and Savannah and disappeared into the crowd of legs and feet.

"Dad!" Terri shouted, turning toward her father, who was entranced by a Victorian family encircling a huge, brightly lit Christmas tree.

"Dad! Ricky ran ahead. You need to get him!"

"What?" Uncle Guy was brought back to the present by Terri's hysterical screams.

A security officer miraculously appeared and offered to escort Uncle Guy to the front of the line to find Ricky.

"But I have two girls here..." Savannah could hear the panic in her uncle's voice of not knowing what to do.

"You go get your boy; I'll watch the girls."

Savannah turned at the sound of a musical and angelic voice. A woman dressed in a gray coat with a fur collar and cuffs stood behind her. Shiny crystal buttons resembling oversized snowflakes shimmered with her every breath. Savannah thought it was the most beautiful coat she had ever seen. Her own mother, who was very elegant, didn't even have one like it, and she made a mental note to discuss this with her father for her mother's next birthday gift.

"Oh, that's so kind of you. Thank you. Girls, please behave. I should be back in a jiffy."

The security guard unlatched the velvet rope, and Uncle Guy stepped onto the side with the displays, looking out of place in his modern-day suit and coat as the Victorian characters celebrated a calm Christmas.

"Are you girls enjoying the Christmas village? It certainly is nice to look at while we wait to see Santa," asked the musical voice.

"We are now that Ricky's gone," said Terri, turning to the woman and smiling her gap-tooth smile.

Savannah laughed at her cousin's comment and turned to smile at the woman. She had her hands on the shoulders of two boys who looked to be around Savannah's and Terri's ages. One was taller, with light brown wavy hair and brown eyes, and the other was smaller with darker hair and grayish blue eyes. The smaller boy looked distracted as if he was trying to conceal something within his hands. The boys were dressed identically wearing their best Sunday coats with scally caps perfectly perched upon their heads.

"I hope your dad can find him," the taller boy said, sounding very serious, as if what Ricky did was something that he, himself, would never do.

"He will. Ricky's always taking off like that, and Dad always finds him," Terri said matter-of-factly, barely turning around to look at the boy. She had her hand on the velvet rope and was fascinated by it.

"Savannah, feel how soft this is!"

"Oh, it's so pretty," Savannah said, running her hand along the thick velvet.

"I wish I could take it home. Don't you think it would make a nice belt for my red dress?"

Terri slid her hand back and forth across the rope, her hand moving along the rope as the line inched forward.

"We're getting there!" Savannah excitedly said as she thought she could see Santa's throne if she stood on her tiptoes.

"Ouch!" cried Terri. Savannah flattened her feet and looked at her cousin who was tugging on her arm.

"My finger is stuck!"

Savannah bent to see where Terri's index finger had disappeared. She could see that it was caught in the end of the rope that contained a latch. It had a little hook under it and Savannah pressed on it, but the latch refused to open.

"Oh, it hurts!" screamed Terri, and Savannah watched her cousin's finger quickly turn a sickening shade of purple.

"Honey, stay calm," said the lady in gray. "Security will be here, and they'll get your finger out. It will be okay."

The woman's calming words seemed to take effect as Terri nodded in agreement.

"Can you wiggle your finger?" asked Savannah, holding onto her frightened cousin.

"A—a little," Terri whimpered.

"I can get it out." Just then the smaller boy with the lady in gray stepped forward and examined the rope. Savannah watched as he took the thing he was fidgeting with earlier and stuck it into a tiny screw near the clasp and worked it steadily, suddenly loosening the screw as Terri's swollen finger was released from its death grip.

"Okay, everyone, move aside!" Two burly security officers arrived on the scene—one with large wire cutters that looked like they belonged in a horror movie and the other carrying a huge bag of ice.

"Wow! They were going to cut her finger off, Mom!" the taller boy exclaimed.

"They were going to do no such thing, Mitchell," said the lady in gray. "They were simply going to cut the brass and her finger would have slipped right out, but Matty beat them to it."

One of the officers took Terri's hand and gave it a look. He removed some ice from the bag and wrapped it in a paper towel.

"Here, you go, sweetie. Just keep this on your finger and the swelling will go right down." The officer turned to the lady in gray.

"Your little girl will be just fine," he said, and went along to his next order of business.

"Thank you, officer," said the lady in gray. She looked at Terri's finger, and the color was already back to its normal flesh tone. Savannah noticed that the lady in gray gave the younger boy who saved Terri's finger from a gory amputation a stern look. She didn't seem mad, but there was something in her eyes in which she was silently communicating with the boy. Savannah knew that look. She was the recipient of that same look many times from her own mother when she had done something that she should not have.

"That didn't take long," said the woman, patting Terri on the shoulder. "Are you okay now?" she kindly asked.

"She is, thanks to him," Savannah said, nodding toward the smaller boy. Savannah wanted to make sure the boy didn't get into trouble later at home.

"What's in your hand?" asked Savannah, pointing to the boy's coat sleeve. She had just seen him quickly slip whatever it was up into his sleeve.

The boy looked at his mother and Savannah noticed what pretty grayish-blue eyes he had.

"Grandpa Max gave it to me yesterday. It's a long car ride and I didn't know if we might need to change a tire or something, so I brought it with me."

"Good thing you did, Matty, or that girl would have had her finger cut off for sure!" Mitchell chimed in, giving Savannah the feeling that he almost wished that happened.

"My finger!" screamed Terri, holding it close to her chest as if she was holding one of her precious baby dolls as she dropped the ice on the floor.

"Your finger is fine, dear," the lady in gray said gently, retrieving the ice. "Oh, look who is here!" she exclaimed as she put the ice back on Terri's finger.

"I got him!" Uncle Guy triumphantly walked through the crowd, carrying Ricky as if he were a prize won at an amusement park. He was perched on top of Uncle Guy's shoulders, holding the biggest multicolored lollipop Savannah had ever seen.

He gets a lollipop for running away? Savannah thought, becoming just the slightest bit angry and a little jealous, as she loved lollipops. Ricky misbehaves, Terri almost loses a finger, and he gets the most spectacular lollipop ever made? The unfairness of it all made Savannah want to cry.

"The jolly old elf himself caught him. Just coming back from feeding the reindeer, and Ricky jumped right up into his arms. Tell everyone what he told you, Ricky."

Uncle Guy lifted Ricky from his shoulders and put him next to Savannah, with that beautiful lollipop right in her face.

"Daddy, my finger..." whimpered Terri, holding up her hand to her father's oblivious face.

"Here," said Ricky, reaching into the deep pockets of his father's overcoat. He handed Terri a lollipop just like his. He reached in again and handed one to Savannah.

"Santa said that if I'm good and I give my sister and cousin a lollipop, then he might give me an extra Christmas wish."

Savannah watched her little cousin turn his attention to the Christmas displays and to his oversized lollipop.

"Thank you, Ricky," Savannah said in barely a whisper, absolutely mesmerized by the lollipop. It had to be the size of a saucer, with swirls of Christmas red and green along with yellow, blue and pink, all melded onto a thick white stick. Savannah thought it was the most beautiful piece of candy ever made, and she was torn as to whether to rip the wrapper right off and eat it or keep it in its present and perfect state forever.

She turned to Terri to ask if she was going to eat hers, but she didn't have to, as her cousin had torn into it with both hands and began licking her lollipop in utter happiness, totally forgetting about her bruised finger.

"Oh, my apologies, I nearly forgot!" interrupted Uncle Guy. He was intently listening to the lady in gray explain about Terri's finger, when he reached into those bottomless coat pockets and pulled out two more lollipops and handed them to the boys with the lady in gray.

"I thought I saw two boys with you, and I explained to Santa that they were keeping the girls company and Santa said they should have lollipops, too."

All remained peaceful for the remainder of the day, with Uncle Guy chatting amiably to the lady in gray as they made the trek closer to Santa. Ricky was quietly working on his lollipop, as was Terri, but Savannah decided to keep hers wrapped. It was just too beautiful and there were many other exhibits to look at before they reached Santa, and she turned her attention toward the joyous and happy displays of Howardson's Merry Christmases of the past, happily clutching her lollipop.

THE YEARS PASSED, AND SAVANNAH RARELY SAW HER COUSINS, AS they all had grown up and their lives had taken different directions. Ricky, now known as Rick, lived in Denver and was the senior partner at the city's biggest law firm, and Terri was an occupational therapist in Tampa. The cousins' annual Christmas cards however never failed to mention Ricky's escapades that day, and Savannah recalled that Christmas, fondly, especially the lollipop, which she finally devoured on Christmas Day.

Ghosts of Christmases past, she thought, watching the lights on the tree near Santa's chair sparkle a pretty blue and white.

"Watch out for that tree!"

Savannah was quickly brought back to the present as one of the elves was about to lose his grip on a tree laden with too many ornaments. A fellow elf quickly flew into action and righted the tree and proceeded to take some decorations from it, placing them lovingly onto a nearby tree that desperately needed additional glamour.

She watched the elves, reminiscent of busy birds feathering their nests, climb high onto ladders into the artificial trees, bedecking them with strands of tinsel and garland, wreaths the size of the moon and spectacular ornaments in every shade of the Christmas color wheel.

Savannah watched as the winter wonderland was erected right before her eyes. In a few short weeks she would be living her own winter wonderland at The Blue Spruce Inn, and she could already taste the cider and roast turkey as she turned toward the escalator to head back to the dull world of her insurance company office. Halloween, however, still beckoned, and Savannah decided to take one last stroll through the sale aisles, looking once again at the happy jack-o'-lantern and absolutely deciding to leave it for someone else's bay window. She felt as if his big black triangle eyes were pleading with her to take him home.

"Oh, don't look at me that way, buddy. We were just not meant to be."

Suddenly, the hair on Savannah's neck pricked up, and she had the strangest feeling that she was being watched, and not by the pumpkin. She turned abruptly but was only met by the eye sockets of the dangling skeleton she passed when she first entered the store. Only shoppers lolled about her, filling their carts with Halloween treasures.

"Too much Halloween," she said, shivering, making her way to the ever-revolving front doors of Howardson's.

CHAPTER 2

"She's perfect," Matthew Buck whispered watching the attractive silver-haired woman glide down the store's escalator. Matthew was desperate and by the looks of this woman, she could be the one to pull him out of this mess, one he created himself, with his insistence on a more up-to-date Christmas display. *The Enchanted Land of Claus* was due to open in a few short weeks, and there was still one piece to his *Enchanted Land of Claus* that was missing, and that was the perfect Mrs. Claus.

Matthew knew when he accepted the position of Creative Director of Special Events he would be solely responsible for the Herculean task of redeveloping a time-honored tradition. However, as much-loved as this tradition was, it was tired and dated. He had the experience to pull it off, having previously been the creative director of McKinnley's, a big box chain store based in Chicago that recently went bankrupt. The call from Corrine Howardson, an old college friend, came at the right time just as Matthew received his pink slip.

"Matty, c'mon, I know you want to come back to the bright lights of Boston. And besides, I heard about McKinnley's going belly up." Corrine was recently promoted to marketing vice president of Howardson's and was ready to give the store the twenty-first century makeover it desperately needed, including revamping the Christmas exhibit, and Corrine knew only one person could pull it off.

Matthew felt the blush rise into his cheeks upon hearing the voice of his college crush through his cellphone. College was decades in the past, but he could still recall the day that any chance he might have had with Corrine Howardson vanished before his eyes.

CORRINE AND MATTHEW HAD MOST OF THEIR CLASSES TOGETHER and casually socialized. Everyone liked Corrine: she was pretty without realizing it, kind to everyone, and a great student. She was also the heir to the Howardson's Emporium throne, the stalwart of Boston's retail kingdom.

"Here ya go, Matty," she said, holding out the stapled set of assignment papers the size of a manuscript.

The gold flecks in her brown eyes sparkled in the shaft of afternoon sunlight that streamed in from the large windows of the lecture hall. Her thick light brown hair was piled high on top of her head as two small diamond studs sparkled in her ear lobes. If any makeup graced her glowing face, it was not noticeable at all, as Corrine's natural prettiness needed nothing to enhance it. She was wearing a light green cowl neck sweater, which brought out the amber in her eyes and the pink of her cheeks, and Matthew thought there was no one as beautiful as Corrine Howardson.

Ask her now, Matthew silently commanded, mustering the courage to ask Corrine on a date. He took a deep breath.

"Thanks, Corrine. Corrine…"

"Ya, Matty?" she asked in her charming Boston accent. She quickly turned away from Matthew and enthusiastically waved toward the door. Colton Duke, a Texas cowboy type, and a big bass out of water in this bucolic New England College town, returned her wave. Colton was on a football scholarship, but during a practice he broke his hip and was on the long road to recovery, a road on which Corrine traveled by his side. The sight of Colton Duke sitting in his wheelchair took the wind right out of Matthew's sails, and he knew he stood no chance with Corrine.

"Were you going to say something, Matty?" She had turned back to Matthew, waiting for a response.

"Oh, no," he said, shaking his head. "I just wanted to let you know I thought your presentation last week was outstanding. Great job."

That beautiful bright smile spread across her pretty face.

"Aw, thanks, Matty! That means so much. And congrats on yours, too. Your designs are amazing. I wish I had that kind of talent. Next assignment we should work together. Easy A." She winked at him as she threw her books and notes into her bag.

"Gotta run. I told Colton I'd push him to his chem lab," she laughed. "Oh, almost forgot this!" Corrine said as she grabbed her pen. She looked at Matthew and smiled, shaking her head and said, "Men are so funny. I know Colton could very well get out of that wheelchair and walk, but I swear, he loves the attention. I told him I was only pushing him until his next doctor's appointment, which is tomorrow, so he better not get used to it. But I really don't mind. He's such a sweetheart." She turned and waved again, and Colton smiled the smile of a man in love.

"Seriously, Matty, next team assignment, you're my partner. Deal?"

"Deal." Matthew smiled as Corrine bounced down the steps of the auditorium and into the hall toward Colton. She lovingly tucked a blue and red plaid Stony Oak woolen blanket around his lap, bestowed a gentle and loving kiss on his lips, and then she happily pushed him down the hall and not only out of Matthew's sight, but out of his romantic reach forever.

Corrine's cheerleader personality and natural prettiness made her popular on campus, and it was obvious to everyone that Corrine Howardson and Colton Duke were meant to be together.

Matthew cursed his shyness with women and was crushed, but no matter how hard he tried, he found it almost impossible to approach a woman in whom he was interested; they, however, had no problem approaching him.

And now Summer Graystone was about to let Matthew in on destiny's little secret.

Like a rescue dog that picked up a scent, women honed upon Matthew's vulnerability, and now as he was at his most low. Unbeknownst to Matthew, his vulnerability was extraordinarily palpable, and he did not see the freight train named Summer Graystone come speeding down the track and heading right toward his wounded heart. "Hi, Matthew." Summer walked down the stairs toward Matthew who sat slumped in his seat in apparent defeat.

"Hi, Summer," he said, turning at the sound of her voice. She sat down next to him, the scent of her exotic perfume assailing his nostrils.

"Corrine sure is devoted to Colton. And it's so obvious he feels the same about her. Don't you think they make a sweet couple?"

"I guess. Must be nice." Matthew shoved the last of his notebooks into his backpack.

"I'm sure it is. I haven't experienced anything like that yet, but I'm hopeful. You should be too."

He looked into her eyes, and he noticed they were the most extraordinary shade of purple, the color of his mother's beloved early summer irises. Summer was a pretty girl, but she wasn't Corrine.

"What makes you think I'm not hopeful?" he asked, putting

his backpack on the empty seat beside him. He couldn't help but smile as he felt her body lean in closer to his.

"Call it women's intuition," she said, smiling. She pulled her long, coal black hair over her right shoulder, running her hand through her shining tresses.

"Sometimes hope is all we have," she said, her hand grasping his. The softness of her skin sent a shock through his blood, and Corrine quickly vanished from his mind.

"I'm going to stop for a coffee if you'd like to join me."

Matthew affably shrugged his shoulders. "I could use a coffee right about now," he said matter-of-factly. He glanced at his watch. "My next class isn't for another hour, so yeah, coffee sounds good."

"Great! Oh, it's my treat, since I asked you."

"Thanks. I'll get the next one," he said, smiling.

Summer Graystone, one of the most gorgeous girls at Stony Oak, just asked him on a date, and he accepted.

Eat your heart out, Corrine, he thought, as he happily followed Summer out of the auditorium.

They dated off and on until graduation when they both decided that they needed to go their separate ways. Matthew headed to Chicago, while Summer accepted an entry-level hotel management position in Minneapolis. They parted amicably when they agreed in only wanting to be married to their careers at this young stage in their lives.

Years later, Matthew was checking into a conference at the Snowton Resort in Minneapolis one cool autumn morning when a stunning woman behind the desk greeted him with a captivating smile.

"Matthew Buck. I saw your name on the registry, and I was hoping it would be you."

"Summer?" Matthew asked incredulously. Summer had always been beautiful, but the passing of time made her even more so, if that was even possible. She still had the same flawless complexion, but now faint lines appeared around her eyes when she smiled, which Matthew thought made her even more attractive. Her jet-black hair was still thick and luxurious, framing her pretty, round face and her eyes were still as violet as those newly bloomed summer irises.

Summer stepped from around the check-in desk, walking gracefully toward him. She was wearing a white skirt and jacket which hugged her curvaceous figure in all the right places. She embraced him in a bear hug and the scent of her perfume took him right back to his days at Stony Oak.

"You haven't changed a bit!" she exclaimed, stepping back, grasping his hands tightly within her own.

Matthew was left almost speechless as he stared at Summer. She was absolutely stunning.

"You haven't either, Summer," he said, feeling the softness of her hands in his. "You look amazing."

"Matthew, we simply have to catch up," she said, dropping his hands and walking back behind the desk.

"I'm off tomorrow night. I can arrange for dinner here in our private dining room." She suddenly stopped.

"Oh, Matthew, I'm sorry. I can be so forward sometimes. I noticed that you were checking in alone, but maybe you're…"

"No," Matthew said, shaking his head and holding up his left hand.

"Not married. Only to work, if that counts."

Summer held up her left hand.

"Me either! And I'm with you—only to work and that does count! So, I can arrange for dinner tomorrow night in our private dining area if that works for you?"

He found himself captivated by her violet eyes and bright friendly smile. Summer was a part of his carefree college days, a part of his happy and treasured past, and Matthew didn't realize how lonely he was until this very minute.

"I'd love that," he simply said.

"Wonderful!" Summer exclaimed as she handed him a card.

"Here's my contact information. You can call me but if I don't pick up, leave a voicemail. We can meet right here tomorrow at eight. Would that work?"

Matthew mentally ran through his conference schedule, as it was jam-packed for the next three days.

"That would. The last session tomorrow ends at six, so eight would be perfect."

"Oh Matthew," she said excitedly. She walked toward him and pressed her lips to his cheek.

"It's so good to see you. I can't wait to catch up."

"Miss Graystone, you're needed in the kitchen."

"Oh, thank you, Hannah. I'll be right there." The young waitress walked back to the dining area.

"Duty calls, but I'll see you tomorrow. And, if you need anything, extra towels, blankets, give me a call. And, oh, there will be no charge for the minibar in your room." She winked and Matthew felt his heart skip ten beats.

"Summer, that's very kind of you. Thanks so much."

"Anything for an old friend. Until tomorrow!" She waved and bounced down the corridor in spectacularly high heels, her shapely hips swaying back and forth with each step to a tune that only Summer could hear.

Matthew watched her lithe body disappear around the corner, as a shakiness that he hadn't felt in years consumed him —the feeling of a woman, and a gorgeous one at that, being kind and simply paying attention to him. He tucked the card into his shirt pocket and headed to his room curious to see how his minibar was stocked.

The following year, on a clear and bright late autumn morning at the quaint St. Theresa's Church in Brightmore, Matthew waited at the altar as Summer gracefully walked down the aisle toward her future husband.

There were still days in his life when Matthew couldn't

believe that he married this woman, but she had swooped in so calmly and gently as Matthew nursed his lonely heart. Matthew wasn't even sure if he was ever in love with anyone before, even then at thirty-six years old, with the exception of Corrine. His job had all but consumed him, and Summer changed all that. She was gorgeous, but more important, she was familiar. They were both New Englanders living in the Midwest. They dated in college, and he felt comfortable with someone who knew him when he was younger and had the same shared experiences. He never thought of her as being his wife while they dated in college, but now, there could be no other woman to be Mrs. Matthew Buck.

THEIR MARRIAGE WAS BARELY TWO YEARS OLD WHEN RIGHT BEFORE Labor Day Matthew was in the midst of finalizing the store's Autumn Festival display. Summer had been working crazy hours at the Snowton's Chicago location, and they were lucky if they grabbed a quick dinner and then fell right to sleep. But Matthew was now under a fierce deadline, and he could feel the pressure mounting.

Matthew's phone rang. He shook his head in agitation, and against his better judgment, he answered.

"Matthew. I need you to come home now."

"Summer, it's insane here. Can't it wait until later?"

"No, Matthew, it can't. Just come home and then go back to work. I need to talk to you about something and, no, it cannot wait."

Matthew heard the sense of urgency in his wife's voice, which put him on edge. Summer had a habit of interrupting his workday with her whims, to which Matthew always acquiesced, but he could tell this was not one of her usual demands.

"You're not asking for a divorce already, are you?" he nervously laughed into the phone, hoping to break the apprehension he was feeling. Their careers had invisibly gripped them, tearing them away from each other, and making a young marriage that much more difficult.

"Not yet, but if you're not here soon, I might have to." Summer's end of the line went dead.

"Matty, you're needed up on the display floor. Something's going on with one of the mechanical scarecrows. There's straw flying everywhere..."

"You'll have to take care of it, Fern. Summer just phoned, and she needs me home immediately. I'll be back later. Can you handle it for now?" Matthew noticed Fern's face distort with agitation. Fern made it clear on many occasions how she felt about Summer.

Fern Rhodes was the McKinnley's seamstress, and Matthew adored her as she was the surrogate mother who listened, counseled, and when needed, scolded Matthew. He wouldn't know what to do without her. But there was always one thing Fern made very clear: She felt as if Matthew was Summer's puppet. Summer called, he ran; Summer wanted something, she pulled Matthew's strings.

"Oh, are we playing Summer Says again?" The sarcasm in Fern's voice cut through Matthew like the proverbial dagger. Matthew could usually shrug off Fern's digs about his wife, but not today. He was leaving. Now.

"I'm not playing anything," he said, furiously whipping his jacket from the back of his chair. "My wife called and said she needs me at home, and that's where I'm going. I'll be back when I can."

He heard the terseness in his voice, and immediately felt guilty for being so curt with his long-time friend. He could tell from the wounded look in Fern's blue eyes that he had gone too far.

"Look, the switch is right in the middle of the scarecrow's back. Turn it off, and when I come back, I'll be bearing gifts."

"As long as they're gifts from Sapphire Sweets, then I can forgive you."

Matthew laughed. He looked at Fern who had pieces of straw stuck to her slick black hair and her ever-present tape measure was wrapped around her neck like a wayward scarf. She might have been small in stature but she was fierce in attitude, and her seamstressing skills were genius. They had worked together for years, and she had proclaimed him her honorary son, as she did not have children or nieces and nephews of her own. She lovingly took Matthew under her wing as he entered the highly competitive world of retail design and management. Fern truly was his right-hand woman, and he would be lost without her, especially being so far from his family.

But Summer was his wife, and she came first.

"Not only will I stop at Sapphire Sweets, but I'll also make sure you have a cup of that peppermint tea you love. It might taste even better if you didn't make it yourself," he laughed, full well knowing that she much preferred making her own anything than purchasing it in a store.

"Well, if there even is such a thing as anything being better than homemade, I'll admit it's Sapphire's tea. And cinnamon scones, wink, wink."

Fern shrugged and pulled the tape measure from her shoulders.

"I'll find that scarecrow switch. And I'll see you later." She waved her nimble index finger at him, and Matthew stood erect and saluted.

"Aye, aye, Madam," he laughed and watched his friend fly back to the production area.

Fern's palpable dislike of Summer was clearly evident to Matthew. Matthew knew Fern had nothing but his own best interest at heart, but her brusque comments about him playing Summer Says could grate on Matthew's nerves. For the sake of their friendship, he chose to ignore Fern's gruffness, but Summer was his wife, and he was going to be there for her.

Summer was demanding, but that was her personality, and it took her far in the professional sphere of hotel management. She had worked her way up from manager to general manager at Snowton in just two years, transferring to the Chicago location when they married, taking even more time away from the young married couple. But they both agreed that if they were going to get ahead, this is what they had to do—work—so that later in life, the financial fruits of their labor would be well enjoyed.

Matthew didn't give Fern a second thought, as he grabbed his car keys and headed home.

"Sit down," Summer commanded, as Matthew announced he was home. She had a glass of his favorite chardonnay ready and handed it to him as he flopped onto the couch.

"Wine, wow. I can't imagine what you're about to spring on me," he said, taking a sip. "But then again, I think I can." He really didn't, but he thought it would be fun to play along with his wife.

"What do you think I'm going to tell you?" Summer asked, sidling next to her husband. She put her head on Matthew's shoulder and he kissed the top of her glossy black hair.

"Well, you've already been promoted, so that's out of the question. I know you bought a new pair of shoes last week, and a bag to match..."

"Matthew Buck!" Summer shot up beside him and Matthew could tell by her stern and hurt look on her face that she was in no mood for games.

"You make me sound like the most materialistic person that ever existed. That hurt."

He pulled her in close to him, placing her head back on his shoulder. He could smell her juniper shampoo and nuzzled his face into the beguiling scent.

"Summer, you know I'd never hurt you. I love you. Now, what

is so important that you had me come home during my work insanity?"

Summer pulled away and looked at her husband's blue-gray eyes. She caressed his face and gently kissed him on his lips.

"You're going to be a father," she whispered into his ear.

Matthew pulled back and looked at his wife. Her smile was as large and bright as a full moon.

"We're having a baby? Oh, my God, Summer." He leaned over and deeply kissed his wife, pulling her as close to him as he possibly could.

"Matthew I've been praying this would happen, and I was so scared when it wasn't, but then I decided to let it go and let Mother Nature take its course, and now we're having a baby."

Matthew caressed his wife's beautiful face and kissed her again.

"Summer," he whispered. "I thought marrying you made me the luckiest man in the world, but now, having a child with you, well, I didn't know such happiness could exist. I love you so much."

"I love you, too, Matty," she said, and Matthew could feel her melting into his strong and protective arms. He wasn't just holding Summer—he was holding their world.

OVER A DECADE LATER, THE WORLD THAT MATTHEW TRIED TO KEEP in his tight embrace was ripped from his arms forever.

"It's just not working anymore, Matthew. I think you know that as well as I do."

It was Athena's twelfth birthday, and she had just gone to bed after a day of horseback riding with friends. There had been tension between Matthew and his wife, particularly for the last few months, but it was growing like a festering wound, and when Summer ignored him all day at the riding stables, Matthew knew what was coming, but he had promised himself that he was going to let her make the first move, and not him. He knew that if he did, it could be detrimental, and he was not going to give Summer any ammunition if he could help it.

"What are you thinking?" he asked cautiously, still keeping his cards close to the vest. *Let her be the one to mention leaving me,* he thought as he sat down opposite his wife at their large dining room table.

Summer licked her lips and tugged at her necklace, an anxious habit. *Buckle up, Matthew.*

"Well, if you're going to make me spell it out, Matthew, what's not working is you and me. Our marriage. Maybe it never did."

"What do you mean maybe it never did? I love you, Summer. When we made our wedding vows there was absolutely no doubt in my mind that we were going to be married for the rest of our lives. Are you telling me that was something that you didn't believe?"

Hurt and anger bubbled up inside of Matthew. Was she telling him she never really loved him?

Summer shrugged her shoulders, another habit which Matthew read as her not caring.

"Of course I loved you. Love you. But I will honestly tell you that I did question myself. Was I marrying you for the right reasons? Sometimes I felt that if you didn't come along, I would never have been married, and I have asked myself if I really loved you or I thought I loved you. I do love you, Matthew, but not in the way a wife should love her husband."

Matthew looked questioningly into those penetrating violet eyes. He suddenly noticed the deep lines etched around them, like lines on a map that now creased her face. He also observed those same deep lines around her lips. *When did those appear?* he thought, realizing he never noticed them until now, thinking perhaps he didn't see them because he loved her. Graying hair and fine lines didn't matter because they were growing older together. And now, Summer wanted to end the journey.

"Enlighten me, Summer. How is a wife supposed to love a husband, because I can certainly tell you how this husband loves his wife. And their daughter. I work the way I do not just for me but for the both of you. I want Athena to see a strong father figure who only wants the best for her and goes to work every day and shows her how much she's loved. I go to work every day to provide the lifestyle you love so much…"

Summer put her hand up.

"Stop right there, Matthew. I work full time as well, and don't forget it's my income that provides for our daughter as well as yours. I know what you do, Matthew, but I don't want to drag this out like it's a competition. We both love and provide for Athena, but it's not enough for me. I'm not happy in this marriage. I am not asking anything of you, Matthew, no money, no child support, no alimony, absolutely nothing. Just that you let me go."

"Let you go? Just like that? Look, Summer, we're both so busy with work, why don't we just take some time off and go somewhere, the three of us?"

Matthew watched as Summer's body heaved with an exasperated sigh of frustration, another telltale sign that Summer had made up her mind, and Matthew knew he'd already lost his wife. But he would fight for his daughter.

"What about Athena? What are we supposed to tell her?"

"I've already spoken to her about the possibility that we may be living apart. She was upset, but I told her nothing drastic would happen, that we are still a family, but just not living together."

Matthew felt the fury boil in his blood, gushing through his body. He had to remain in control because he knew Summer enjoyed a good fight, and he was not going to give her one. Not for his sake, but most importantly, not for his daughter who was soundly sleeping in her bedroom down the hall. No. He would handle this with a cool head and not provide Summer any ammunition whatsoever.

"You were always good at tidying messes, Summer. The most important thing right now is Athena's wellbeing. I want her vacation plans to remain the same—staying with my mother in New Hampshire." There was no way Summer was going to ruin Athena's favorite six weeks out of the year.

"Absolutely. I know how much Athena loves her New Hampshire summers, and I would never take that away from her."

Round one, Matthew thought. He and Athena had a close relationship, and although Summer would never jeopardize that, he knew it was extremely important he and his daughter spend time together to help her realize that the failure of her parents' marriage had nothing at all to do with her.

"So how does this work? Do I leave or do you leave?"

"Well, I have made arrangements at the hotel to stay in the penthouse suite. There is more than enough room for the two of us."

"The two of you?" Again, Matthew could feel his blood rage. It was very clear that Summer had been planning this for a while, and that she planned to take Athena away from him.

"I'm not so sure I like Athena living in a hotel."

Summer rolled her eyes and let out an exasperated sigh.

"Matthew, you know the penthouse is bigger than our condo, and I managed the interior decorating so it is homey and not just some sterile hotel room." She waved her hands in frustration.

"Athena's home base will be here, but I want her to feel she can be at home in both places. Until I'm settled."

"And when do you plan on settling, Summer?" *Keep your anger in check, guy. You don't want her throwing anything at you. Her memory is a steel trap.*

"Not sure," she said, shrugging her shoulders."I'm still figuring that out." She held up her hand as if it could stop any words from escaping from Matthew's mouth.

"And don't worry about the money. Again, I'm not asking you for anything that has to do with me. I am solely responsible for this decision, and I am more than capable of taking care of my financial needs. And then some."

Matthew winced at her last remark. Along with her promotion she also received a hefty raise, catapulting her annual salary into the six-figure stratosphere. Matthew was nearly there himself, but not quite, and he knew that since she had taken over the financial lead professionally, she would never let Matthew forget.

"Fair enough. We can have our attorney hash something…"

"I have my own attorney now and I can have her send everything to Nella. She's still your attorney, right?"

"Nella is still our—my attorney, yes." Matthew said, thinking that he shouldn't be surprised at all that Summer had acquired her own attorney. There was nothing she didn't think of.

"I do just have one question, Summer." Matthew felt his mouth go dry as he almost did not want to ask, but he had to know.

"Anything," Summer said, smoothing her skirt, anxiously squirming like a trapped rat, ready to jump.

"Is there someone else?" He could barely get the words out as his heart stammered in his chest.

"No one else, Matthew. I'm quite surprised you asked."

"Why wouldn't I ask? You work long hours, we hardly see each other. When I try to make time for us, you're always busy. How could I not think that?"

"I could ask the same of you, Matthew."

Her violet eyes penetrated his gray-blue ones, and he felt the heat of her anger boring straight through to him. Matthew never realized until this moment how cold and icy those beautiful eyes could be. Had they always been like that? Or did they turn stone cold because she just changed the course of their family's life?

"Matthew, we've been trains running on separate tracks for a long time now. You can analyze things until the cows come home. That's exactly what I've been doing, asking myself what went wrong. The answer is much easier than we think. We simply grew apart. And I believe you've known that, too, and neither one of us is to blame. The should haves, could haves, would haves won't make any difference in the way our marriage ended, and I'm not going to beat myself up and neither should you. We have a wonderful daughter that we will both continue to raise, albeit separately, and I'm only going to think of the good that can come out of this for Athena. I hope we are in agreement on that."

"We are, Summer. Athena's wellbeing is most important for me as well."

"Okay then. I'll be staying at the hotel tonight and since it's been so busy, I'll move my things out next weekend and we can start fresh from there." Summer stood up and smoothed the invisible wrinkles from her silk skirt.

Wrapping it up, just like a business deal, Matthew thought as he watched his wife grab her suitcase-sized, chocolate leather tote bag, her five-inch heels clicking loudly on the newly polished hardwood floor.

"I'm just going to give Athena a kiss and then I'll leave. I'll see myself out."

And Summer Graystone Buck saw herself out from their condo and out from their marriage.

"It's okay, Dad," Athena said to Matthew. They were driving out of the city and into the serene countryside to Carousel Stables where Athena celebrated her birthday party just last weekend, the weekend that changed all of their lives forever. This presented the perfect opportunity for Matthew and Athena to talk, especially since she was begging to return for more lessons.

Matthew glanced at his daughter, her black hair shimmering in the sunlight. He watched his sweet little girl sip on her hot chocolate, her lips puckering to blow on the steam rising from her cup.

"My only concern, Athena, is that you are okay. Your wellbeing is my only concern, and your mother's too. I'm sorry this happened."

"Don't be sad, Dad." He felt the soft touch of his daughter's hand on his shoulder.

"I know that things will be different, but I know things will be the same, too. You're still my dad no matter what, and I love you." He heard her slurp her hot chocolate, and he felt the gentle touch of her hand on his shoulder.

"But I do have to be honest," she said, and Matthew could feel her gaze descend upon him, making him turn for a quick moment. Athena was the perfect blend of her parents—her mother's fair complexion and her father's sea blue eyes. Her thick black hair was twisted in a perfect knot perched on top of her head, and Matthew could see that his little girl was turning into a young woman right before his eyes.

"You know honesty is our only policy, sweetie. Shoot."

Matthew heard Athena inhale and take a deep breath.

"I think you and Mom will be happier not living with each other. I think I've known for a long time that things were not right between the two of you. I can't explain it, but I don't think you've been happy with each other for a long time. At first, I thought it was something I did…"

"Athena, never think that," Matthew quickly interrupted. "You are the one thing your mother and I did that was right. You are the best thing that has happened to both of us. Sometimes it's no one's fault. Things happen in a marriage, and sometimes it's best to move on. But always remember that no matter what happens between me and your mother, we will always love you. You got that?"

There was nothing sweeter than the sound of his daughter's delighted giggle, signifying immediately to Matthew that Athena would be fine.

Athena quickly unbuckled her seatbelt. "Don't tell Mom," she said, as the straps fell from her shoulders, enabling her to quickly kiss her father's stubbled cheek.

She buckled herself back in just as quickly and patted her father's cheek.

"You need a shave, Mister!"

"Well, if you didn't get me up so early, I would have had time. I can shave later. Look, here's the exit to the stables. You ready?"

"Can't wait, Dad!" Athena shouted excitedly, as they made their way down the lane to the horse farm Athena had fallen in love with on her birthday. Little did Summer or Matthew realize, their birthday gift of a day at the stables would set Athena's and Summer's life on a different path, and away from Matthew.

AND NOW, THREE YEARS LATER, MATTHEW WAS IN BOSTON, AND Summer and Athena in London, where Summer was the general manager for a hotel conglomerate, and Athena, attending the Cobble Brooke Riding Academy of England, one of Europe's premier equestrian schools.

MATTHEW WATCHED THE SILVER-HAIRED WOMAN SAIL DOWN THE escalator, knowing he had to act fast or he'd lose her in the lunch-time crowd. He ran down the nearby staircase, dodging hordes of shoppers until he was close enough to tap her on the shoulder. Matthew reached out but instead of his fingertip reaching for her shoulder, he found himself flailing as his foot caught on a stray piece of garland. He quickly lost his balance.

Matthew instinctively braced himself and outstretched his arms to break his fall, but his hand caught the strap of the woman's bag that was fastened tightly to her shoulder. A howling scream pierced the air, and shoppers turned and laughed, thinking a Halloween display had been set off. Instead, shoppers witnessed a man violently thrashing behind a woman, grabbing onto her bag. Shouts of *thief! help her!* rang through the store as the Howardson's plain-clothes detectives descended upon Matthew, now lying prone on the cold, hardwood floor. One of the detectives, a former professional wrestler, was just about to cuff Matthew when he heard, "Brock, it's me, Matthew Buck. I tripped and fell."

"Oh, Mr. Buck, so it is. What in the world? I'm sorry I didn't recognize you, but I usually see you face to face, not face to store floor."

Brock helped Matthew to his feet and quickly put away the cuffs.

"Entirely my fault, Brock. You were just doing your job, and very well I might add. Howardson's is lucky to have you." Matthew brushed himself off and extended his hand in friendship to Brock, who gripped it like a vice.

"I'm glad you think that, Mr. Buck. You understand how I reacted, a woman screams, and—oh my gosh, ma'am, are you okay?"

Brock quickly turned toward the woman, who was watching with a stern look on her face as these two men congratulated themselves on a job well done.

"Well, thank you for finally asking," the woman replied with an edge of annoyance in her voice. Matthew watched as Brock's face fell at the cold curtness of her tone, making Matthew realize she was truly the 'victim', not him.

"I am so sorry," he said, extending his hand in greeting."I'm Matthew Buck, creative director for Howardson's, and—and I hope you accept my sincerest apologies for the 'attempted robbery'. I didn't mean to frighten you."

He smiled and turned the charm level up as high as he could, detecting what he thought was a faint smile gracing her lips. She was actually quite stunning, with her platinum hair framing a round face, and eyes the color of emeralds shimmered in her pale and flawless complexion. She accepted his hand and a buzz of electricity shot up his arm.

"Savannah Brady. Nice to meet you. I think."

Matthew smiled. "It doesn't sound like you're too upset, and I hope that you're not, but I'd like to make this up to you somehow."

"That's not necessary, Mr. Buck. Your apology is more than enough. Now, I've got to get back to work."

Savannah Brady pulled her soft hand away from his strong one, and Matthew became instantly aware of how long he held it as she headed toward the revolving door.

"Ms. Brady," The command of his own voice surprised Matthew as she abruptly turned around, but he couldn't afford to lose her now.

"I'm sorry, I know I'm keeping you, but, well, there's a reason I fell for... on you."

Nervously, Matthew dug his hands into his trouser pockets for his talisman. His left hand found the worn handkerchief, one of many his mother had bought for his father and his brother to carry. His grandfather, Maximillian, always had a neatly starched white one with the initials MB embroidered in blue thread in the bottom right-hand corner in every pocket of every coat, pair of pants, and work shirt. In carrying on with family tradition, Matthew's mother always presented her husband and sons with monogrammed handkerchiefs every Christmas, and now Matthew couldn't be without one in any of his coats, pants, or shirts. He ran his fingers over the raised embroidery, feeling the curve of the letters M and B and felt the strength of his grandfather and father each time he touched it. And now, when he especially needed it, Matthew could feel their love surge through him via the handkerchief.

"Ms. Brady, truth be told, I was actually following you."

Matthew watched as she twitched her head from side to side and furrowed her brows, as if not understanding him.

"Following me? Do you find following female customers in your department store amusing?"

Matthew shrugged his shoulders. "Absolutely not," he said, gripping the handkerchief even tighter.

"It was not my intention to frighten you. I saw you walk from the Christmas display, and well, ah, I just thought you'd be perfect." There. He said it.

She stepped toward him and narrowed her emerald eyes, and Matthew instantly felt the heat of her anger penetrating into his own.

Matthew instinctively backed up, now realizing this was not a woman who joked easily.

"Oh, it's not a pickup line or anything like that," he laughed trying to diffuse her obvious anger. "It's a proposal, a job proposal I have for you, if you are interested, and I hope you are."

"I already have a job, one which I am very late for," she said, turning again toward the door, her silver hair bouncing with each step.

"Wait, please hear me out, for just one minute, I promise."

Matthew watched as her shoulders appeared to relax, and she slowly turned around toward him. He sensed a possible opening, and he knew he had to tread lightly and keep the charm turned on high.

"It's an opportunity for you to become part of the Howardson's Christmas tradition, but I don't want to keep you any longer, so perhaps we can meet for coffee when you're done at work today? Five o'clock at the Yellow Pumpkin Cafe? I think you'll find what I have to say quite fascinating." Matthew fumbled in his jacket pocket and pulled out a business card.

"If you can't make it, please call me, as I don't want to waste your time, but I'm hoping to see you at five?"

"The card's not necessary, Mr. Buck. I'll see you at five." She turned on her heels and stomped through the revolving doors of Howardson's and out of Matthew's sight.

Matthew's brows furrowed in disappointment thinking perhaps that with that snooty attitude, she was actually not his perfect Mrs. Claus.

"Gotta find out," he whispered as he headed in the opposite direction, deeper into the store and into his office to prepare for his five o'clock business proposal.

CHAPTER 3

Savannah glanced at the clock on her computer, as four forty-five flashed a bright green. Her afternoon was busier than she'd expected, and before she knew it, she was pulling out her antique, silver compact, a birthday present from her son, and dabbing on Midnight Mauve, her favorite lipstick, which immediately pinked up her pale face. She spritzed on some perfume, grabbed her tote, and was on the elevator and out the building door walking towards the Yellow Pumpkin Cafe, located just around the block from her office. Savannah walked quickly in her wedges, as she didn't change into her usual running shoes, which were pretty shabby-looking. Work shoes would make a much more favorable impression, although the tote she carried was a worn cotton bag she'd picked up in Hilton Head on a girls' weekend many summers ago. The bag was sentimental and every time she carried it, which was most days, she could still smell the ocean salt and sand. She had intended on going back someday, but her budget was tight, especially with The Blue Spruce Inn vacation quickly approaching, but maybe in the next year or two. Savannah had a lot of maybe next year moments these past few years, and she was tired of it. No more maybe next years. Her new mantra was now or never, and her Blue Spruce Inn Christmas was definitely a now and would not be a never. She now applied this mantra to meeting this Mr. Buck and seeing what his 'being part of Howardson's Christmas tradition' meant. No harm done in simply chatting. Savannah knew it was time to start to open up and to not shut life down anymore. She had done that for too long, and though Savannah couldn't imagine what Mr. Buck had in mind—maybe some freelance administrative work, or perhaps playing a silly little elf—it was time to start taking chances again.

Well, I'm about to find out, she thought as she saw the handsome Matthew Buck give her a wave from his window seat. She waved back and headed into The Yellow Pumpkin and to a date with destiny.

"I HOPE YOU DON'T MIND THAT I'VE GONE AHEAD AND ORDERED, but The Yellow Pumpkin has the best hot chocolate in town," said Matthew as a teenage girl arrived at the table just as Savannah took off her coat. The waitress put down two extra-large mugs of steaming cocoa along with a dish of freshly whipped cream, and small bowls of crushed peppermint candies, sprinkles, and maraschino cherries.

"Enjoy," she smiled and walked away.

"Exactly what I was going to order," Savannah said, taking a seat. The delectable chocolate aroma immediately put her at ease, and she spooned a dollop of pure white cream into her cup and took a sip.

"Best I've ever tasted, that's for sure."

Savannah watched as Matthew spooned two fluffy white dollops of whipped cream into his cup and topped his with a sprinkle of crushed peppermint.

"Very close to my mom's," he said, the whipped cream capping his nose. He took a napkin and brushed it from his face. " Happens all the time," he laughed.

Savannah smiled and took another sip, surveying the man sitting opposite her. He was attractive enough with immaculately groomed salt and pepper hair wavy strands just touching his shirt collar, and his blue-gray sea-glass eyes twinkled as he smiled. She felt the charm ooze from him as he heaped more whipped cream into his cup.

"So, what's this opportunity you have for me, Mr. Buck? Extra seasonal help?"

Matthew smiled. "You could say that," he said, stirring the peppermint sprinkles into the hot chocolate.

The sparkling eyes now looked straight into her green ones.

"Well, when I saw you, Ms. Brady, I knew immediately you were the person I was looking for to complete *The Enchanted Land of Claus*, that's the theme of this year's Howardson's Christmas display. All of my staff have been hired, but there was one very important piece missing. Until today. And when I saw you, I knew I had found it."

Savannah shook her head, puzzled, not quite knowing at all where this was heading.

"First, please call me Savannah. Second, what in the world could I possibly be perfect for? I'm an insurance clerk. does this *Enchanted Land of Claus* need a policy—anyone under the age of sixteen driving a sleigh without a license?"

"Ah ha! A sense of humor. A bonus." Matthew laughed, taking another draught from his oversized mug. Savannah felt his look turn more serious and she watched as he rubbed his hands together, as if he was about to make a fantastic proclamation.

"You, I believe, would make the perfect Mrs. Claus."

Savannah felt her back turn rigid against the booth, sitting upright in astonishment, her head almost hitting the wooden top of the seat. She stared incredulously at the smiling man sitting across the table from her. She wasn't sure if he was insulting her or complimenting her in some bizarre manner.

"Mrs. Claus? Are you serious? I know I'm a woman of a certain age, but I certainly do not look like the wife of Santa Claus." Savannah pushed the cup of cocoa away from her and stood up with indignation. "Thank you for asking, Mr. Buck, but the answer is no. I most certainly would not make the perfect Mrs. Claus."

Matthew quickly rose from the booth, almost spilling the hot chocolate into his lap. He found himself face to face with Savannah Brady, and he felt her ire extraordinarily apparent. He instinctively searched for the reassuring comfort of his handkerchief.

"Ms. Br— Savannah, please don't leave. I meant no insult, and I apologize if what I said came off the wrong way. I didn't mean it to. I know it sounds way out there, but if you just give me a few moments to let me explain. That's all I ask. And that I buy you another hot chocolate?"

Savannah grabbed her tote bag and looked at Matthew, not knowing if she should dump the remainder of her cocoa over his head and give him a few choice words of her own, but when he rose from the booth Savannah felt herself soften, and her anger slowly diminished. Maybe it was the way his shoulders stooped in defeat when he stood up, easing one hand into his pants pocket. Or that the tone of his voice was endearing and apologetic. Or that she noticed his cheeks turned a bright red when offering to buy her another hot chocolate. She couldn't put her finger on it, but there was something about his now sheepish demeanor that embarrassed Savannah about her own rude behavior. Savannah, by her own admission, knew she was becoming grumpy, especially during this past year. There had been so much she had to contend with, and hard as she tried to keep her emotions in check, sometimes she couldn't, and the lid blew off her kettle. This was one of those times she knew she had to put the lid back on and simmer down. Mr. Buck meant no insult, and she knew she'd overreacted. After all she was a woman in her early 50's, and comparing her to Mrs. Claus, who was no spring chicken either, bruised her already fragile ego.

"Well," she said sitting down at the booth, "I never pictured myself as the Mrs. Claus type, but what do you have in mind, Mr. Buck?"

"First another hot chocolate," he said, waving the waitress back to their table.

"A hot chocolate bribery will get me every time. I'll listen with a more open mind and a mugful of delicious hot chocolate. With extra whipped cream of course."

Savannah smiled as the waitress took the order and quickly returned with two more piping hot mugs of cocoa. She spooned the cloud-like whipped cream into her cup and this time decided to help herself to crushed peppermint.

"Although I still cannot imagine me as Mrs. Claus." She sipped the hot chocolate. "Oh, the crushed peppermint really adds that…"

"Extra Christmasness?" Matthew laughed. "It's subtle, but definitely makes it extra special." Savannah liked the sound of his laugh and settled in to hear Matthew Buck present his proposal on why he believed Savannah Brady was the perfect Mrs. Claus.

CHAPTER 4

"New twists on old traditions?" Savannah pushed her empty mug toward the center of the table. Matthew had talked for almost half an hour about his vision for giving this year's Howardson's Christmas display a twenty-first century makeover.

"With all due respect, Mr. Buck, when it comes to Christmas traditions, people rarely like change, never mind 'new twists.'" She was beginning to wish she had left after the first cup, as she, herself, was one of those people who was not fond of twisting old customs into new ones. But she not only promised Matthew she would hear him out, she knew she needed to do this for herself, too. Savannah was well aware that along with her unhappiness, she had become rigid, not liking to stray from the comfortable and familiar. She had always been a traditionalist herself and was constantly the butt of her family's jokes, especially when she took out her grandmother's life-sized red velvet Easter bunny right after Valentine's Day, as that was what her grandmother and mother did. Her husband and son hated that well-worn, crazy button-eyed rabbit, but, as she would say, 'it is a family tradition.'

"Better for Halloween," Patrick always joked.

"I agree, Savannah," Matthew said, still animated, "but

generation after generation has seen the same thing, and while that's heartwarming to see grandparents with their grandchildren share in those memories, sometimes things do get old and tired."

"I hope you're not referring to Santa! Or Mrs. Claus for that matter," Savannah laughed.

Savannah saw a smile illuminate Matthew's face and he shook his head no.

"Santa old and tired? Never. And that's how I envision this year's production. Kids are smart and they know a fifty-year old robotic figure when they see one. Sure, their parents and grandparents love to walk down memory lane, but we want to excite all generations, while still maintaining that old familiarity, but update it for a younger generation. And that's where you come in."

"I'm all ears, Mr. Buck." Savannah tightened the scarf about her neck as a cold breeze blew in when the cafe's door opened and several members of that young generation flew in, chatting excitedly about what to order from the Yellow Pumpkin menu.

"If you're cold, I am happy to switch sides with you," Matthew offered.

"I'm fine, but thank you," she said, thinking his offer was very kind and chivalrous.

"I just can't wait to hear how I fit in with all of this. But, if you are looking for a young, say thirty-ish year old Mrs. Claus, then I don't think I'm your woman. That's one thing I know I am certainly not!"

"Oh, I know that..." She watched Matthew's face twist in embarrassment as he cut himself off. She thought he must have realized that he might stick his foot in his mouth again about her age, and if that was the case then her being part of his twenty-first century vision would melt like snow on a mild winter day right before his eyes.

"I mean that I don't want a young..." He stopped again.

Savannah watched amused, thinking that it's a careful line to walk when broaching the subject of a woman's age, especially when a man was doing the talking. She smiled and decided to give Matthew some help.

"Mr. Buck, I'm a woman in my early fifties, and I have no problem letting the world know that's what I am. Age is a gift not given to many, or something like that. I don't look back and wish I was younger. I look forward to everything that's yet to come—my son getting married, giving me a grandchild or two, and retiring to my namesake city. I try to look forward, not to look back. So go on. Why me?"

"Well, it was actually your hair."

"My hair?" Savannah's hand instinctively flew to her head, and she ran her fingers through her hair, thinking some silly Halloween decoration was caught in it. But that was out of the question because Bea Burns, her nosy co-worker, would have taken great joy in letting Savannah know she had something sticking out of her hair.

"I know I need a cut, but my stylist has been..."

Matthew's laughter interrupted her." No, it's very becoming..." He stopped himself again, and Savannah saw the heat rise in his cheeks. She thought she really must be getting to him for some reason because everything that had come out of his mouth made him sound as if he thought it was offensive, which it wasn't at all. She didn't mean to have that effect on him, especially after checking her own attitude, but still, there was something that she felt he was scared of in her presence.

"It was actually the color that caught my eye. It reminds me of a frozen waterfall."

"Oh, thank you," Savannah said. Now it was her turn to feel the color rise in her own cheeks, feeling somewhat embarrassed by his sweet compliment.

"No one's ever referred to it like that before. I'm either gray or white to most people, although I prefer platinum myself. But there are tons of women who have this hair color. Why me?"

Savannah sensed a hesitation in Matthew, almost as if he knew he had to choose his words very carefully.

"Well, like I said, new twists on old traditions. Mrs. Claus is an old tradition, but you'd be the new twist. A more modern Mrs. Claus. One who is still warm and caring, but, well, I'll just say it, not dowdy and ah… pleasantly plump. You're the one who looks like she can take care of the big guy in addition to running the castle, keeping the elves on task, and is ready to hitch up the reindeer to the sleigh in the beat of a heart. Not to mention bake and construct gingerbread houses at the drop of a snowman's fedora."

"I think I like it. Keep going…"

Savannah saw that from the mischievous twinkle in Matthew's eyes he was in his glory depicting how he perceived his *Enchanted Land of Claus*.

"Mrs. Claus has the same color hair as you, but that's where the similarities end. The traditional Mrs. Claus is always portrayed as an older lady and sort of subservient, and her hair pulled into a matronly bun, I suppose you could say. My Mrs. Claus has long flowing ice colored hair just like yours, and although she might be a woman of a certain age, she's more contemporary and, well, not frumpy. I think you know what I'm trying to say?"

"What you mean to say is that some of Mrs. Claus' traditional physical attributes are good, but some could use some updating. That right?"

Matthew nodded his head in agreement, taking a sip of his hot chocolate, and winced in disapproval and waved for the waitress.

"Oh, it's warm chocolate, not hot."

"Wow," said Savannah, marveling at his ability to down yet another Yellow Pumpkin hot chocolate. These were not simply cold weather beverages, but desserts in and of themselves. As much as she loved them if she had a third one, she would burst right at the seams. But not Matthew.

That's a guy for you, she laughed to herself as the waitress placed another cup in front of him and she watched as Matthew spooned two big dollops of the whipped cream and crushed peppermint into his cup.

"So, I think I have found the perfect Mrs. Claus. What do you think?"

"Well, what makes you so sure you found her? I like the idea, but I'm still not convinced," she said playfully, realizing she was enjoying their conversation and that it was actually nice to sit and chat with a charming man. It had been so long.

"Well, it is my job to convince you that being part of Howardson's *Enchanted Land of Claus* is an opportunity that you just cannot refuse."

"Hmm, but aside from the color of my hair, what makes you so sure I'm the one?"

He shrugged his shoulders.

"Just an instinct. I've been doing this for a long time, and I think I have a good feeling about whether something, or someone, will work or not. Full disclosure. I was upstairs in the store, and I saw you watching the display rolling out, and well, you just had this look of wonderment, if you will. It was as if watching the Christmas display unfold was something you look forward to every year. You looked like you were happy to see it return."

Savannah found herself shocked at Matthew's perception of her earlier in the day. She had felt exactly as he just described —happy.

But she didn't want to let him on to this fact, so she maintained an expert poker face.

"I am happy to see it return. Like a lot of people, I came here when I was a child, and I brought my son, too. I guess you could say it's like an old relative you see only during the holidays. You know it's Christmas when Howardson's starts decorating. It does make people happy. Including me."

"My vision for Howardson's this year is Christmas Present with a Dash of Christmas Past. Santa will be a little less rotund, not a lot, but a little more athletic. You know, like a pro wrestler type."

Savannah laughed picturing Santa in a wrestling ring.

"Sure, I can just see Santa smacking down Jack Frost and the Abominable Snowman."

Matthew laughed.

"Well, he probably could because our Santa is actually a former pro wrestler—you met him earlier—Brock, our chief security guard. So, of course, this Mrs. Claus I'm thinking of would be like minded."

"A wrestler?" Savannah smiled, full well knowing that's not what he meant. "If that's the case, I don't think I fit the bill."

"You're funny. Mrs. Claus will have that caring and sweet personality, but be more athletic as well. You know, lots of skiing and snowmobiling and lots of walks around their castle with the reindeer. Outdoorsy and healthy, but while still maintaining the jolly old souls of the Clauses, hence *The Enchanted Land of Claus.*"

Savannah furrowed her brows in thought. She still wasn't convinced that she could pull this off.

"I do like the idea, it does still seem traditional, which is very important, but perhaps less tired. Revived and refreshed, I guess you could say."

"Exactly! A bit more modern but in keeping with the sweet hot cocoa and gingerbread cookies we all know and love. And will continue to love. And eat."

"And you think I could pull this off? Because I'm not so sure."

"I do. I think customers would be drawn to you. You did mention you have a son, so I'm assuming you like children?"

"I love children, Mr. Buck, and maybe someday I'll be lucky enough to be blessed with grandchildren. But not now."

Matthew's hands flew up in excitement, sending the spoon flying to the floor.

"Well, see, as Mrs. Claus, children will be your biggest customer! And they go home with their parents at the end of the day—a perfect situation."

"I don't know, Mr. Buck. I work all week and the thought of going to another job…"

"Hours are flexible. Santa and Mrs. Claus arrive the Saturday before Thanksgiving, and you'll be there on the weekends only until December 10, but after that it does tend to get hectic and busy, but it's only for about two weeks. *The Enchanted Land of Claus'* final day is December 23. I promise, I'll make it worth your while. All the cookies and hot chocolate you can eat and drink, plus a generous Howardson's discount."

Savannah laughed. "Well, so much for your athletic Mrs. Claus!"

"I think you'll really enjoy it, Savannah. You really seem like you would fit the spirit of Howardson's *Enchanted Land of Claus.*"

"Well, I guess I'd be a fool to turn that down, now wouldn't I, Mr. Buck?" Savannah extended her hand. "I'd love to be your new Mrs. Claus."

CHAPTER 5

ON A GUSTY SATURDAY MORNING ONE WEEK AFTER ACCEPTING Matthew's offer, Savannah walked the mile from her home to Howardson's. Cyclones of dried brown leaves swirled about her as she tightened the scarf around her neck, warding off the morning chill. Savannah enjoyed the brisk cold air, a little cooler than most early November days, and the air was tinged with the unmistakable autumn earthy aromas of woodsmoke, pumpkins, and dried apples. She deeply inhaled the invigorating clear air, filling her lungs and blowing up her cheeks like a squirrel's stocked with nuts, and exhaled a cleansing breath. Feeling even more energized, Savannah picked up her step and walked more vigorously, as the walk gave her time to think about what she had committed herself to for the next several weeks. At the time of Matthew Buck's offer, it sounded fun and he was willing to pay her $20 an hour, plus a 75% store discount. She needed a new parka for her trip and had been eying a snow-white puffer coat with a faux fur-trimmed hood and cuffs since Labor Day. This winter luxury was well out of her price range, but with this part-time gig and the discount, she could afford the coat and maybe even the matching mittens. Savannah envisioned herself walking on The Blue Spruce Inn's miles of wooded trails, with a dusting of fresh snow falling from a winter sky, with one of the inn's golden retrievers by her side. In her mind's eye, she could see and hear shiny black-capped chickadees and downy gray titmice singing, tweeting, and fluttering like tiny winter angels from pine tree to pine tree, chirping their own avian yuletide carols in the sharp cold December air, all the while tucked into her cozy new coat.

The sudden blare of a loud bus horn jolted Savannah from her daydream, and she realized she was standing at the front door of Howardson's. Even at nine o'clock on a Saturday morning the revolving doors were spinning faster than a tornado, with shoppers thrusting each other in and out at a dizzying speed. Savannah grasped the brass vertical handle and pushed herself inside the store and stopped in her tracks in utter amazement.

Every trace of autumn and Halloween had been wiped clean from the counters and floors. At each end of the main information desk stood two ten-foot Fraser fir trees. Icy white lights were expertly threaded throughout the trees, creating the illusion that the teeny sparkling diamonds were sifted like confectioner's sugar onto each dark green branch. In lieu of tinsel and garland was a thick silver and gold sash artistically woven through the branches proclaiming "Howardson's Celebrates the Season." Savannah truly felt she had walked onto a Christmas movie set, and she suspected that this was only a tease. The real extravaganza would be on the third floor, where merchandise had been removed to accommodate *The Enchanted Land of Claus*. It was not yet open to the public, but Matthew had given her the code to the employee elevator which would take her directly into *The Enchanted Land of Claus*, where she had a starring role.

The elevator dinged and the doors opened and what she saw before her eyes took her breath away. Savannah was no longer in Howardson's Emporium. Like Dorothy being whisked over the rainbow, Savannah found herself magically transported to a Christmas wonderland the likes of no other she had ever seen.

Two enormous wooden doors, decorated with winter greenery, stood open to a large area. On each side of the doors were two additional Fraser fir trees festooned with glittery ribbons of red, green, gold and silver and every holiday decoration imaginable. A plush red carpet lay on the floor that would eventually lead customers into *The Enchanted Land of Claus*. A large hand-painted sign was positioned above the doorway proclaiming *The Enchanted Land of Claus*, and like Dorothy stepping on to the first yellow brick of the road leading to Oz, Savannah stepped onto the red carpet and made her way down, according to the giant peppermint candy sign, *Peppermint Stick Stroll*. Walking slowly, she gazed in wonder at this magical transformation. Aisles of computers and electronics had magically morphed into Christmas vignettes—animatronic figures of children skating on frozen ponds, and reindeer and foxes gently bobbing their heads up in holiday greeting. Electric fireplaces festooned with multicolored stockings blazed in hearths. Ambling further down *Peppermint Stick Stroll*, Savannah found herself in front of two of the most magnificent thrones she had ever seen, reminiscent of a museum exhibition. They were identical except for the color—one was upholstered in a rich, red velveteen and the other in a dark pine tree green. They were adorned with faux-gold trim, with snowflakes and Christmas trees carved into gold. A large cushion sat in the middle of the thrones, with two smaller ones at each side, ensuring plenty of room for children to sit upon to tell Santa and Mrs. Claus their most magical Christmas wishes. Huge chandeliers in the shapes of three-dimensional stars hung from the ceiling, glowing bright white, pale yellow, icy blue, and Christmas red, as the serenades of winter birds could be heard among the decorated life-like trees. Savannah thought this could rival one single New York City department store, and

Matthew Buck was nothing short of a creative genius. A feeling of pride surged through Savannah as she recalled what Matthew had said to her about being a part of this cherished tradition and its pure Christmas magic. Savannah then knew she made the right decision in accepting the role of Howardson's Mrs. Claus.

"I hope I can live up to it," she said, still gazing in awe at the momentous display.

"Oh, I think you'll do just fine."

Savannah quickly turned around toward the voice but saw no one, and then, out of nowhere, a woman tiptoed from behind a giant candy cane. She had a bright yellow tape measure hanging around her neck and one of those old-fashioned pin cushions wrapped around a skeletal wrist like an oversized wristwatch. It looked like a huge ripe tomato with multiple pins and sewing needles stuck into it, poking up from inside. She seemed familiar to Savannah, and then Savannah recalled she was the woman who had been tying the bow on the moose's neck shortly before Matthew mugged her.

"Matthew described you very well, I might say. I maybe have to take in the waist a bit and hem the dress a tad, but yes, very good job indeed."

"You must be Fern Rhodes," Savannah said, extending her hand. "Matthew emailed and said you'd be ready to meet with me at 9:30. I know I'm a bit early, so I'm happy to wait." She looked up at the lighted stars and thought she could wait there all day if necessary. It was too beautiful to leave.

"No time like the present," said Fern, marching toward Savannah. "My seamstress workshop is back here. I have your costume already made, and I do believe all I have to do is tweak it a bit and you'll be Mrs. Claus in a jiffy!"

Savannah obediently followed Fern towards the back of *The Enchanted Land of Claus*. Fern slid open a pocket door and proceeded into a small work area full of fabric swatches, measuring tapes, dress mannequins and a large, old-fashioned sewing machine.

"This way, please, and watch your step. I can get a bit messy when I'm working, and I tend to throw things helter skelter. I don't want you to trip, but then again, I guess that's how you ended up here. A fortuitous fall on behalf of Matthew Buck I'd say."

"You heard?" Savannah asked, feeling the heat rise in her cheeks with embarrassment, as it did cause quite the scene that day.

"Of course I heard, and I think it's actually charming." She stepped close to Savannah and got right to work, encircling the tape measure around Savannah's hips.

"Matthew's brilliant, but he can be socially awkward," she said through a mouth full of pins. Savannah worried that Fern may accidentally swallow them, but she adeptly removed them from her mouth and stuck them safely back into her bracelet-like pin cushion.

"Looks like I got your measurements very close to right," she said, walking over to a rack full of costumes hanging on felt hangers. Fern pulled a hanger from the rack containing a dove gray silk covering and plopped it into Savannah's arms.

"Dressing room's right in there," Fern said, pointing to a blue door. "Put it on then come on back out and let's see if it fits properly."

Savannah got the immediate impression that Fern Rhodes was quite the task master and when she discharged an order, it was to be obeyed. Immediately. Where Fern was small in stature, she seemed the type who received the respect she commanded—intimidating but also encouraging. Savannah remembered a vague sort of warning in one of Matthew's emails.

"I've known Fern Rhodes for years, and there's no better seamstress, but she can be a little eccentric. Bear with her and once she warms up to you—and she will—she'll treat you like royalty."

A shiver of excitement coursed through Savannah's hands as she gingerly unzipped the silk dress cover. She already felt she had been given such extraordinary treatment just by having someone create a custom-made dress for her, as everything she bought was straight off the rack. There had never been an occasion in all of Savannah's fifty-three years that she needed something custom made, not even her wedding dress, which was a pretty, white, lace, tea-length dress she purchased in Howardson's bridal salon thirty years ago. It was Savannah's decision to keep her wedding simple, as she and Bradley had just enough money saved for a down payment on a small house outside of Boston. Bradley always told her she never looked more beautiful than she did in that dress, and every year on their wedding anniversary, with the exception of the year she was pregnant with Patrick, she wore the dress for their annual dinner date.

"You never change, Savvy," he'd tell her every year with their champagne toast, she recalled closing the door of Fern's dressing room.

"To my favorite girl in my favorite dress."

Savannah cut a tiny swatch of fabric from the dress and had placed it into Bradley's hands before his casket was closed at his funeral, a piece of their lives together to keep with him for eternity.

"Are you almost done?" Fern's high-pitched squeak of a voice brought Savannah immediately back to the present.

"Just a sec," she breathlessly answered in anticipation of what was inside the silk covering. She pulled down the gold zipper to the end of the bag and spread it aside. Savannah let out a gasp of delight as she gently pulled the dress from the bag. It was spectacular.

The dress was reminiscent of a 1950s swing dress, with a long-sleeved fitted top and a skirt that flared from the hips. The top was crushed velvet while the skirt was a gorgeous silk that was soft as a puppy's fur. The dress was the most beautiful shade of blue Savannah had ever seen, reminding her of a clear winter sky after a snowstorm.

She quickly shed her sweater and jeans and carefully stepped into the dress, sliding her arms into the sleeves and pulling the top over her shoulders. She was just able to reach the zipper in the back and gently pulled it up to her neck. Savannah looked in the mirror, marveling at the reflection before her. The dress hugged her in all the right places, accentuating her hips and bust, but without being too tight or revealing. It hit right at the knee, the skirt billowing and swinging with every move, as snow-white faux fur trimmed the hem and tickled her knees. The collar and cuffs had the same trim as the hem, with tiny glistening white seed pearls sewn under and above the trim giving off sparkles of light, giving the illusion that twinkling stars were sewn into the dress. A rhinestone belt embellished with clear crystals had fallen onto the floor, and Savannah picked it up and fastened it around her waist, making her shimmer like a frozen winter pond. It was a simple design, but the details made it extraordinary.

"I didn't forget your feet," Fern called, "but you'll have to come out of that dressing room to get them."

"I'll be right there," Savannah replied, unable to take her eyes from the mirror's reflection. She hadn't felt this magical since her wedding day.

"Now that's the ticket," Fern said, her head nodding in approval at Savannah's appearance as she walked from the dressing room. "Almost perfect," she declared as she grabbed a large shoe box and handed it to Savannah.

Savannah waded through what seemed like a whole package of white tissue paper before she unburied what was in the box.

"An old cobbler friend of mine made them. They won't be too small, but if they are too big you can wear extra socks. Although something tells me these will fit perfectly."

Savannah pulled out a pair of shearling boots, white as a fluffy winter cloud on a clear cold day. The lining in the boots was the color of the dress with pretty tassels just a shade darker than the dress hanging from the sides. She heard a very faint jingle, and upon taking a closer look, she discovered minuscule silver bells discreetly embroidered into the tassels. Savannah slid them onto her feet and looked into Fern's magic mirror. She was no longer looking at Savannah Brady. She was looking at Mrs. Claus.

"I think just a nip here and a tuck there," Fern said, her hands pulling on the dress and stretching it around Savannah's waist, tugging on the sleeves and puffing out the shoulders.

"Not quite perfect yet, but it will be tomorrow. Are you able to come back then?" asked Fern as she shooed Savannah back into the dressing room to change.

"I'll be here," she told Fern, carefully slipping from the dress.

"Don't bother putting it back in the bag," Fern said."I'll get to work on it soon. Oh! One more thing. How could I have forgotten?" She ran to her sewing table and grabbed a long rectangular white box which she handed to Savannah.

"Totally optional, but I think it completes the outfit." Savannah removed the lid and waded through more endless white tissue to find a pair of white silk gloves. She pulled them onto her hands and the softness was incredible, feeling as if she were not wearing anything at all.

"Might not be too practical when decorating cookies, but I think it adds a nice touch when meeting and greeting," Fern said, watching as Savannah extended her hands in admiration.

"They are just beautiful. I promise to be extra careful," Savannah said, removing the gloves carefully, finger by finger, and gently replacing them inside of the box.

"See ya tomorrow!" And with that, Fern disappeared deep into the back rooms of *The Enchanted Land of Claus*.

"Just like a Christmas elf," Savannah laughed, a feeling of giddiness washing over her. She had something to look forward to now instead of just another weekend of running the same errands and collapsing in front of the TV as the dulcet tones of a home shopping channel anchor droned on about frozen cookie dough and six-foot-long mops until she fell asleep. Soon she would be putting on that most beautiful and magical dress and greeting Howardson's customers as the official Mrs. Claus of *The Enchanted Land of Claus.*

SAVANNAH'S PHONE PINGED AS SHE UNLOCKED THE DOOR OF HER apartment. She had stopped at the grocery store and now her arms were full of bags, almost dropping the bag that contained the eggs. She managed to push the door open with her foot and set the bags on the counter that separated the kitchen from the living room. Thinking it was Patrick, she excitedly pulled the phone from her pocket but saw an unrecognized phone number. As she read the text, she couldn't stop a smile from spreading across her face.

"Fern said the dress was perfect. Get some rest, Mrs. Claus. MB."

"That I will do, MB," she said, smiling, returning the text. A happy excitement she hadn't felt in a long time flooded Savannah, and even the mundaneness of putting groceries away seemed a little more thrilling.

CHAPTER 6

THE SATURDAY BEFORE THANKSGIVING FINALLY ARRIVED. Savannah peered from behind the forest green velvet drape that separated *The Enchanted Land of Claus* from the rest of Howardson's. Excited squeals of children pierced the already charged air, with parents trying to hush them, asking for patience as Santa was almost here.

"Fern," whispered Savannah from the concealed corner behind the thick drape, "there's got to be over one hundred people out there! What have I gotten myself into?" Self-doubt began to seep deeply through Savannah's psyche and suddenly the idea of portraying Mrs. Claus became more mortifying than merry. She was never one for large crowds, but this was no crowd, it was a deluge of holiday shoppers waiting to enter *The Enchanted Land of Claus* and expecting an extravaganza nothing short of spectacular.

"You've gotten yourself into a stunning dress," said Fern, adjusting the seed-pearl collar. "Here, put this on. I just whipped it up last night." Fern handed Savannah a wad of her infamous white tissue paper. Savannah carefully unwrapped it and uncovered a stocking hat made from the same soft velvet of the dress. It was a shade darker blue and had snowflakes embroidered on the top with the effervescent seed pearls sewn intricately into each flake, giving off a sparkling effect. It was trimmed in white faux fur, exactly matching her dress and a huge white pompom dangled from the tail.

Fern stood on a stool and adjusted it on top of Savannah's head.

"You know, I'm not really a hat person," said Savannah as Fern pulled down hard to get the effect she wanted. She tugged the triangular part of the hat down to the left and fluffed up the pompom so would fall right at Savannah's ear, where glittery diamond earrings hung from Savannah's lobes.

"That's the ticket!" Fern said and quickly flashed a mirror in front of Savannah's face.

"See? The finishing touch." Fern whipped the mirror back into her pocket before Savannah could even get a look.

"Five minutes 'til showtime!" Fred called. "Places everyone!" His booming voice and loud hand clapping sent the elves scurrying in different directions—some to the hot chocolate stands, and some to the *Reindeer Village* where mechanical reindeer practiced their take-off skills.

"Mrs. Claus, a word please," Fred took Savannah aside.

"When I pull on the cord, the curtain will slowly open, and you'll be standing in front while the elves will be right behind you ready to escort our guests into *The Enchanted Land of Claus*. When you hear me ring the bell," his large hand pointed to a huge gold bell off to the side, "you'll say 'Welcome, Everyone to *The Enchanted Land of Claus*!' Then the elves will take it from there."

"What? You want me to make an introduction?" Savannah could feel her heart race and her hands start to shake. Public speaking terrified her.

"It's seven words," Fred said counting out the words on his sausage-thick fingers. "Oh, sorry eight. Didn't anyone tell you this?"

Leo suddenly crept up behind him and whispered, "two minutes, Sir."

"No, no one told me anything. Fern..." Savannah turned to ask Fern for some kind of explanation, but she had disappeared, no doubt conveniently hiding behind one of the life-sized candy canes.

"Too late now," said Fred, his burly hands grabbing onto the thick heavy velour rope, slowly pulling it down like Quasimodo in the bell tower. Savannah watched in horror as the drapes slowly opened.

Savannah closed her eyes tightly. This was a once-in-a-lifetime chance for which she was personally chosen, and she wouldn't let Matthew, Howardson's, and most importantly, herself, down. She then heard her mother's voice whisper the words that always encouraged Savannah when she was nervous about presenting projects in elementary school.

"Time to shine, my dear Savannah."

The bell clanged loudly, and two elves suddenly appeared on each side of her. The drapes opened and Savannah found herself extending her arms open in pure delight. Upon seeing what seemed like thousands of smiling faces, any fear or inhibition that consumed Savannah for the last few moments completely vanished. With outstretched arms she happily greeted the eager Howardson's Emporium Christmas customers.

"Welcome, everyone, to *The Enchanted Land of Claus!*"

Savannah Brady's chance of a lifetime had officially begun.

CHAPTER 7

Six exhausting but thrilling hours later, Savannah sat in the employee lounge, her feet propped up on Fern's stool. They were sore and tired from standing for so long, but as weary as she was, Savannah was also exhilarated and felt that with a little rest she could start right back up again—which she would, tomorrow at twelve.

Shoppers still lingered in the store, as it closed at eight pm on Saturdays, but *The Enchanted Land of Claus* closed at six giving the elves plenty of time to spruce up for the following day.

"Oh, thank you," Savannah said as Fern brought over two steaming mugs of peppermint tea.

"This smells heavenly." Savannah inhaled the fragrant scent, and her tiredness melted into relaxation.

"It's my favorite pick me up, next to chocolate," smiled Fern. She was still in her costume of a red velvet sweater and green velour pants and red Santa hat. Savannah had changed out of her dress to keep it clean for tomorrow and was in comfy lavender fleece lounge pants and matching top.

"Fern, it just occurred to me that I didn't see Matthew all day." She took her first sip of tea and was immediately comforted by its warmth as it slid down her throat and into her belly, warming her from the inside out. "You would think of all days he'd be here."

"Oh, he was," Fern replied matter-of-factly. "You were so busy with customers he didn't want to interrupt you from your Mrs. Claus zone, which, I might add, you played with sheer perfection. Well done." She hoisted her teacup in a toast.

"Mrs. Claus zone, I like that. Well, you know how gun shy I was especially…" as Savannah cleared her throat in an 'a-hem,'"no one told me I had to make the first introduction to *The Enchanted Land of Claus*. If I had known that, I may not have done it."

"Oh, precisely," Fern said, gulping the last of her tea. She got up and opened the tea box to make another cup.

"That's why I didn't say anything. As you can probably tell, this is not my first rodeo, and sometimes I find it better to let the important things slip at the last minute and spring it on people when they're not at all expecting it. That's when they deliver, and you most certainly did."

"Not your first rodeo, huh? How many have you ridden in, if you don't mind me asking?" Savannah liked Fern's style of not letting the proverbial cat out of the bag until the last minute; it worked wonders on her because had Savannah known, she would have been grasped by a full-blown anxiety attack that could have rendered her speechless.

"You said you've known Matthew for a long time, too. Did you meet in Chicago?" Savannah still found it strange that Matthew wasn't here, and despite Fern's claims that he was, she still wasn't sure.

Savannah was about to get up when Fern raised her hand.

"Sit. You've done enough for today. Let me get this, as this calls for another cup of tea."

"Thank you, Fern. My feet feel like they are on fire. I don't think they've ever felt this tired!"

"You'll get used to it. Feet are tough."

Fern brought another mug of tea and set it in front of Savannah, who gratefully closed her eyes and let the peppermint scent waft into her nose. Fern sat down opposite her and put down her own oversized mug. 'World's Greatest Seamstress' was painted on it along with a large silver needle with a bright purple piece of thread hanging from its eye.

"Great cup," Savannah said, lifting her own Howardson's mug to her lips. "Where on earth did you get that?"

"Matthew, of course. He gave it to me shortly after I first met him, so many years ago. I was a seamstress at McKinnley's, you know that big chain that rivals Macy's, especially with their own Thanksgiving Day parade? Anyway, I was in my tailoring department. The store had their own line of women's clothing, very popular I might add, and I assisted in designing and sewing. It was a small line and the store wanted everything made right on the premises. It was a little pricier, but top quality, I assure you. One day, this befuddled young man came in wearing the most awful fitting suit I had ever seen. The regular tailor was out sick that day, and I was tasked with measuring him and altering his suit. So, of course, while doing so, we chatted, and he was told by his boss that even though he had talent, he also had to look the part and have a well fitted suit. Well, long story short, you get to know someone very well when you are tailoring a suit for them, and an hour later, we were fast friends. He likes to call me his unofficial aunt, as he was far from home. From the moment I met him I knew he'd work his special magic at McKinnley's, and he most certainly did. His displays became legendary. Look up McKinnley's on that internet of yours and you'll see. Anyway, still making a long story shorter, McKinnley's went bankrupt and we were each awarded the dreaded pink slip. Matthew's college friend then offered him the job here. He negotiated me into his contract, knowing that I had a sister in Boston, and voila, here I am. Couldn't be happier, either." She stopped to sip her tea. "And that, my dear, is the story."

"Wow. That must have been difficult moving from Chicago. It sounds like you lived there for a long time." Savannah said, rubbing her tired feet.

"My sister and I were Army brats so moving around was no big deal. I never married or had a family of my own, and I've quite enjoyed watching Matthew evolve into the star that he has most deservedly become. I know he's very close to his family and he misses his daughter terribly, so I'm glad he finds me that elder person in his life that he can talk to. He's quite the young man, well, maybe not as young as he was, but compared to my seventy-three years, he is."

Savannah almost did a spit take as she was just about to swallow another delicious sip of tea.

"Seventy-three?" Savannah was incredulous. The woman did not have one line on her face and her figure was as lithe as a ballerina's. Her makeup was expertly applied, and she flew around the store as if she had wings on her feet.

Fern smiled. "I know. I owe it all to genetics. My mother was ninety-seven when she passed away, God rest her soul, and she still looked like a spry seventy-five-year-old woman. Still drove her car, too, until she was about ninety-six."

Fern stood up and stretched.

"I also keep working, walk as much as I possibly can, and drink plenty of peppermint green tea. And it keeps me sane, too. Helping to put this together is no easy feat, but like my mother always said, keep your mind thinking and your body moving and you'll have a happy, long life. I think there's absolutely truth in that."

"Fern, you are certainly proof of that," Savannah said, making a mental note to stop at the store for peppermint green tea. If today was any indication of what the next several weeks was going to be like, she needed to buy a case!

"Well, that said, time for me to say good night and see you

tomorrow. Sunday hours start at twelve, so we get a little more shut eye, which, you Mrs. Claus, I think could use."

Fern winked at Savannah. She grabbed her coat and the invisible wings on her feet flew her out of the lounge door.

CHAPTER 8

MATTHEW BUCK WAITED OUTSIDE, HIS CAR RUNNING TO STAVE OFF the cold dark November evening. He glanced at his watch. 7:30 pm. He thought he would have caught Savannah by now, especially after the day she had. He made sure to go unnoticed, disguised as one of *The Enchanted Land of Claus* security guards. Fern designed the Santa's Sheriffs' costumes to look like Christmas cowboys—crushed velvet wine-colored vests over denim shirts and black pants. All the security guards wore trim, short, white beards with green satin Stetson hats trimmed with white fluff, as a black velvet band complete with a shiny, silver buckle wrapped around the brim of the hat. Fern had outdone herself again, as the Howardson's security team made their festive presence known, albeit disguised, just in case they were needed.

Matthew always concealed his presence in all of his displays. He felt if his employees knew the boss was on the floor, they would become self-conscious and not be themselves. This way, he could observe not only the employees' actions, but, even more importantly, the customers', and today, he saw nothing but happy, smiling faces. Of course, there was the occasional toddler who screamed when put on Santa's knee, but other than that, from what he surveyed from underneath his Santa's Sheriff's Stetson, the first day of *The Enchanted Land of Claus* was a huge success.

Matthew especially took note of Savannah. He knew all of the elves, Brock did a marvelous job of portraying Santa, and of course with Fern on the floor, he knew everyone else would be in order. Matthew had taken a huge chance on Savannah, based solely on the color of her hair, but when he saw her greet the visitors that entered those majestic wooden doors, he knew he had made the right choice.

Fern worked her seamstress magic with the dress. It could not have looked more perfect, and its femininity made Savannah all the more attractive. Her hair shimmered like ice against the winter blue velvet as the skirt flowed gracefully over her hips, swishing and swaying with her every move. Her silk-gloved hands greeted customers for hours and her engaging smile never once left her friendly face. He knew when she opened her arms and announced the official opening of *The Enchanted Land of Claus* that he literally stumbled upon the perfect Mrs. Claus. He now wanted to thank her by taking her to dinner, but he had been waiting for almost an hour and still no sign of her. Of course, he could have easily gone into the employee lounge, but even now, at fifty-one years old, Matthew still found himself tongue tied when in the presence of a woman he found captivating. He was professionally successful and had the business world at his feet, but when it came to romantic relationships, he professed himself an utter failure, especially since his divorce, which left him much less confident than he had been when he was younger, and that wasn't saying much either.

Although he had been married and raised a daughter, Matthew still felt like an awkward sixteen-year-old boy about to ask his crush on a date. He never had any confidence in himself when it came to women, but for some reason, he knew women found his shyness attractive. These women Matthew dated had no clue of his insecurities with the opposite sex, that queasy feeling in the pit of his stomach when he was about to meet a date. But Savannah seemed different. He still felt nervous in her presence, but there was also something calming about her demeanor. In the safety of his car, he could always chicken out and zoom off and not be seen. However, if he walked into the lounge and saw her there, Matthew knew he could easily become tongue-tied and would say something insufferable, which he had already done on several occasions in the short time of knowing her. He decided to spare himself any potential humiliation and hunkered down in his car. Thinking he must have missed her, he was about to head for home when a sudden flash of silver caught his eye, and he saw Savannah swing out through the revolving doors of Howardson's.

"Now or never, stupid," he said rolling down he windows of his car.

"Savannah!"

Savannah turned toward the car parked in front of the store. Matthew fumbled with the door and stumbled over his too-long legs upon getting out and almost fell on the curb. He quickly straightened himself up and walked over toward her, hoping she didn't notice his gangly approach.

"Matthew, hello!" Her smile illuminated her face like a starry Christmas night. "I was hoping to see you at some point today, but it was so busy! And, I have to admit, I had a great time. I'm really looking forward to tomorrow. But I am exhausted," she said, dragging out the word, indicating that she was truly bone tired.

"How about a ride home then, the least I could do after a day like today." Dinner was off the menu, for now. He didn't want to keep her out late, and he scolded himself at his foolishness of thinking she'd want to have dinner after such a hectic day, but a ride home might suffice.

"Oh, thanks, that's so sweet. But I need to stop at the store, and I don't want you driving me all over town. I don't mind walking. My feet are rested, and the fresh air would do me some good."

Savannah's green eyes shone with enthusiasm and she didn't seem tired at all. Even after this long first day she was eager and Matthew believed her when she said she couldn't wait to do it all over again tomorrow.

"Walk? After being on your feet all day?" Matthew opened the passenger door of his ten-year-old red Subaru Outback. "It's no imposition. It's the least I could do for such a performance. You were a hit with everyone, Savannah. The feedback has been tremendous."

"Feedback?" Savannah questioned, accepting his offer and getting into the car. "Already?"

"Already," Matthew said, and walked quickly to the driver's side.

"On opening day when customers are leaving, we ask them to fill out a quick survey—the old fashioned way—that's the way Old Man Howardson, I mean, Oliver Howardson, the founder prefers; on a card with a pencil. This gives us a good gauge of what the customers thought. All tens! Everyone loved *The Enchanted Land of Claus* and you as well." He rubbed his cold hands to get the blood circulating.

"I guess your old traditions with new twists were just what the customer ordered." Savannah settled herself into the passenger seat.

"You're what the customers ordered. Where to?"

"Oh, Queensbury Street, but I was going to stop at the Sunflower Market first. I'd like to pick up some peppermint green tea."

"Let me guess," Matthew said, putting the car in drive and taking the first left toward Sunflower Market. "Fern has you addicted."

"She certainly has. And if today was any indication of what tomorrow is going to be like, I'm going to need a storeful!"

The green light turned yellow, and Matthew was glad as it gave him a few extra moments with Savannah. The awkwardness he felt earlier dissipated like falling snowflakes on a Christmas tree. His confidence never failed him when he was talking business, and he could go on forever.

"Well, it's on me. It's the least I can do for such a brava performance today, and as I am sure it will be for the next few weeks." He pulled the car up to the curb, put it in park and let the motor run to keep the car and Savannah warm. "You stay here. I know exactly what to get."

Matthew dashed into the store and straight to the coffee/tea aisle. He purchased this tea for Fern many times, and it did seem like Fern could go through gallons of it, so much so that he told her she was starting to turn as green as the peppermint leaf printed on the box. There were two boxes left so he grabbed them both, paid, and headed back to the car.

"Only two left. Fern must have raided the place already," he said, getting inside and turning toward Savannah. She had fallen asleep. Her silver hair cascaded over the black upholstery of the passenger seat, looking peaceful and angelic.

"C'mon, Mrs. Claus," he said, guiding the car into the street." Let's get you home."

CHAPTER 9

With her thermos of peppermint tea, Savannah was ready for the day. Having the thermos would enable her to slip into the break room for a quick sip whenever she felt the need for a pick me up, along with a bite of some homemade biscotti or chocolate drizzled pretzels that the elves kindly left in the kitchen. Her assignment today was to command the central hot cocoa stand, and when she arrived, huge sterling silver urns were already in place on each end of the table, full of creamy thick hot chocolate delivered from the Yellow Pumpkin. There were several smaller cocoa stands scattered throughout *The Enchanted Land of Claus*, but Savannah was stationed at the main one, where hot chocolate would be served, as well as huge gingerbread cookies ready to be decorated.

"May I decorate a cookie, please?" Savannah had been busy setting out the cookies and decorator icing when she glanced around and saw herself looking down into the prettiest pair of brown eyes she had ever seen. They were perfectly round with gold flecks and large black pupils, like sweet balls of milk chocolate. The little girl had hair to match that was pulled into a long ponytail and tied with a festive, red ribbon. She was dressed in her holiday finery—a pretty tartan red and black skirt with black tights with tiny, embroidered candy canes. She had on a red woolen coat with a reindeer pin at the collar of brown fur, that perfectly matched her eyes and hair. Savannah felt her heart give the familiar tug of melancholy that only a child could do to her, as it made her realize how much she missed her son, her little boy son, especially at this time of the year.

"You certainly may. I'm just about done setting everything up and you, young lady, are my first customer." *The Enchanted Land of Claus* had just opened, and the crowds were yet to come. Fern told her, from experience, not to expect a large crowd until later on the second day and Savannah had to admit she was grateful for the quiet.

Savannah stepped out from behind the table, and saw the little girl held the hand of a teenage girl.

"Are you Mrs. Claus?" the little girl asked. Savannah looked up at the older girl who smiled.

"Why, yes, I am." Savannah couldn't help but smile herself. For a quick moment she felt silly referring to herself as Mrs. Claus, but when a bright smile spread across the little girl's face, the feeling vanished and her motherly instincts kicked in, as she bent down and was eye level with the girl.

"May I ask what your name is? I love your coat. I had one like that when I was little except mine had black furry cuffs and collar."

The little girl looked up to the older girl, who nodded affirmatively.

"I'm Sylvene. And this is my neighbor Molly. She takes care of me sometimes when my mom's at work."

"Well, I am pleased to meet you, Sylvene. And you as well, Molly."

Savannah turned her attention back to Sylvene.

"That's a very pretty name you have," Savannah said softly. It was unusual, but it seemed to fit the little girl.

"Thank you. It's my grandmother's name and my mom's. My grandma is Sylvia and my mom is Jolene. That's how I got named Sylvene!" She smiled a sweet, toothless smile.

Savannah almost blurted out the history of her own name but caught herself as she remembered she was not Savannah Brady while at Howardson's. She was Mrs. Claus.

"Can you make wishes come true, like Santa?" Sylvene's brown eyes became as wide as chocolate saucers.

"Well, you can tell me your wish, Sylvene, and then I can let Santa know what it is. How's that?"

"But this isn't a Christmas wish," Sylvene said, knitting her brown eyebrows together in seriousness. "It's a Thanksgiving wish!"

"Sylvene, I think Mrs. Claus only helps with Christmas wishes," Molly said. Savannah noticed the gentle shake of Molly's head as if she was trying to let Savannah know she did not have to grant a Thanksgiving wish.

"I'd like to hear your Thanksgiving wish, Sylvene." She winked at Molly, letting her know that she was happy to hear Sylvene's wish.

"See, Molly, I told you she'd want to know!"

Savannah was level with Sylvene's chocolate eyes. Her cheeks had a faint blush on her pale face as she leaned in closer to Savannah.

"Mrs. Claus," she whispered, "my mom is hurt, and she won't be able to cook our Thanksgiving dinner. My wish is for my mom to have a nice Thanksgiving. She loves it so much and she loves cooking it, but she can't. Not this year, anyway." Sylvene put her head down and a tiny mittened hand wiped away a tear.

"Who wants to decorate a gingerbread cookie?" Fern's twinkly voice sang from behind the giant snowman from where she seemed to have magically appeared.

"I heard there was a little girl here who wanted to do a little Christmas cookie decorating." Fern held out a large gingerbread man. "This guy here needs some eyes, a nose, a mouth, some toes…"

"Oh, I'll help!" Sylvene danced behind the table with Fern, who also supervised the sprinkling of colored sugar, among other cookie decorating delights. Sylvene then stopped and turned to her babysitter.

"Is it okay that I decorate a cookie, Molly?"

Molly looked toward Savannah for approval, "Mrs. Claus, can Sylvene decorate cookies?"

"She sure can, as long as she makes one for me, too. I get almost as hungry as Santa!"

"Wow!" Sylvene exclaimed excitedly. "Then you might need at least ten!" Fern took the child's coat and gently hung it over a chair, which she moved far enough from the table so no stray icing would hit it. She then took one of the many red and green aprons she had sewn and tied it around Sylvene's waist.

"I'm sorry about that," Molly said, looking over at a very busy Sylvene. A couple of other children were invited to join Fern's decorating party.

"Oh, don't be sorry. What's the matter with her mother?" Savannah felt her heart break at the little girl's wish for her mom.

"Jolene is a nurse and she hurt her knee. She was lifting a heavy patient last week when she tore her anterior cruciate ligament in her knee. She's on bed rest at least for another few weeks and then she needs a series of tests for possible surgery. But right now, it's strictly rest. We live in the same apartment building, and I babysit Sylvene when her mom works late. I go to City College and when I get home, I try to spend time with Sylvene so Jolene can get some rest. As good as Sylvene is, she's still a kid, and Jolene is adamant that she not stay in and worry about her all the time. And I love being with her. She's like the little sister I never had."

"Do they have any family nearby to help?" Savannah asked as she watched the little girl carefully frost a cookie under Fern's expert direction.

"No. Sylvene's dad isn't in the picture and Jolene's parents live in Tennessee. Jolene hasn't even told them that she's hurt. Jolene's sister lives in Texas, and is having a high-risk pregnancy right now, and she didn't want to worry them. They're both so sweet and Jolene is so kind. Sylvene's her whole world. I try to help as much as I can because I really love both of them. We'd have them for Thanksgiving, but we're visiting my grandparents in Rhode Island. My mom's going to bake some pies for them, that we'll drop by before we leave on Wednesday as Jolene said that was all she wanted. I just wish there was more I could do."

Savannah was touched by the young woman's concern for Sylvene and her mother, and she patted Molly's shoulder in understanding.

"Of course you do," she said thoughtfully, watching the little girl laugh with Fern as if she didn't have a care in the world.

"Molly, I'd love to help them. I know you don't know me but I'd like to help them with their Thanksgiving meal…"

"You're Mrs. Claus," Molly interrupted with a bright smile, "It would mean everything to Sylvene if her mom has a happy Thanksgiving. If you give me your number, I can text you Jolene's information."

Savannah pulled out her phone and the two exchanged numbers.

"Well, if Mrs. Claus has anything to do with it, they will have a wonderful Thanksgiving." Savannah resolved that it would be nothing less.

Fern sent Savannah home that evening with two large gingerbread cookies and filled her empty thermos with hot chocolate.

"I hate to waste it, and I don't think you had much to eat all day. Take this home, take off your shoes, and put your feet up and enjoy."

Fern was correct about Savannah not eating, as the day was as busy as ever, and there was no time, save for a sip of tea here and there, for Savannah to take a break. Not that she wanted to—being Mrs. Claus—walking amongst the shoppers, talking with them, decorating cookies, and even listening to the wishes of the younger children who were too scared to visit Santa himself.

It made Savannah realize how much of life she had been truly missing out on, especially during this time of the year when the sun sank lower and faster with each passing day, and darkness descended by four thirty, quickly turning afternoon into evening all too soon. This time of the year was Savannah's hibernation time, as she referred to it. Like an old mother bear, as soon as she got home from the office, she put on her pajamas, curled up with one of Patrick's old stuffed animals for company and slept for no less than ten hours each winter night. But *The Enchanted Land of Claus* was alight in shimmering colorful Christmas lights that glimmered festively throughout the store like the aurora borealis on a northern winter night, instantly brightening Savannah, and she felt herself awakening from her hibernation as if it was springtime again, albeit in December.

Savannah switched on her small electric fireplace and watched the orange flames dance merrily behind the screen. The soothing heat surged onto her bare feet and she felt her muscles loosen and her body relax from the flow of warm air emanating from the heater.

After speaking with Molly, images flashed throughout Savannah's mind of the little girl's face, those eyes the color of Hershey kisses and hair as brown as a baby mink's, and the simple wish of a happy Thanksgiving for her injured mother. She hoped it had not distracted her too much from the other customers, and as Fern predicted, the afternoon was much busier than the morning.

At least she had a few days off now and could recuperate until *The Enchanted Land of Claus* reopened on Friday afternoon. Fortunately, Savannah was able to arrange her work schedule, working longer days Monday through Thursday and leaving earlier on Friday, enabling her not to dip into her vacation time, which she saved so hard for so she could spend a relaxing two weeks at The Blue Spruce Inn.

She abruptly jumped up and grabbed a notebook and pen from her desk as holiday dinner ideas suddenly popped into her head. She had no Thanksgiving plans this year, but now things had changed. Suddenly, there was a turkey to roast, potatoes to mash, and cornbread to bake. At least Sylvene and her mom would feast like royalty if Savannah had her way, and she quickly began making a list of Thanksgiving Day items she would need at the grocery store.

As visions of stuffing and turkeys danced in Savannah's mind, she was deep in thought about Thanksgiving preparations when the shrill ping of her phone made her jump. She reached over the ottoman to retrieve it and saw Matthew's name flash on the screen.

"Another great day, Mrs. Claus. Rest up these next few days. You're gonna need it. Thanks for a job better than well done. MB."

"Rest?" Savannah laughed. "Not Thanksgiving week. I have a dinner to prepare!" Any holiday doldrums that had previously seized Savannah were suddenly unlocked, as the thought of preparing a Thanksgiving feast invigorated her, and her melancholy mood dissipated into simple joy.

Savannah always loved holiday cooking and baking when Patrick was growing up, and never even minded the post-feast clean up. It was the moments she fondly recalled like showing Patrick the turkey in the oven every half hour when she basted it, watching it turn from a light brown to a golden honey bronze to always bestowing the honor of giving her son that first piece of tender roasted meat. The look of appreciation and gratitude on her little boy's face and his oohs and ahhs were all Savannah needed for a happy Thanksgiving. Now, she could do this for a little girl and her mother, making Savannah feel thankful, realizing that her life had taken a most unexpected turn—one for the better, for a change—and she couldn't wait for Mrs. Claus to make her first delivery of the holiday season.

CHAPTER 10

THANKSGIVING MORNING DAWNED BRIGHT AND COLD. SAVANNAH slid the big beauty of the bird into the hot oven, ensuring plenty of leftovers for Sylvene and Jolene at least for the next week. The evening before, Savannah whipped up several pounds of mashed potatoes, stuffing, and butternut squash. Molly and her mother baked pies, and Savannah also made sure to get plenty of cider and a special vintage of Thanksgiving wine for Jolene. Molly alerted Jolene to Mrs. Claus' delivery, but Savannah made them promise not to tell Sylvene, as this was a special surprise for the thoughtful little girl; a visit from Mrs. Claus on Thanksgiving Day.

A tingle of happiness raced through Savannah as she set the timer and made sure she had plenty of basting stock. It was one of those fleeting feelings of happiness that only lasted for a moment and didn't come very often but when it did, Savannah had the feeling that anything that once seemed impossible was now the exact opposite.

"Oh, if only that feeling could be bottled," she said, wiping her hands on her apron, bagging the fancy paper plates and utensils. It was a feeling quick as a shiver, and no phrase described the feeling better than 'live in the moment'—a brief and ephemeral twinkle of happiness, which could easily be forgotten until the next flutter, and when that would happen was impossible to predict.

That quiver of happiness was enough to sustain Savannah as she prepared her feast. Tomorrow, Howardson's would be ramping up the Christmas spirit, and Mrs. Claus would have her hands more than full. She eagerly anticipated her own holiday grand finale, and as soon as *The Enchanted Land of Claus* closed for the season, she would be off to The Blue Spruce Inn.

"It's going to be a busy month, Hon," she said to the photo of Bradley that she kept on the kitchen windowsill above the sink. Her finger gently traced the outline of his face, and Savannah suddenly noticed something was missing—there was no sting of tears at the back of her eyes when she looked at his handsome face—but instead a feeling of gratefulness. She was grateful that she and her husband built a life together, raised a child, and knew the love of a family. Bradley would always be with her, but right now there was no sadness when Savannah looked at the photo, and the deep, dark feeling of anguish she usually felt in the pit of her stomach was replaced by a flash of happiness. She felt the touch of his celestial hand guiding her out of grief and showing her the way back to some kind of peace and tranquility.

Savannah took the photo from the windowsill and gently kissed the picture of her husband.

"Thank you, my love. I know you are always with me." And this time, no tears fell when she looked into the loving face of her deceased husband.

SAVANNAH GAVE HERSELF THE ONCE OVER IN THE FULL-LENGTH mirror bolted behind her bedroom door. *The Enchanted Land of Claus* costumes were not allowed outside of Howardson's, but Fern gave Savannah special permission to take the dress home with her on Wednesday evening. She never really got to see how she actually looked in the dress as she was just jetting to Howardson's from her full-time job, quickly shedding her work clothes, and slipping into costume. She barely remembered how it looked during the first fitting, as so much had happened since then, but now she had the chance to really see what others saw. Fern was an absolutely brilliant seamstress, and she had sized Savannah perfectly simply from Matthew's description. The billowy skirt hit just at her knees and made a pretty swishing sound as she moved. The velvet top shaped her nicely and the seed pearls sparkled like starlight. It was a masterpiece created just for her, or actually Howardson's Mrs. Claus. She spun around and the skirt billowed in the breeze it created, and she felt like Cinderella at the ball.

"Amazing how a dress can transform plain Savannah Brady into glamorous Mrs. Claus," she laughed, the skirt rising and falling like the ocean tides as she spun. It was nothing short of magical, and although she still felt like old Savannah Brady, she swore she could feel the spirit of Mrs. Claus. Somehow this legendary lady Savannah invoked entwined with her own psyche, and with the combination of the two, Savannah felt as if she could grant wishes and perform miracles while wearing that dress. It was most definitely infused with an extraordinary sort of Christmas magic.

"Don't forget the hat," she told herself as she placed it on her head and adjusted the snowball of a pompom until it was perfect, just as Fern would.

"Here goes nothing," she said to her Mrs. Claus reflection, and giving herself the thumbs up, Savannah carefully packed the holiday dinner into large bags, and she was off to make a little girl's Thanksgiving wish come true.

CHAPTER 11

Matthew slammed the brakes of his car and came to an abrupt stop. He was about to run the yellow light, but past experience taught him there was the very strong possibility that a city cop was lying in wait for the one leadfoot to blow through the light on a holiday, even though traffic was practically non-existent. Matthew thought better of it and decided the risk wasn't worth it, especially since he had been lax in getting his Massachusetts driver's license and was still driving with his Illinois one, which might constitute even more grounds for an unwanted and very expensive ticket.

"C'mon, my food's getting cold," he muttered as he impatiently tapped his fingers on the steering wheel. The red light seemed unusually long. Matthew looked from side to side, and making sure there was absolutely no one around, he made the snap decision to go through the light. He was just about to accelerate when a flash of blue caught his eye.

"What the—"

The red light finally turned green, and Matthew steered his car to the curb, towards the blur of blue that beamed before his eyes.

"Savannah?" Matthew said aloud. She was retrieving several shopping bags from the trunk of her car, placing them on the steps of the building in front of her.

Matthew turned off the ignition and jumped out of his car. He shivered fiercely as the cold air slammed through his light fleece jacket, and assailed his body. *What on Earth is she up to?* He thought as he walked over to this woman in blue.

"Well, if it isn't Mrs. Claus," he said, as Savannah sprung around, looking surprised to see him there.

"Well, Happy Thanksgiving, Mr. Buck," she smiled. He laughed to himself as he watched her cheeks turn to the shade of the pink beach roses near his family's home.

"Fern gave me permission to wear the dress outside of the store just for today. I'm doing a favor for one of your most loyal customers," she said tilting her head towards the bags.

"Making a special delivery? I'm happy to help if you need it." He silently hoped she did.

Savannah looked toward her car, and Matthew was struck at the shine of her long silver hair flowing in the late autumn breeze.

"Four hands are better than two, right? I'd love a little help, but I don't want to keep you from any plans."

"No plans for me. Just going to the Yellow Pumpkin to pick up my own dinner." A dinner to eat alone. He couldn't get home for Thanksgiving as his family was a three-hour drive up north, and he needed to be in Howardson's later to prepare for the post-Thanksgiving holiday crowds. Unlike other stores, Howardson's didn't pull all-nighters on Thanksgiving night. The staff would be busy enough for the next few weeks, and Thanksgiving was sadly becoming a forgotten holiday. Employee time with family, according to Corrine's great grandfather Oliver Mathias Howardson, was worth more than a few thousand dollars which the store might or might not make in the wee hours of Black Friday morning. The store was opening at seven thirty, and

Matthew knew he had a long night ahead. A quick takeout at the Yellow Pumpkin would have to suffice for this year.

"Smells like Thanksgiving," he said, grabbing two of the heavy bags from the steps of the building.

"I have to warn you, it's a walk up, no elevator. Can you make three floors with a twenty-pound turkey?" *For that smile,* he thought, *I would walk up twenty-three floors.*

"Let's go," he said, motioning with his head toward the building's doors.

"What in the world are in these?" he laughed, walking into the foyer, shifting the heavy bags in his hands.

Matthew followed as Savannah led the way up the three flights of polished cherry wood stairs.

"Only a gigantic turkey and enough food to last a week. Almost there," Savannah announced as they approached the third and final set of stairs.

Matthew paused on the landing and turned to Savannah, who looked as if she hadn't even broken a sweat.

"These must be some special people," he said, as he felt the perspiration break out on his forehead. He could hear the pounding of his heartbeat in the drums of his ears, and Matthew couldn't determine if it was from the stair climbing with ultra-heavy bags or from being in such close proximity to Savannah.

"I think they are. They gave me a reason to cook Thanksgiving dinner, something I didn't think I'd be doing this year." She looked back at him and smiled. "They gave me a reason to be happy and not be so lonely."

No wonder people are so drawn to you, he thought, turning around and finishing the final flight. *Including me.*

"What number?" he asked as he stopped to catch his breath.

"326. Oh, right here." Savannah knocked on the door and turned to Matthew with an excited smile. He shrugged his shoulders and went along with Savannah's game.

"Mrs. Claus! What are you doing here?" A very pretty little

girl with long, brown hair answered the door. Her wavy chestnut ponytail and big brown eyes instantly reminded Matthew of Athena when she was that age, and for a brief moment he felt flung back in time and was with his little girl once again. The sadness of missing his daughter at the holidays suddenly swelled within him.

Savannah stooped down to the little girl's level.

"You wished for your mom to have a Happy Thanksgiving and Mrs. Claus wanted to make sure your wish came true."

"Come on in, Mrs. Claus," called a voice from inside. Savannah turned her head to Matthew and nodded toward the inside of the apartment.

"What smells so delicious, Mrs. Claus?" asked Sylvene, running excitedly into the dining room where a woman, who Matthew presumed to be Sylvene's mother, was sitting. The girl and woman were mirror images of each other.

"I'm so glad you think it smells good because it's all for you and your mom. Happy Thanksgiving!" Savannah said and started to pull the contents from the bags.

"Oh, I'm sorry, this is Matthew Buck. He's one of Santa's helpers at *The Enchanted Land of Claus*."

Sylvene sidled close to Matthew and examined him from head to toe.

"I've never seen you there," she said. "Fern told me who all the elves were, and I know I've never seen you."

Matthew had almost forgotten what it was like to speak to a child and to one who truly believed in the magic of Santa Claus. He bowed to Sylvene.

"You are correct. You haven't seen me. I am there at night when the store is closed making sure that everything is in order for the next day."

"Oh, you make sure there's plenty of hot chocolate and cookies and decorating stuff?"

"Exactly." He was out of practice talking to children, so he decided to keep his replies short and to the point, lest he slip up, but he had the feeling even if he had, Mrs. Claus would catch him.

"That's right, Sylvene. Mr. Buck is very important and has a big job to do while we are all asleep."

"Thank you, Mr. Buck. I really love it there." She turned and ran toward her mom and gave her a huge hug.

"Happy Thanksgiving, Mom. I wished for you to have a Happy Thanksgiving, and Mrs. Claus made my wish come true."

Sylvene ran toward Savannah, throwing her arms about her, engulfing her in a hug.

"You are very welcome, Sylvene. Now, let's get you two settled so you can eat until you burst!"

"Can you and Mr. Buck stay and have dinner with us," Sylvene asked as she helped Savannah take the food from the bags and set them on the dining room table.

"That's so kind of you, Sylvene, but Mrs. Claus has to give the reindeer their Thanksgiving dinner, and I think Mr. Buck is probably having dinner with his family. This is for you and your mom. You two girls deserve a nice day together."

"That's going to be quite a feast," Matthew said looking at all the food, and thinking the golden-brown turkey looked especially delicious, as did the mashed potatoes, stuffing and cornbread. He suddenly remembered his own dinner order which needed to be picked up, but he didn't want to rush Savannah.

"You two have a wonderful day," Savannah said, as if on cue.

"Mrs. Claus, thank you so much," called Jolene from the dining room table. She began to gingerly get up and Matthew quickly noticed the crutches she was grabbing from behind her. He dashed across the floor to stop her.

"Please, don't get up. We will see ourselves out. Happy Thanksgiving."

The look of gratitude in the woman's eyes was all the thanks Matthew needed.

"Thank you, Mrs. Claus," Sylvene softly said as she wrapped her arms around Savannah's waist. "Thank you for making my wish come true for my mom."

Matthew watched as Savannah hugged the little girl, bending her head to the girl's hair and giving her a sweet kiss.

"Don't eat it all at once," Savannah laughed. "Happy Thanksgiving!"

"Happy Thanksgiving," Matthew said as he joined Savannah at the door. Savannah turned and blew a kiss to the little family and closed the door behind her.

"That was quite the wish," Matthew said as they reached the sidewalk outside of Jolene and Sylvene's apartment. "You cook all that yourself?" Matthew again remembered the dinner he had waiting to pick up.

"I did," Savannah said as she pressed the pad on her car key. "My Thanksgiving plans were waylaid this year, so it was nice to cook for someone else. She's such a sweet girl and when she asked me if I could help her mom have a happy Thanksgiving, well, who could resist those big brown eyes?"

"She certainly is a sweetie," Matthew said. The sky was growing grayer and even had a faint scent of snow. He zipped the collar on his fleece as unexpected words suddenly flew from his mouth.

"If you have no plans, why don't you join me for dinner? I'm picking it up from the Yellow Pumpkin and there will be at least enough for five. What do you say?" There. He asked. He watched her face contort, as if she didn't quite know how to answer.

"Oh, that's very nice of you, but I couldn't. I..."

"If you're going to say I can't impose, well, you're not. There's a common area in my building and we can have dinner there. There's a big fireplace, and it's even decorated. What do you say?" He couldn't believe he not only asked her for dinner but was somewhat insistent upon Savannah accepting. It was as if a holiday spell was cast over him, having him doing things that he most definitely would not even have thought of doing with anyone else. Matthew watched her smile brighten her wind-kissed face and felt his heart skip a beat.

"Well, I was going to say I think I need to rest up for tomorrow, but did you say fireplace? That's something that I really miss. I had one in my old house and there was a fire almost every night from Halloween to St. Patrick's Day. And there's nothing like the scent of woodsmoke."

"I had you pegged for a fireplace type of girl, and I had a feeling that might get you to say yes," Matthew laughed, digging his hands into his pockets to warm them and to secure the handkerchief that always gave him confidence when he needed it most, and this was one of those times.

"Well, I am getting hungry—for both food and a fireplace. I'd love to. Thank you very much."

"Fantastic. I'll pick up the food, My address is 508 Triton Terrace." Matthew gesticulated with his arm on how to get there from Sylvene's house.

"Got it," Savannah said, getting into her car.

"Just let the concierge know you're my guest, and he'll let you into the common area. I'll see you there in about twenty minutes?"

"Twenty minutes," repeated Savannah as she slid into her car. Matthew watched as she turned her car around and headed toward 508 Triton Terrace.

"Thanksgiving dinner with Mrs. Claus," he chuckled as he headed toward his own car. It wasn't going to be such a lonely holiday after all.

CHAPTER 12

"BY THE WAY, THAT IS QUITE THE DRESS YOU'RE WEARING."

Savannah suddenly became aware she was still wearing the Mrs. Claus dress. It didn't occur to her to stop at home to change. Even though it had only been a little more than a week since *The Enchanted Land of Claus* opened, Savannah felt it belonged to her, like her 'second skin' which was how her mother referred to a favorite old sweater: navy blue with loose threads hanging from the cuffs. Savannah could hardly remember her mother being without it from fall to late spring, and now this is how Savannah felt about the dress. It had become a part of her, totally forgetting she had it on.

"I probably should go back and change," she said, watching Matthew pull out the Yellow Pumpkin Thanksgiving dinner fixings. The food smelled heavenly as pangs of hunger thrust through Savannah's stomach. That dry piece of toast at six am no longer staved off her hunger.

"Don't be silly. People don't dress up anymore these days, plus how many people can say they had Thanksgiving dinner with Mrs. Claus? Besides," he said, peeking into the other bags, "aha, plenty of napkins." Matthew pulled out a wad of bright orange-

and chestnut-colored napkins and laid them with a flourish in front of Savannah.

"No worries. And spills or stains can be blamed on me. Just enjoy."

Matthew's smile sent a tiny shock through Savannah, and she hoped he didn't notice the heat she felt creeping into her cheeks. She watched him take out containers of gravy, mashed potatoes, butternut squash, stuffing, and cranberry sauce. He reached into another bag and pulled out a cellophane wrapped platter of carved turkey.

"Ah, and my personal favorite," he laughed as he put two huge, golden-brown turkey legs on the table.

"Those look like something out of King Arthur's court," Savannah chuckled as she helped unwrap the food.

"No kidding," he said, sitting down and helping himself to a huge spoonful of mashed potatoes. "I feel like I need to wear my suit of armor when I eat them. And I'm not kidding—I actually have a suit of armor."

"Oh, I love medieval history. My first dog was a chocolate lab I named Morgaine Le Fay, after King Arthur's half-sister. How did you come across a suit of armor?" she asked, spooning apple-raisin stuffing on top of her sliced turkey.

"Funny you should ask," Matthew laughed, unfurling a napkin and placing it on his lap. "I won it. A knight, or lancer, was my high school mascot and it stood in the entryway of the school. Every graduation one was raffled off—I have no idea where the school got these things—and the year I graduated, I won. And no matter how many times I've moved over the years, Sir Lucan, or Luke, has moved with me. Kind of like my own personal knight in shining armor."

"Sir Lucan?" questioned Savannah. She grabbed another napkin and tucked it into her collar, ensuring that not a drop of gravy would drip on the precious dress.

"One of Arthur's less famous knights, known for his loyalty, especially devoted to Arthur during his skirmishes with Lancelot. Faithful to the end."

Savannah lifted her glass in a toast.

"To Sir Lucan, the most faithful wearer of armor a king could ask for."

"To Sir Lucan," smiled Matthew, clinking his glass of amber cider with Savannah's.

Matthew reached for a handful of napkins.

"Laura, the manager, knows I'm a slob, so she really stepped up for the holiday," he laughed, handing Savannah more napkins.

"Well, thank you, Sir Matthew," Savannah replied, rising from her chair and bowing in a curtsey before him.

"One can never be too careful," Savannah said, seating herself, taking several more napkins and heaping them on her lap.

"I might look ridiculous, but this dress is going to see a big day tomorrow and no one wants to see Mrs. Claus with gravy stains on her dress. Besides, Fern will kill me," she laughed, helping herself to the potatoes and gravy.

"So," Savannah said in between delicious mouthfuls of turkey, "you need to be back in the store later tonight?"

"I do," he said, taking a sip of cider. "I'll be back at about three am, with a small crew just to make sure everything is in working order. Believe it or not, we still haven't seen the crowds yet, as there are some people who absolutely refuse to Christmas shop until the day after Thanksgiving. Those are our hard traditionalists that we want coming back, hence the old traditions part of old traditions, new twists. So, you'll need your rest tonight, Mrs. Claus."

"Well, I intend to get it. Just me and my book then lights out." Without warning, a bolt of debilitating melancholy struck. Savannah bent her head and put her hands to her eyes. She inhaled deeply, trying to focus on her dinner, but she was overcome with a sudden sadness—something she thought she had conquered, but evidently that was not the case.

"I'm sorry, Savannah. Did I say something to upset you?" asked Matthew. She could hear the concern in his voice, and as quickly as it struck her, the sadness suddenly evaporated.

"No, it's not you. It's me." She took a deep breath and feeling that Matthew was someone she could talk to, she began her confession.

"I've been widowed for two years now, and holidays have been hard since my husband passed. And this year, my son started a job in Switzerland, and it's the first time we've spent a holiday apart. Cooking for Sylvene and Jolene was such a welcomed distraction. I guess this room, so festive and with a fireplace, well, it reminds me of happier times, I thought I would be able to make it through the day without crying, but, well, I got close." She forced a smile but when feelings of loneliness suddenly took their siege, Savannah was rendered powerless in stopping them.

"Well, that makes two of us," Matthew said, pulling his chair closer to the table and resting his elbows on the side of his plate.

"I'm divorced, and according to my wife, or ex-wife, she and I should never have married in the first place, but we did, and I can't say I regret it because I have a beautiful daughter. She's with her mother in London. My ex manages one of those huge hotel chains there. Summer, my ex-wife is a good mother, and she and Athena are very close. It hurt like hell when Athena told me she wanted to try and live in London instead of staying in the States, but turns out she loves it. She's a horse lover, and she is becoming quite the equestrienne. I visited before I started at Howardson's, and it's as if she belongs there. You know, the quintessential English country house with the greenest fields imaginable for riding all day. I miss her like crazy, but I'm glad for her, too. I know she's happy, but, well, call me selfish, I'd give anything to be spending the holidays with her."

Savannah's sadness lifted, realizing she wasn't the only one alone on Thanksgiving.

"When my son moved earlier this year, and I knew he wouldn't make it home for the holidays, I booked a Christmas vacation in the wilds of the White Mountains at The Blue Spruce Inn. It sounds like a fairy tale Christmas, and I could use that right about now. The family who runs the inn raises golden retrievers who hike with the guests. I especially can't wait for that. I miss my own dog so much."

Savannah noticed a slight smile form on Matthew's face.

"Have you heard of The Blue Spruce Inn?"

"It sounds very familiar. My family lives a few hours north in the middle of nowhere." Savannah watched as his face brightened with the mention of his family.

"I'm glad you have family relatively close by. I think that helps. Especially during the holidays."

Savannah poured herself another glass of cider.

"Me and my Christmas fantasies. Please stop me if you've heard enough."

"I love Christmas fantasies—obviously, as I created one—and dogs too." Matthew said, "but with my lifestyle right now, especially trying to get to London as often as possible, well, there's barely time to breathe. But my mother has dogs up there in the mountains, and they're mine again whenever I visit. Best of both worlds, you could say."

Savannah turned toward the bonging of the huge clock above the fireplace. It was already five o'clock and darkness was quickly descending, as the soft glow of candlelight descended upon the room, and another couple arrived and sat in front of the fire.

"Well, Matthew, I think I should get myself home. It's going to be a busy day tomorrow."

Matthew rose from his seat, brushed his hands on his pants and put his hands inside of his trouser pockets, immediately comforted by the handkerchief.

"Let me help you clear…"

"Absolutely not. You were my guest, and great company for

this single dad. Plus, you cooked an entire Thanksgiving dinner for people you hardly know and did me the great favor of sparing me a holiday spent only with Sir Luke. That's very selfless of you, Savannah. I should be thanking you."

Savannah was touched by his words and a bit embarrassed, and she felt her cheeks turn warm at his words, leaving her almost tongue-tied herself.

"Well, good night and thanks again." Savannah walked toward the front door.

"Savannah, wait!" Matthew shouted as she opened the door. A cold breeze ripped into the entryway, sending shivers through Savannah's body. Or was the quavering more of a result of hearing him call her name?

"My mother would box my ears if she found out I didn't escort a lady to her car. And Mrs. Claus at that!" He took the door from Savannah and let her step outside. The air was frosty and the sky arcing from the light lavender of sunset to the inky blue of dusk. Bold hues of dark pink and purple fringes could be seen on the horizon, but for all intents and purposes, the pleasant Thanksgiving afternoon had morphed into Thanksgiving evening, and was ending all too quickly.

Savannah pressed the car keypad, sounding the loud beep and the click of her car opening. Matthew opened the driver door for her, and she got inside the frigid car.

"Thanks again, Matthew. You certainly made my Thanksgiving less lonely." She smiled, her heart lifting in happiness.

"Likewise," Matthew said, closing the car door.

Savannah rolled down the window. Her eyes locked with his, as her heartbeat accelerated. What was happening?

"M'lady, I thank thee for a lovely holiday and bid you a fond farewell." Matthew took Savannah's hand that was resting on the car door and gently raised it to his lips and lightly kissed it.

Savannah trembled as she slowly slipped her hand from his and turned up the soft fur collar of the dress.

Did he feel it too? She thought as a current of sharp electricity ran through her body.

"Fare thee well, Sir Matthew," she laughed, inserting the key into the ignition.

"What a couple of nerds, huh?" Matthew laughed as he pulled away from Savannah's car, his smile lighting up the dark late autumn afternoon.

"Mrs. Claus is no nerd, Sir. Savannah Brady well, that's a different story. See you tomorrow. Happy Thanksgiving and thanks so much again!"

Savannah gave a little wave, rolled up the window and pulled out into the street toward home. She could see Matthew in her rearview mirror until she signaled and took the turn that would take her home, and out of his sight.

Later that evening, Savannah snuggled under her thick quilt, a gift from Patrick, a constant reminder of the love of her son. It was the afternoon of his departure, and they had strolled past Howardson's. The window display featured a bedroom decorated in the most pretty and calming hues: Light green fluttery curtains the color of newly sprouted grass hung from a window. A glider the color of pink sherbet was nestled in the corner near the window, but it was the bed that was the main feature of the window display, and it was adorned with the most beautiful quilt Savannah had ever seen. It had a pale blue background the color of an early morning summer sky with big bright sunflowers stitched into the corners with an extra-large one right in the center. The sunflowers' tender brown faces were framed by delicate triangular petals the color of summer sunshine and their long slender emerald stems and leaves stretched as if reaching for the sunny sky.

Savannah's grandmother was a master quilter and as many

times as she tried to learn from her, Savannah didn't have the patience. She became easily disgruntled when her stitching wasn't straight, or if the simple design of a five-pointed star looked more like a meteor shower, and she would throw down her needle and thread and thump off in frustration. As much as she wanted, Savannah just was not able to sit still and sew. If she was going to sit, she'd prefer to have a book in her hand, where she could solve mysteries alongside Nancy Drew or pretend to be the fifth March sister. Reading brought Savannah instant joy and gratification, but stitching irritated her, and she was unable to see the prospect of beauty that little stitches would eventually create. But, oh, how she wished she possessed the fortitude it took for the simple patience of her grandmother to create an heirloom to last generations. If only she could make that beautiful quilt in the window.

But Savannah couldn't. The day after their farewell lunch, a Howardson's delivery truck left a large package at Savannah's door. She couldn't imagine what it could be, and when she opened it and removed the beautifully wrapped quilt, tears instantly sprang from her eyes. A large envelope had been taped to the package. She opened this just as carefully, and gently pulled out a card. It wasn't the run of the mill flat type but one that was three-dimensional. She folded it according to the directions, and she soon had a sweet bouquet of sunflowers tucked inside of a blue wooden box. There was a flap on the center of the box part of the card, and when she flipped it open she read:

A bouquet that will last for every season of the year. Enjoy your new quilt.

All my love, Patrick.

It was as if her little boy's arms were wrapped around her whenever she ensconced herself in her quilt. And now, this peaceful Thanksgiving evening, she was able to reflect on the holiday, grateful being able to grant the wish of a child and grateful as well to have had an unexpected holiday dinner with a soul as lonely as her own.

Savannah knew sleep was a necessity tonight, but she was restless and too excited to get to bed just yet and decided to do a little prepping for the long day ahead. She pulled out a foot bath from her closet she received a couple of Christmases ago in a Yankee Swap at her office.

"Maybe some foot massaging will relax me, oh, and some candles, too," she said, lighting sea blue ocean-scented candles.

"I never thought I'd use this," she laughed, the rippling warm water gently soothing her feet. She sat on her couch and closed her eyes, imagining herself standing in the surf at magical Tybee Island. Her parents brought her there for their fifteenth wedding anniversary when she was fourteen, so many years ago. She could still recall standing right at the shoreline with the salty ocean water tickling her toes and the breeze of the spraying ocean mist on her face and hair. The sea breeze candles worked to recapture the atmosphere of the coastal city for which she was named.

Savannah then recalled her mother's favorite story of the city in which she met the love of her life.

SAVANNAH'S MOTHER, CECILIA, PLANNED A WEEKEND VISIT WITH her best friend, Delphina, who had moved to the city when she married the previous year. As the warm water lapped at her feet, Savannah could hear her mother's wistful voice recall the day, as her mother always said, "that changed my life forever."

"It was the last weekend in April," Cecilia would begin, "and the weather could not have been more perfect. The sun was shining, and the sky was a brilliant blue. The air was warm, with just a touch of humidity, nothing like what would follow in the summer. It was just wonderful weather and all I wanted was to be outside.

"Such sweet tropical exotic scents I never experienced rode in on every breeze. Camellias, and the azaleas, oh, the azaleas. The prettiest pinks, purples, and even red and yellow. And the tea olive trees. Their scent is indescribable, and I can only say it is the scent of heaven. And when I stepped off that train and saw my first palm tree swaying gracefully in the Georgia breeze, I just fell in love.

"Delphina and I were walking down ultra-fancy Broughton Street, happily window shopping, which was all we could afford, when the pretty, bright spring sky suddenly turned coal black. Out of nowhere, thick sheets of rain slashed from the sky, but we were lucky enough to be able to duck under the awning of a storefront. Of course we were not the only ones with that brilliant idea. I was so mesmerized watching the huge slate gray clouds scurry through the sky that I lost sight of Delphina. Just as I realized this, I felt myself being pushed onto the wet pavement, falling down as hard as the rain. I can still feel that unexpected sensation of losing my balance and landing right on my backside. Very fortunately, not so hard that I broke anything, thank the Lord, but hard enough that I was sore for days.

"'I'm sorry, I'm so sorry,' was all I heard and when I looked up, I thought the storm had passed and the sky cleared as I was staring into the brightest pair of green eyes I had ever seen. Eyes just like yours, Savannah, dear.

"This pair of green eyes got closer to mine, as strong arms gently took hold of my shoulders and pulled me upright. This green-eyed man was being so polite and careful and ever so apologetic, never mind handsome as could be. Those green eyes sat in a ruddy-complected face surrounded by hair that was as black as the stormy sky. His smile was so sweet and friendly, well, I knew then and there, this was the man for me.

"Then next thing I know Delphina appears calling 'Sean Gallagher, what in the world!' She hadn't been in Savannah a year and she had already picked up a Southern accent, and I almost didn't recognize her voice. 'What have you done to my friend?' I could see the smile behind her feigned anger but decided to play along.

'Delphina, all this talk of Southern gentlemanly-ness and chivalry. This man knocked me off my feet!'

I saw the twinkle in those emerald green eyes of his, and I knew right there this man would be my husband.

"Well, Delphina was blathering on about something but neither I nor Sean heard her, we were just lost in each other. Evidently, he had been invited to the little party she was giving me before I headed back to Boston, and she invited Sean because he was heading up north in the fall for a job, and Delphina wanted to be sure he knew at least one person in the cold unfriendly North. That night at the party, if there was anyone else there, we didn't notice.

We exchanged addresses and we wrote to each other until he arrived, and from that moment on, we were inseparable. My parents were none too happy about me spending all this time with someone I barely knew, but they were ever so wrong. I knew this man the moment I first looked into his handsome face, and we married on the day we met one year later. We thought we were happy until you came along, and then we really knew what happiness was. I always told your father if it's a girl we are going to name her Savannah Georgia Gallagher. I always joked with him, telling him that way he'd never forget where we met. And he'd always say back to me, 'I would never forget where I met the love of my life.'"

Savannah's eyes moistened with tears, recalling her mother's face whenever she told Savannah the story of how her parents met, that pure and honest look of love that always softened the sadness behind her mother's eyes when she spoke of her husband after he passed away. Sean and Cecilia were married fifty years. Cecilia was never quite the same after Sean's death, and Savannah swore her mother died of a broken heart, joining her beloved husband in heaven one year later.

Savannah missed her parents terribly, and she needed them so much when Bradley died, but she was always certain of two things: That they were now and forever together, and that Savannah knew they were with her during those dark days after Bradley's passing.

Run-of-the-mill grotesque horrors of girlhood such as snakes, bee stings or the boogeyman never terrified Savannah as they did her friends. But one thing did: her parents dying. She prayed she would be married with children of her own when that day came, which it did when Savannah was a wife and mother, but throughout her childhood, losing her parents was the stuff of her nightmares.

During one especially petrifying nightmare that Savannah could still recall to this day, she woke up in a cold sweat, having just dreamed her parents were dead. She woke up screaming uncontrollably and sobbing so hard she could not catch her breath and found herself in the throes of a full-blown anxiety attack. Her eyes were shut so tight they hurt, tears streaming down her face, and she could not control the violent shaking of her body.

Cecilia rushed into her daughter's room and flicked on the light, trying to console her daughter. Savannah opened her eyes and her heart slowed. The clean scent of her mother's perfume, and the comfort of her soft arms safely in her mother's embrace, brought Savannah out of her nightmare and back into reality. It was nothing but a horrible dream. Her mother was at her side, and her father, who could sleep through a hurricane, was tucked under the blankets in his bed, and her mother gently rocked and soothed her daughter.

"I know it was a bad dream, Savannah, dear, but I want you to remember one thing." Her mother's voice was calm and loving and she kissed Savannah's tear-stained face, while listening to her daughter relive the terror of her dream.

"Your father and I are not going anywhere for a very long

time, and when we do, you will have a family of your own who will be there to comfort you. But take comfort, my sweet daughter, in knowing that your father and I might not physically be here for you, we will still always be with you. Any kind of help you may need, you just call on us, and we will be there for you. Never, ever worry about that."

Savannah's mother had kept her promise. Whenever dark times descended upon Savannah, a sign from her mother would unfailingly appear. Cecilia's birthdate, June 27, was important to her mother and she always used it for her pin number and occasionally played it in the lottery. Shortly after Bradley's death, when Savannah was in the dark grips of grief, 627 suddenly appeared everywhere—in the license plate of the car in front of her when she was sitting in traffic, in the phone number of a TV infomercial, or the expiration date of a box of pancake mix. Savannah knew it was never a coincidence—whenever Savannah felt at her lowest—627 would appear, and she knew her mother was with her so much so that whenever she glanced at the clock in the morning or evening and it was 6:27, or if the number appeared on a receipt, she always smiled and said "Hi, Mom." Even in death, Cecilia Gallagher kept her promise to her daughter.

Savannah glanced at the clock. 6:27 pm.

"Hi, Mom," she smiled, sighing aloud, thinking of when she could return to her namesake piece of paradise. All of her extra cash she made at Howardson's just paid for her Christmas vacation, so if she had any left over, she would start a Savannah, Georgia fund for her next vacation.

"One has to have something to look forward to," she said as she inhaled the calming sea-salt scent of the candles. She closed her eyes and let her mind unwind, thinking of the majestic wooden doors opening on the biggest shopping day of the year, and *The Enchanted Land of Claus*, Black Friday edition, would spring to life. As busy as it was before Thanksgiving, Savannah had a feeling Matthew was right, and that the crowds at Howardson's pre-Thanksgiving would be nothing compared to the truly official start of the Howardson's Christmas shopping season. Savannah knew, as she felt her eyes grow heavy, there was no place she would rather be than *The Enchanted Land of Claus.*

CHAPTER 13

THE LINE BEGAN TO FORM AN HOUR BEFORE *THE ENCHANTED LAND of Claus* officially opened, and snaked all the way back to the escalator, seeming endless. Savannah couldn't ever remember seeing a store so crowded on the start of Black Friday weekend. Matthew's overnight crew had done an outstanding job by adding several more hot chocolate stations as well as extra cookie decorating tables, along with make-your-own ornament crafts tables, and gift-wrapping exhibits. Additional lights had been strung and more animatronic creatures were added, including a family of penguins skating on a frozen pond, a polar bear with a tartan ribbon tied festively about its neck that jingled as the bear slowly moved its head back and forth, while Christmas red cardinals chirped from the ceiling high decorated trees.

"This is really what the North Pole must be like," Savannah laughed during a short break, when she caught Fern in the lounge chugging down a cup of peppermint tea.

"The elves are working their Christmas butts off!" Fern exclaimed in between sips. "Break time's over!" Fern declared, rinsing her empty cup in the sink and dashing back out to the front lines.

That was the first and last time Savannah chatted with Fern the entire day. Photo ops with Santa enabled her to sit for short periods, but for much of the day she was on her feet greeting customers, serving hot chocolate, and decorating cookies. It was non-stop, and Savannah loved every second of it, even though her feet and legs ached in places she didn't even know existed. During that rare moment of slow down, she had searched for Matthew but figured he must have been busy with the engineering and computers, and she was so busy herself that even if she did see him, there would be no time to chat.

A small sting of disappointment nipped Savannah at not seeing him, but any thought of Matthew was quickly forgotten when one of the hot chocolate spigots got stuck and chocolate oozed all over the floor, creating a muddy chocolate river right in the middle of *The Enchanted Land of Claus*. A tall gangly elf magically appeared with a roll of paper towels, and the mess was instantly cleaned as another urn was brought into action. Savannah loved those little moments of mishaps because, they not only made her laugh, thoughts of Matthew, like the muddy floor, were wiped clean from her mind. He had *The Enchanted Land of Claus* so well run, that when sprinkles were spilled, or thrown, and more cups or cookies were needed, the empty supply was filled practically immediately, and that was no small feat. *The Enchanted Land of Claus* staff were absolute professionals, and their dedication to ensuring all customers' happiness was above and beyond, and that was all thanks to Matthew Buck. It was he who hired everyone, including Savannah, and he expected nothing less than perfection, and what he wanted was absolutely delivered.

. . .

LATER THAT EVENING, SAVANNAH PULLED HER FEET OUT OF THE foot bath and dried them with a fluffy blue towel. She massaged some peppermint foot cream into the soles of her feet, letting the tingling cream warm and relax her tired aching muscles. The comforting scent made her want a cup of peppermint tea to warm and tingle her insides as well, so Savannah slid her feet into cozy shearling slippers and padded to the kitchen. With tea in hand, Savannah flicked on the TV and found an old nameless Christmas movie in which Santa was having trouble packing his sleigh, and that was the last thing Savannah remembered as she drifted into a deep sleep full of dreams starring snowmen, pine trees, giant candy canes, and Matthew Buck.

"ANOTHER BIG DAY," FERN SAID, PEEKING FROM BEHIND THE THICK drapes. "Hope you got your beauty sleep last night, Mrs. Claus."

"I most certainly did," she said, putting on her best Mrs. Claus voice. "Mrs. Claus is ready to face another day in *The Enchanted Land of Claus*. Let's roll!"

Fern straightened the red ribbon around her neck, and Savannah couldn't help but think she had to have been an elf in another lifetime. She looked just like one, acted like one, and her elfin hands could whip up a Christmas hat or mittens in what seemed like minutes. Fern herself was pure Christmas magic.

"Have you seen Matthew lately?" Savannah innocently asked as she looked at herself in the mirror, straightening her own hat. Although she had seen him two days ago, she was looking forward to thanking him again for not only what turned out to be a wonderful meal, but for his company as well. Delivering Thanksgiving to Sylvene and Jolene had only taken up part of her day; after the cooking and cleaning had been done and the delivery made, Savannah was still faced with a long holiday afternoon spent alone, and she knew if she couldn't keep herself busy, she could easily wander into the past where she had lived the quintessential Rockwellian Thanksgiving, surrounded by the people she loved most. Pangs of despair had stabbed at Savannah as she parked in front of Sylvene's building. She wanted to make the delivery short and sweet, as she wanted the day to be just for Jolene and her daughter, and the thought of returning to a lonely and empty apartment was something Savannah dreaded. And then, like an angel descended from heaven, Matthew was by her side helping her unload her car, saving her from the sad prospect of a holiday spent alone, by inviting her to Thanksgiving dinner. Savannah's Thanksgiving holiday morphed from sad and lonely to warm and wonderful, and she felt she owed Matthew a debt of gratitude.

Savannah knew Matthew was here most of the night and that he was probably fantastically busy, but she wouldn't have minded saying hello to those sea-glass eyes that merrily crinkled when he smiled.

"Oh, he's around somewhere," Fern said matter-of-factly as she grabbed onto the handle of the wooden door."I'm sure he'll come up for air at some point." Fern looked at her watch. " Twenty seconds and counting," she announced as everyone lined up to greet the visitors anxiously waiting to enter *The Enchanted Land of Claus*. Fern turned toward the elves and sheriffs and lifted her arms up for the opening cheer.

"Okay everyone! Hands in the middle. Five, four, three, two one! Howardson's Christmas season has begun!" With an exaggerated flourish of arms, Fern pulled the drapes open as excited patrons rushed into *The Enchanted Land of Claus*.

Savannah was replenishing the cookie station when she felt a tug on her skirt grabbing her attention. She turned to see Sylvene, once again dressed in her holiday finest. This time the little girl had her brown hair in two ponytails tied with frosty thick blue ribbons imprinted with pictures of reindeer. She wore a pretty white coat, with an old-fashioned Santa pinned to her lapel. Savannah remembered she had a similar pin when she was

Sylvene's age, and when the red string under Santa's beard was pulled, his nose lit up a bright cherry red. Jolene was standing protectively behind her daughter, her hand resting on Sylvene's shoulder, with a crutch under the opposite arm.

"Sylvene, I'm so happy to see you!" Savannah was delighted her new friend had stopped by and she slipped a cookie from the tray into the little girl's hands.

"A little surprise from Mrs. Claus," Savannah whispered. A pure look of delight spread across the little girl's face, and once again, Savannah felt Sylvene's small arms engulf her waist in a grateful embrace.

"Thank you again for Thanksgiving. We ate it all up!"

"Well, we're getting there. And quickly!" Jolene laughed. "We truly cannot thank you enough, Mrs. Claus."

"You are both very welcome. Now, let's get ready for Christmas! Sylvene, have you visited with Santa yet?"

Sylvene shook her head, her brown ponytails swung with each shake. "Not yet," she whispered, looking up toward her mother.

"She's a bit nervous talking to Santa," Jolene said, leaning on her crutch.

"Could I tell you instead of Santa?" Sylvene's Hershey kiss eyes never failed to tug at Savannah's heart. It was nearly impossible for Savannah to refuse the child, but she also didn't want to let Sylvene believe she could grant her every wish. Cooking up a Thanksgiving dinner was one thing, but Christmas wishes were reserved for Santa.

"Why don't we go together and visit with Santa?" Savannah said, stretching her hand toward Sylvene.

"No thank you," she said. The little girl looked downcast, but then suddenly her eyes twinkled with mischief, and she looked toward her mother and then Savannah.

"What if I wrote Santa a letter and gave it to you to give to him for me? Would that be okay?"

Whew, Savannah thought. *Off the Christmas ornament hook for that one!*

"That's a wonderful idea. Next time you come by you can give it to me, and I will personally take it to him myself. How's that?"

Savannah watched as Sylvene's smile, bright as a string of Christmas lights, illuminated her face.

"Yeah! C'mon, Mom," Sylvene said, tugging at Jolene's coat hem. "We have to go home and write to Santa!"

Jolene hobbled closer to Savannah, out of Sylvene's earshot, who suddenly became mesmerized by a mechanical reindeer.

"Thank you so much. Sylvene says that Santa reminds her of her great-granddaddy, who passed last summer. My grandfather had a white beard and glasses, but was only 140 pounds soaking wet. But nonetheless, talking with Santa she says will make her miss great granddaddy."

"I understand," Savannah gently said, giving a comforting squeeze to Jolene's shoulder. "Whenever she's ready, I'll be here."

"Oh!" Savannah exclaimed, it dawning on her that Jolene was out of her apartment. "It's good to see you up and about! Are you feeling better?"

"Oh, I am. I got the okay from my doctor to get out a bit. It took a while getting down the stairs, but as you know, I have my own little nurse-in-training, and as long as I go slowly, I'm fine. Besides, I was not going to miss all of this!"

"It's quite amazing, isn't it?"

"No wonder Sylvene can't stay away. And thank you so much again, for Thanksgiving. It was beyond thoughtful."

"You're very welcome." Savannah kept her response short to keep her own emotions in check.

"Bye, Mrs. Claus," Sylvene sang, taking hold of her mother's hand, walking through the wooden doors of *The Enchanted Land of Claus.*

"Your number one fan, I see."

Savannah couldn't suppress the smile that began to form on

her face upon hearing Matthew's voice behind her. She gave her skirt a twirl around only to find herself face to face with a mustachioed man dressed as one of Santa's Sheriffs. If it weren't for the familiar voice, she would never have recognized him, as he was decked out in the Howardson's Christmas security costume.

"Sheriff Sugar Plum?" Savannah couldn't help but laugh at Matthew's Santa Security name tag. "I think that fits you very well for some reason."

"Okay, okay, Ms. C.," Matthew laughed and leaned in closer to Savannah's ear. She could feel the goosebumps rise on the back of her neck at his nearness, and the smell of his aftershave awoke the dormant butterflies in her stomach, a sensation that shocked and surprised Savannah.

"You know that if I had my way, I'd be Sheriff Candy Cane, but Fern bestowed that honor upon Leo."

He sighed exaggeratedly. "Ah, what can you do? She must think I look more like a sugar plum than a candy cane. What is a sugar plum anyway?"

Savannah laughed. "Well, Leo is taller and definitely more shaped like a candy cane. Plus, he has that mop of red hair, so I'd say Fern absolutely made the right choice."

Matthew conceded and shook his head in agreement, the tiny round silver bells hanging from the brim of his cowboy hat jingling musically as he shook his head, making Savannah laugh even harder. Just the other day they were chatting solemnly about missing family and now, this stoic man was dressed like an over-the-top country superstar with bells on his hat, no less.

"I see our little friend has been by to say hello."

"Sylvene is definitely our number one fan, although she's not the only one. I do see many repeat customers," she said, waving to several familiar faces.

"She's too shy to speak to Santa because he reminds her of her great grandfather who recently passed away." Savannah felt a tug of sadness pull at her heart, as she certainly could empathize with Sylvene over the loss of a loved one.

"Well, I get that," Matthew said, straightening his mustache. "My own grandfather's been gone for quite some time now, and I still miss him. He was my best friend growing up."

Savannah took a deep breath, desperately wanting to change the subject of the losses of loved ones.

"On a happier note, she is writing her letter to Santa, and she has chosen me to be her personal postmistress."

"Well, I couldn't think of a better courier." The static of Matthew's walkie talkie broke into the air. He reached from his pocket and pulled out a red walkie talkie with a flashing green screen.

"Sheriff Sugar Plum copy, Sheriff Sugar Plum." The static stopped and Matthew spoke.

"Matthew here, ah, I mean Sheriff Sugar Plum. What's up, Leo, oh, I mean Sheriff Candy Cane," he asked, giving Savannah a conspiratorial wink, which furiously jolted the butterflies in her stomach, their wings beating furiously against her insides.

"Copy Sheriff Sugar Plum. One of the mechanical snowman's arms is swinging wildly and is out of control, throwing snowballs everywhere. The customers think it's a riot and are starting to throw the snowballs back, and this is presenting a dangerous situation. He's lobbing styrofoam snowballs left and right, Sheriff Sugar Plum. Location is 4B."

"I'm on it, Leo—Sheriff Candy Cane," Matthew put the contraption back in his pocket.

"Duty calls for Sheriff Sugar Plum," he announced, saluting to Savannah.

"By all means," Savannah laughed. "We can't have any wayward snowmen tearing up *The Enchanted Land of Claus*."

"No, Ma'am, we cannot." Matthew bowed with an exaggerated flourish and was off to save the patrons of *The Enchanted Land of Claus* from a snowman run amuck.

CHAPTER 14

"I'LL PUT ON THE PEPPERMINT TEA KETTLE," FERN WHISPERED TO Savannah. It was almost closing time and the last of the day's customers were slowly flocking from *The Enchanted Land of Claus*, waving goodbye to the elves and Mrs. Claus, and promising to return soon.

Savannah said goodbye to everyone before retreating to the lounge for her cup of tea when the familiar music of a girl's voice made her turn back toward the doors.

"Mrs. Claus, Mrs. Claus!" It was Sylvene with Molly trailing closely behind her. She was out of breath but still jumping about excitedly.

"Here's my letter, Mrs. Claus. I wanted to be sure Santa got it tonight. I hope it's not too late."

"Sylvene insisted we get the letter to you tonight," Molly said apologetically. "The store is about to close, so give your letter to Mrs. Claus, Sylvene. I'm sure Mrs. Claus is very tired and would like to get some rest."

"Yes, Molly," Sylvene replied, handing Mrs. Claus her letter.

"Could you make sure Santa gets this tonight?"

Savannah knelt so she was face to face with the child.

Sylvene's face was so full of hope, and those wide brown eyes shown with the innocence that only can be seen in children who believed in the magic of Christmas.

"As soon as Santa returns from tucking the reindeer into bed, I will put this right into his hands. I promise."

Sylvene threw her arms about Savannah's neck.

"Thank you, Mrs. Claus," she whispered. "You helped make my Thanksgiving wish come true. Maybe you can help with my Christmas wish, too."

"Santa always does his best, and I will try my best to help him, too." Savannah hoped that would suffice as she had no idea what was in the letter. The last thing Savannah wanted was to promise something to Sylvene that she or Santa could not deliver.

"I know you will." Sylvene handed the letter to Savannah.

"I'll put it safely in my dress pocket, and when I see Santa later, I will hand it right to him and tell him it's very important." She carefully tucked the letter deep into the folds of the dress pocket.

"Thank you, Mrs. Claus," called Molly as she took hold of Sylvene's hand and headed out toward the main area. Savannah watched Sylvene turned around, brightly smile and give her the thumbs up. Savannah returned the gesture as the two left, and the elves closed the wooden doors on another day in *The Enchanted Land of Claus*.

Savannah shuffled her overworked feet to the lounge where she could prop up her tired soles and indulge in the warmth of a cup of Fern's peppermint tea. She also hoped some biscotti or a cupcake or cookie was left, as the elves were always baking treats. She made a mental note to whip up some fudge as she patted her dress pocket, knowing Sylvene's letter was safe and headed into the lounge for a bit of post-workday crowd relaxation.

CHAPTER 15

After hours, Savannah and Fern enjoyed their pot of peppermint tea and biscotti in the employee lounge and traded tales about the customers they encountered throughout the day. They were laughing hysterically over one young boy who couldn't get the knack of how to hold the icing bag and ended up squirting icing onto everyone who passed by, including Fern, who got a shot right in the eye.

"Ah," she said, sipping the last of her tea. "It wouldn't surprise me if that kid turned into some kind of top chef someday. It's always those who have no idea of what they are doing in the beginning who end up mastering it in the end."

Savannah burst into laughter.

"Fern, the look on your face when that icing shot into your eye. For a second I couldn't determine what was redder—the frosting or the color your face turned after you were hit!"

Fern shook her head, joining in with Savannah in the laughter.

"And then the kid had the audacity to shrug his shoulders and squirt the darn frosting into his mouth!"

"Seriously, Fern, I think just between the two of us, we are going to have enough stories to write a book. We can call it *The Un-enchanted Land of Claus.*"

"Right," said Fern,"or *My Secret Life as an Elf in Santa's Workshop: True-Life Holiday Hazards of Working in a Department Store Santa's Village.* Or something silly like that."

"Even better," Savannah said, getting up to wash her teacup.

"Well, my dear, I'm on my way home. Thanks for the chat and laughs. See you tomorrow. Oh, just leave the dress in the usual place and I'll press it when I get in. See you then!" And as quick as a snow bunny, Fern vanished.

Savannah was more exhausted than usual, her arms and legs feeling heavy as lead, as she hung up the dress on the silk padded hanger. She lovingly straightened it, and closed the closet door, thinking only of how amazing her soft bed was going to feel after this fun but frantic day.

"OH NO!" SAVANNAH BOLTED UPRIGHT IN HER BED, ABRUPTLY waking from a deep sleep."Sylvene's letter!" She picked up her cell to check the time. Four o'clock am. The store didn't open until eleven on Sunday morning and *The Enchanted Land of Claus* an hour later. Savannah couldn't wait seven hours to get into the store—that was practically an entire workday. Her hands worked faster than her brain and before she realized she had texted Matthew. Almost immediately after sending the text, her phone pinged his reply.

"Talk about dedication. I will be at the store at 5:30 as there are some other mechanical problems besides the wayward snowman that I need to work on. I'll meet you at the front entrance. Can it wait until then?"

Savannah exhaled a huge sigh of relief, and she fell back onto the down pillows. She texted Matthew that she'd see him at 5:30, which was still ninety minutes away. Savannah was too restless to stay in bed and got up to put on a pot of coffee, having the distinct feeling that today would be longer than usual, and her mind could only relax when she had Sylvene's letter safely within her own hands.

CHAPTER 16

"She's either very dedicated or very... I don't know." Matthew paused talking to himself as he put the key into the ignition and waited for the car to heat. It was still pitch-black outside at almost five thirty am and it may as well have been the middle of the night. There was a time when he loved the shorter days and the colder air, and as much as he loved winter, he did miss the longer days of early sunlit mornings and late sunset evenings. New England winter days were short. Matthew recalled his grandfather telling him the shorter days meant more time for stargazing. Grandpa Max's house was a few miles down the road from Matthew's family home, and had a large deck surrounded by tall pines and oak trees. There were no streetlights at all, and Matthew remembered deep dark nights camping in his grandparents' backyard. He and his brother spent a lot of time with their grandparents, as their own parents were busy getting their business up and running. Matthew couldn't wait to get to Grandpa Max's house for a weekend of backyard camping and searching for heavenly constellations.

Nights were not as dark living in the city. The bright beams of the streetlights blocked out the twinkling of the stars, not that

Matthew had much time to stargaze lately. But on those lonely nights, especially when he lived in Chicago, he'd step out onto his balcony to see if constellations were visible, and he felt lucky if he saw even just a few stars sprinkled in the city sky. It was the same in Boston, with too many artificial lights blocking out the natural glow of a clear winter sky. Although barely visible, he thought he could make out the Big Dipper, and then out of nowhere, he felt his stomach take a nosedive into a longing he hadn't felt in a while—a longing to return to the backyard of his boyhood, standing behind the telescope on the deck and looking up into the skies for his and grandfather's stars.

"You'll be there at Christmas," he said, turning up the heat to as high as it would go. "If you had accepted the job in Charleston you wouldn't be freezing on a cold December morning," he laughed, as the car started to warm up slightly. As much as Matthew enjoyed the warm weather, he knew that he couldn't last in the South, as much as he'd like to think he could. He would miss the cold air tinged with woodsmoke, the bright red and orange leaves of a New England autumn, and, he was loath to admit, he would miss the snow, the very same snow that his family depended on during this time of the year. But city snow was definitely more difficult to navigate, with plows blockading the roads and the streets narrowed from the towering snowbanks. When he was at his grandfather's place, they would always hop into the little Caterpillar plow and burrow their own path to wherever they needed to go and thought nothing of it. The happy joys of childhood—country stargazing and snowplowing.

Pangs of guilt churned in the pit of his stomach, and he thought of Athena. Matthew was so busy during Athena's childhood making a name for himself they never made it up to Grandpa Max's during the winter for a ride on the snowplow. There was no time for stargazing either, even on the little balcony in Chicago. Athena's mother filled up any free time with dance classes, gymnastics, extra tutoring, whatever it took, as she would say "to get Athena to the next level." This, of course, became the impetus for many heated arguments over the years between Matthew and Summer, eventually leading to Summer's and Athena's exodus.

"YOU HAVE EVERY MINUTE OF EVERY DAY SCHEDULED FOR HER, Summer." It was the week before Athena started school, and Matthew was able to take a rare few days off, an extended weekend at Labor Day. He planned to take his daughter back to New England for a family visit, and Athena was looking forward to it.

"I can't wait to play with the dogs, Dad, and Gramz sent me a picture of all the cookies and pies we're going to bake. It's going to be awesome."

Matthew couldn't wait to get his daughter back East where she could enjoy the simple joys of life and just be a kid without having every minute of her day scheduled to the second, even if it was just for a long weekend.

"Matthew, you are so dramatic," Summer had said, rolling her eyes in exasperation.

"You know how competitive everything is these days, and in order for our daughter to succeed in life, she needs all these extracurriculars. Before we know it, she'll be applying to colleges. I don't understand why you don't get that, Matthew."

"I get it, Summer, but she is so young, for God's sakes. She needs a break, and more importantly she needs to be with me. I'll be there by tomorrow at twelve to pick her up. Our flight is at four so that will give us plenty of time to get to the airport."

"What are you talking about?" Matthew's ex-wife's voice sounded more annoyed than usual.

"What do you mean? We're heading to my mother's tomorrow. Remember? We spoke a couple of months ago about it and I emailed you the itinerary." Matthew felt his heart beat faster as anger started to build.

"So help me, Summer, if you've sabotaged this..."

"Matthew, I'm not sabotaging anything. Stop being so dramatic, please. I remember the email and I emailed you right back letting you know Athena wouldn't be able to take the time off due to a gymnastics recital. Don't you remember?" Matthew heard her accentuate the word 'you' blaming him for not paying attention to her.

"Summer," he said, calming himself. Matthew knew her better than she realized, and he needed to tread carefully. He raised his voice to her once in another disagreement about Athena, and she was on the phone to her lawyer as quick as a fastball pitch. Matthew checked his emails constantly, and he absolutely would have remembered such an email from Summer. He knew she was lying. Again.

Matthew decided not to pursue the matter and get into what could be a very heated argument with his ex-wife. It just wasn't worth it, nor was it worth a possible call from her attorney.

"I don't want to fight with you, Summer," Matthew said, trying to keep the defeated tone from his voice.

"Athena hasn't seen my mother or her cousins in too long. I understand she's getting older and her activities are important to her, but so is her family."

"Matthew," Summer began, with her tone of impatience. He could hear she was trying to keep her emotions in check as her voice became quiet and her words measured.

"We agree on two things, Matthew. One, that we both love Athena more than anything in the world, and two, that we only want the best for her. Do you concur?"

Concur, he thought, as she turned on her icy-cool corporate 'let's make a business deal' voice.

"I concur," he said, trying his hardest to keep the sarcasm at bay.

"Then you need to understand that in order to stay competitive, Matthew, Athena needs to be involved in as many activities as possible. It's not the same as when you and I were her age. These school applications are like a business prospectus, detailing their entire lives, and if there's any kind of a gap, it's noticed, hence her heavy schedule. Besides, you know where I'd like her to end up for college." Summer was very impressed by elite college degrees. Maybe it was because she didn't have one herself.

Matthew could see the fiery embers burning in Summer's deep violet eyes. It was that look of determination he noticed when they first met—that look of always getting anything that Summer Graystone wanted, including him as her husband.

"Her choice of college is up to her. Not you."

"Well, I'm trying to gently influence her," she said, flashing Matthew one of her smiles immediately sending the hairs on the back of his neck straight up. Matthew knew Summer was up to something.

"I might as well tell you now. I've been hired to manage The Jenkins-Mint hotel. At their headquarters. You do know where that is." It wasn't a question; it was a statement.

This was it.

"I do. London."

"I've accepted and I'm due to be in London after the first of the year. And I want Athena to go with me."

"You can't be serious," Matthew said, feeling for his handkerchief in his pocket. He knew he had to keep his composure or the consequences could be great if he did not.

"Of course I'm serious," she said, as if he had a head full of rocks and had some kind of comprehension problem. Summer's condescending tone irritated Matthew to no end, and it was a huge part in the collapse of their marriage. She played on his insecurities and was as manipulative as she was beautiful, but Matthew knew her better than she realized. She wanted a fight, something she thoroughly enjoyed, but like an expert chess player, Matthew knew what his next move was going to be. What it had to be.

"I think Athena would love London." He couldn't believe what he was about to propose, but if it would keep the peace for Athena's sake, Matthew would do it.

"What?"

Matthew watched Summer's face distort; her perfectly arched black eyebrows knitted together in astonishment, making the horizontal line embedded on her forehead, which he knew she hated, even deeper. Her lips pursed, causing the small dents around her mouth to become even more pronounced, and Matthew laughed to himself as he thought no amount of botox could stop Mother Nature. Matthew knew every line and curve of his ex-wife's body and what she didn't like about herself, one of those things being the fine lines on her face. Matthew thought the older Summer got, the more beautiful she became, and other men thought that as well, for she never lacked a man's attention whether he was in his twenties or eighties. But the beautiful ones are always the most insecure, and Summer was no exception, and he would not give in to Summer's temper.

"This would be the experience of a lifetime, and I'm not going to deny Athena this opportunity. As long as concessions are made for her to come back to the States during school vacations, I'm okay with it. And I'll fly over any chance I get."

Matthew watched his former wife twist the huge rings on her fingers and pull at the large green emerald about her neck, a nervous habit of Summer's whenever she felt she wasn't getting what she wanted. What she wanted was a fight, a chance to put Matthew down, telling him how he works all the time, never having time for his family. He knew she wanted to scream at how he was more dedicated to his career and not his wife and daughter, but he didn't give her the chance, not one little opening where she could berate and condemn him. She had done that enough during their years of marriage, and he was done. Everything he did he did for Athena.

"Fine."

"Excellent." It was done. And this time, Matthew was the victor.

"If it's okay with you, I'd like to pick Athena up and take her for ice cream. I want her to know I'm on board."

"Of course." Summer glanced at her white gold Cartier watch.

"She's done with practice in half an hour. Do you have the address?"

"Please. I'll have her home early."

Matthew let himself out, leaving Summer sitting on the couch, knowing Summer had no idea what just happened between them, and that was exactly how Matthew wanted it.

"This is a great surprise, Dad." Matthew and Athena were tucked into their favorite booth at Kandy Kanes, a popular ice cream parlor on the outskirts of the city. It was always decked out for Christmas, but no matter what time of the year, there was always a little seasonal flair—a bouquet of spring flowers on the giant stuffed snowman's hat, a pair of trendy shades perched upon Rudolph's red nose in the summer, and now, with fall quickly approaching, pumpkins of all sizes and shapes bedecked the booths, with garlands of autumn leaves encircling Santa's neck, and wreaths of dried sunflowers and cranberries hung on all the windows. It was their favorite place to go after a practice, or if Athena just needed to talk, and Matthew knew that this was one of those times.

"Well, it's been a while since we've done this, and Kandy's is the best at this time of the year."

"Dad, Kandy's is the best any time of the year."

Matthew looked at his growing daughter. Her thick mane of jet black hair was just like Summer's, and that's where the mother-daughter similarities ended. Athena had Matthew's facial bone structure and the same sea-glass eyes, albeit a shade more gray than Matthew's. She had the natural slim build of her father, but where Matthew was gangly and awkward, Athena was graceful and elegant. She was passionate for her love of horseback riding, just as her own parents were about their careers, and Matthew secretly hoped it wouldn't be her downfall It was all Athena could talk about, and Matthew worried about alienating friends who had other interests. But right now, she was happiest perched in a saddle upon a horse.

"I know about London, and I want you to know that I am on board with you living there. Chance of a lifetime, kid."

Two huge ice cream sundaes were placed before each of them, Athena with her favorite of chocolate chip ice cream, hot fudge, butterscotch, marshmallows and whipped cream. Matthew had coffee ice cream, hot fudge, extra whipped cream, and crushed peppermint candy.

"I was afraid to tell you, Dad," Athena said, digging into her sundae, melted marshmallow dripping down the side of the sundae glass.

"That's not your responsibility, Athena, that's up to me and Mom, and we talked and there was no way I wasn't going to agree. It's a great opportunity for both you and your mother."

"What about you, Dad? I hate leaving you here. I guess that's why I feel so afraid and kind of guilty. Mom's really built it up and makes it sound so wonderful. She even promised me horseback riding lessons. Now Mom says I can do that every day."

The coffee ice cream was smooth and cold and tasted absolutely delicious and helped Matthew concentrate on what he needed to say to Athena.

"Athena, the last thing I want you to do is worry about me. My job is to worry about you, not the other way around."

"I know, but you're the only dad I've got and you're also the best dad anyone could ever have. Will you promise to FaceTime every day?"

"No, can't promise you that," Matthew said, picking up the sundae glass and drinking the rest. He put the glass down and looked directly into his daughter's eyes.

"I promise to FaceTime you five times a day, how's that?"

Athena smiled, her sterling silver braces glittering in the sunshine. "Like I said, you're the best. I love you, Daddy."

"Love you more." Matthew said, feeling his throat start to choke. "You better finish. I promised your mom I'd get you home early." He reached for his handkerchief and regained his composure. The last thing he wanted was for Athena to see how much he was going to miss his little girl.

"Here," he said, taking the handkerchief, dabbing away a bit of hot fudge sauce from his daughter's chin. Athena took the handkerchief from him and grasped it in her hand.

"Can I have this, Dad, to keep with me? It will be like having you with me when we leave."

"Of course you can, Sweetie," Matthew replied, touched by his daughter's thoughtfulness.

"Plus, I know you have a lot more at home, thanks to Gramz," Athena laughed, as she carefully tucked it into her little purse.

Matthew and Athena had grown closer, even with his daughter an ocean away. Matthew was determined to keep all lines of communication always open with Athena—Skyping, FaceTime, emails and texts, and through these wonderful twenty-first century modes of communication, Matthew learned things about Athena he may not have otherwise, like her growing passion for horseback riding and competing. While the car was still heating up, Matthew scrolled back to one of her more recent texts.

I know you probably get tired of hearing me drone on about Gemini, but he's just so exquisite, Dad. It is like he and I were meant to be. The minute I saw him. I knew we would be riding together for years to come. He's so gentle, and all I have to do is pull on the reins subtly and he knows exactly what to do. LOL—it sounds like I'm describing a boyfriend! No worries, Dad, none of those in sight. The only men in my life are you and Gemini. Mom said you might be able to fly over after the New Year...

Athena had also included a photo of her perched upon the back of a beautiful jet black stallion, a wreath of silver bells hanging around his great neck. He had miniature Santa hats perched on each ear with green velvet ribbon threaded through his glossy mane. Although dressed in her full equestrian attire, he could see how Athena was no longer a little girl, but now a young woman. Her face and body had thinned and she seemed taller as well. Her beautiful black hair cascaded over the front of her shoulders and had small green and red ribbons pinned throughout her own beautiful mane.

"My little girl is still there," he said, looking at the photo of his daughter. He missed her, but he wouldn't want her to be anywhere else, as he could see she was flourishing. If he had to share his little girl, he was glad it was with this magnificent horse.

Matthew put his phone in his pocket as the car was finally warmed, and he pulled out onto the street toward Howardson's.

I'd never be able to take her away from this life she has now or from this horse, he thought, stopping at a red light. He did mention to Summer that he would visit after the busy season, and he and Athena could celebrate a belated Christmas and New Year. He couldn't wait to see Athena ride Gemini.

Summer emailed him about Gemini in the fall, wondering if it would be possible for him and Summer to split the cost and purchase him for Athena's Christmas present. He agreed on the condition that he had to be there to let her know, and Summer had agreed, even though it would be after Christmas.

As much as he was looking forward to his visit with his daughter, Matthew's thoughts turned to Savannah, musing that if he did accept the position in South Carolina, he would never have met her. The more he got to know her, the more his feelings for her intensified, which totally surprised him and threw him off kilter. He dated his share of attractive women in Chicago and Boston, but they were only attractive on the surface—plenty of cosmetic surgery and frozen faces, with professionally manicured claws clutching onto designer handbags. Not one of these women possessed any depth. He felt they feigned interest in him because of his profession, and even for the fact that his daughter lived overseas—translation being no kids in the picture. He asked one woman who had a mutual friend why she wanted to be set up with him. She giggled sillily and said "you're cute." That was it—cute—like a baby hamster was cute.

"Cute?" Matthew looked across the table at the woman whose name he couldn't recall. Was it Mindy? Mandy? Maddy?

He watched Mindy/Mandy/Maddy fidget in her seat, like a school girl who had been asked by her teacher if she did her homework when the answer was an obvious no. Matthew wasn't even sure that he was looking at an actual woman—her hair looked like a peroxide experiment gone wrong, looking like a dried out haystack. It fell over her shoulders and down past her waist, almost unnaturally long. Must be those extensions, Matthew thought, recalling Athena once wanted them, to which he and Summer both adamantly said no.

Mindy/Mandy/Maddy also had huge bee-stung lips, lipsticked in a blood red color that matched the polish on her claw-like nails. When she picked up her wine glass, her nails clicked like an old-fashioned typewriter, making Matthew grimace as it was if she was running those blood-red claws across a chalkboard. Her perfectly sculptured nose was as tiny as a button, and her face had an unnatural sheen of a fresh botox injection. Her eyebrows were two perfectly arched triangles perched unnaturally over hazel eyes. Matthew thought they were hazel, as it was very difficult to even see her eyes because her tarantula-like false eyelashes were so thick and long.

"Yeah, cute." She put her drink down and stared intently at

him across the table and asked in all seriousness, "do you know what cute means?" Her heavily made up eyes opened wide, revealing large round black pupils, indicating to Matthew she might be on something.

"Because if you don't, well, I'm sure I can better explain it to you. At your place. Or mine." Another giggle. "You know what I mean?"

Matthew flashed one of his charming smiles, knowing full well there was never going to be a 'your place or mine' tonight or ever with Mindy/Mandy/Maddy.

"I wish I could, but duty calls. I have to be at work at 5 am." Not wanting to hurt her feelings and being ever the gentleman, he added, "Maybe another time."

Her mouth molded into an exaggerated pout and reached out a clawed hand that gently stroked his. "Oh most definitely."

Mindy/Mandy/Maddy spent the rest of the evening talking about her online profiles and the many hits and swipes she received every hour. She went so far as to even demonstrate on her phone how online dating worked.

After what seemed like an eternity, the waiter brought the check, finally freeing Matthew from this disastrous date. "I'll walk you to your car," Matthew said as he put his hand on her chair and gently pulled it out for her so she could get up.

"Oh, so chillavis!" Matthew tried his hardest not to laugh at her ridiculous mispronunciation of the word his mother ensured he and his brother had been brought up to be.

"That's okay. I'm going to have a seat at the bar. Someone just swiped me and said they were nearby and could meet up for an after dinner drink. I Ubered anyway. Ta!" She wobbled away on shoes that reminded him of stilts he saw in a circus clown parade years ago with Athena. She seated herself at the bar, and within seconds a young man casually sauntered over to the stool next to her, took a seat, and motioned for the bartender to bring drinks. Matthew watched as those lacquered nails caressed the man's cheek, slowly moving upward to his temple where she raked them through the man's curly brown hair, and Matthew silently said a prayer of thanks that he was going home alone.

Matthew shook that dreadful memory from his head as he maneuvered his car through an alley at the back of Howardson's toward the garage. A security guard flagged him in and Matthew parked in his usual spot. He got out and was hit with such a blast of cold air his teeth started to chatter, and he rushed for the elevator to take him inside. He punched in the security code and was let into the main floor of the store. He glanced at his watch: Five-fifteen. He still had fifteen minutes before Savannah arrived and decided to walk through the empty store, something he quite enjoyed, as he was able to see the store as no customer ever did. It was as quiet as a winter night in the country and although the store lights were dimmed, he was still able to see every piece of merchandise the ground floor offered to entice shoppers to the upper levels, including *The Enchanted Land of Claus*. Upon entering Howardson's, customers were greeted by several information associates who were able to answer any question that was fired their way. Every prospective employee had to pass the infamous "Howardson's Emporium History Quiz" in order to be hired. Matthew recalled the day Corrine handed him a piece of paper resembling the academic tests from high school, filling in a minuscule oval with a number two pencil.

"Are you kidding?" he asked incredulously. He didn't even interview for the position as it was handed to him on a silver platter, and now he had to take a test?

"No." Corrine answered him seriously. She shook her head, her diamond earrings, catching the light streaming in from the huge picture window in her office, sparkling like stars on her earlobes, just like the day in the auditorium when Matthew knew she belonged to Colton. She was still as beautiful as she was in college, and very obviously still in love with her husband, as her office was brimming with photos of him and their three children.

Their children, two boys and a girl, were the perfect blend of both their parents.

Corrine laughed. "C'mon, Matty, we need to make sure you know the store. My great grandfather still scores these tests himself, so I hope you pulled an all-nighter."

Matthew filled in the circles to the best of his ability and saw a red arrow on the bottom of the page, indicating to flip the sheet over. On the reverse were lines that looked as if drawn with a pencil and a ruler, along with a short statement: *Please describe what being a Howardson's Emporium employee means to you, in no less than 50 words. The more the better. Words, that is.*

Matthew chuckled as thought for a moment and began to write:

Being a born and bred New Englander, I know as far as department stores go, it doesn't get any more prestigious than Howardson's Emporium. In an era of cookie-cutter, big-box stores, Howardson's has retained its charm and personal shopping experience well into the twenty-first century. Having lived in Chicago for longer than I care to admit, and being employed by one of those above-mentioned cookie-cutter big box stores, it is beyond refreshing to know old-fashioned charm and personal attention still thrive and drive at Howardson's Emporium. I would be honored to be a part of this New England tradition.

Sincerely, Matthew Buck

Two days later Matthew found an envelope in his office. He unfolded the contents and found his test scored with a big A+ written in red china pencil. He flipped it over and saw a comment in the same red pencil under his "essay:"

Dear Matthew,

Welcome to Howardson's Emporium! We are proud and blessed to have someone like you overseeing our much beloved Christmas extravaganza. Your comments, though brief, truly demonstrated your love for tradition, and the traditions of this wonderful part of the country, especially at Christmastime. I wish you all the very best and look forward to meeting you in the New Year.

Cordially,

Oliver Mathias Howardson V or as most people refer to me

OMH—Old Man Howardson

Matthew was so touched by OMH's response he had it professionally framed and displayed it proudly in his office. OMH spent most of his time in Florida, but he did still make it back up East during the summer. Perhaps they could meet then.

Matthew was snapped from his deep thoughts, turning toward a tapping sound on the glass door. Savannah waved at him on the other side of the revolving door. He immediately unbolted the top and bottom locks and motioned for her to push on the large brass railing so she could enter the store.

"Wow, it's cold out there!" she said, holding a cardboard tray in one hand and a white bakery bag in the other. Matthew was struck at how beautiful she looked at this early hour. She wore a navy blue wool coat with her head ensconced inside of the coat's hood trimmed in gray fur. Silver hair shimmered like platinum silk under the dim fluorescent lighting when she shook the hood from her head. Her green eyes sparkled with mischief, and her smile was dazzling. Ever since Thanksgiving he had wanted to be able to see her again and not as Mrs. Claus, but as Savannah Brady, so, of course when she texted him, he jumped at the chance.

"The heat's just starting to kick on in the store, so it should be warmer soon," he said.

"Oh, sounds good," she said.

Savannah extended the tray that contained two large coffee cups to Matthew.

"A thank you. It's just coffee, but I really appreciate you letting me in. Oh, and donuts!" She shook the bakery bag in her other hand.

"Half a dozen assorted. I hope that's okay with you?"

A donut made of dirt would taste just as good as long as it was you who brought it, he thought, accepting the bag.

"All my favorites. I'm sure."

"Great!" she said smiling.

"Let me grab my letter and then we can dig in. How's that?"

"Let's get that letter," he said, taking the coffee and leading the way to the employee lounge.

"I wasn't sure how you take your coffee, so I have cream and sugar in the bag along with the donuts. My not-so-subtle attempt at thanking you for giving into my paranoia."

Savannah pushed the button for the elevator. They rode up to the employee lounge in silence however broken by the grumbling of Matthew's stomach.

"Sorry, the smell of those donuts reminded me that I hadn't eaten since sometime yesterday. I can't even remember when."

"Here, take one now. Why wait?" Savannah smiled. "I can't have the man who rescued me starve now can I?" Matthew felt his heart give a little twitch. Between her smile and her thoughtfulness, he was officially smitten.

"I will," he said, plunging his hand in the bag and pulling out a honey dipped donut sprinkled with red and green jimmies.

He bit into the freshly made still warm donut. "This is heavenly. Thank you." The gooey glaze stuck to his fingers and he looked just like a kid who got the first weekend donut.

They jerked to a stop on the third floor, and Savannah raced out as Matthew headed for the lounge and some extra napkins. He turned to see her dashing toward him waving an envelope in her hand.

"Looks like you got what you wanted," he said, the scent of the strong coffee making him realize how much he needed caffeine. A look of happiness and relief appeared on Savannah's face.

"I did." Savannah carefully put the letter in her coat pocket and zipped it securely, tugging on the zipper pull a few times just to be sure it was safe. She sat down and took the lid off her coffee cup, and inhaled one of her favorite scents.

Matthew grabbed his cup and poured five containers of cream into his coffee, swirling it with a red plastic stirrer as it turned a light and pretty caramel hue.

"Wow. How's a little coffee with your cream?" laughed Savannah. "It's always astounded me how anyone could take their coffee with all that cream and sugar. Guess it's just me!"

"Well, I'm no coffee purist like you, obviously," he laughed, nodding toward her steaming cup of black coffee. He emptied several packets of pure white sugar, stirring furiously, creating a tornado-like funnel inside of the coffee cup, ensuring the sugar was appropriately dissolved. Matthew took a sip and stirred again until he finally got the texture and taste he wanted.

"Mission accomplished. The color is a perfect shade of cafe au lait, and there are no sugar granules. The perfect cup of coffee."

"I suppose if I brought whipped cream and peppermint sprinkles, you would throw those in, too?"

"Give me a little credit, Savannah. I can be discerning when it comes to my hot beverages. Sometimes," he laughed as he helped himself to a second donut, a delicious Boston cream.

"What's so important about that letter that it dragged you out of bed in the middle of the night? Or at least 5:30 am?" He chewed his donut thinking that he would have come out for her at two in the morning if she asked.

Savannah wiped her mouth with a napkin and swallowed the last bite of her snowy coconut donut.

"It's Sylvene's letter to Santa, and I promised to personally deliver it to him. She and her babysitter ran in right before closing time last night, and I put it in the pocket of my dress, but I was so exhausted after Fern and I finished our tea, I hung up the dress and headed home. Without the letter. I knew it would be safe, but I just got a little nervous that's all. It's special and the last thing I'd want to do is lose it or forget about it. It must have been playing around in my subconscious because I woke up out of a dead sleep, and I just had to get it into my own hands. And now I do, thanks to you," she said, gulping down the rest of her coffee.

"That's dedication for you," Matthew said, raising his coffee cup in a toast.

"Well, as I hope you know, I take my role as Mrs. Claus very seriously." Savannah tucked her napkin and stirrer inside of her coffee cup and got up to throw it away.

"So you're a little like Spiderman, then? With great power comes great responsibility?"

"Oh, a Spiderman fan, are you? My son was constantly throwing his fingers out to me expecting webs to shoot out of his fingertips when he was little, so I do know a thing or two about Spiderman. So yes, you could say some customers may think I have great powers, but more importantly for me, I do have a great responsibility." Savannah sat down and looked Matthew directly in the eye.

"When you hired me I thought it would be a way for me to take my mind off of my own loneliness during the holidays and earn some extra cash. Which it has on both counts, but it has become so much more. I'm not only representing Howardson's but I'm also representing one of the most beloved characters of Christmas. You've enabled me to bring Mrs. Claus out of the shadows so to speak."

"Out of the shadows? How?" Matthew asked, almost reaching for a third donut, but decided against it, although he could have inhaled an entire bag. And he would when she left.

"What I mean is we all know Mrs. Claus, but she's always secondary, if even that, and I don't think she had much attention paid to her over the years. But because of your incredible vision of old traditions with a twenty-first century twist, I've been able to make her so much more than one dimensional, not just someone who bakes cookies and feeds the reindeer. Although I do a lot of that, too!

But it's more, so much more, Matthew, and playing Mrs. Claus has made my life, during a time that I was dreading, happy. And if I can help make someone else happy at Christmas, then that's a bonus."

"See, the perfect Mrs. Claus," Matthew said. And if anyone would ever ask him when he knew he was absolutely head over heels in love with Savannah Brady, Matthew would tell them it was the day she brought him coffee and donuts and the importance of a child's letter to Santa. Savannah glanced at the clock above the microwave.

"It's six forty-five! I can't believe I bent your ear for that long, and I know you have so much work to do. I don't want to keep you any longer, so I'd better get a move on!"

Time seemed to evaporate whenever Matthew was with Savannah. It flew on Thanksgiving or any other minute they had spent together, but he wasn't ready for her to leave. He also knew that if he wanted to see her more and get to know her better, he was going to have to take a leap of faith himself and be the pursuer. Matthew sensed Savannah was not the type of woman to be the aggressor in a relationship, and he didn't have to know her for that long to pick up on that. Matthew had an ex-wife and one too many blind dates in which the woman was always the initiator, and he was never comfortable with being chased. On the other hand, it was not Matthew's nature either to be the pursuer. Summer chased him down as a predatory cat would an unsuspecting mouse. When it came to professional matters, Matthew had no difficulty at all being the aggressor, albeit politely, but aggressive wasn't even the correct word, as he always associated it with negative connotations. Matthew likened himself as more assertive and emphatic. He always tried to channel his Grandpa Max's manner of doing business.

Neighbors constantly brought their broken tractors or snowplows to Grandpa Max's garage and expected repairs right on the spot with nothing in return. As nice and neighborly as

Grandpa Max was, he always let them know he'd be happy to fix whatever they brought to him, but there would be a price.

Cleet Hardwood, a farmer who owned more acres than anyone could count, came to the barn and expected service from Grandpa Max immediately.

"C'mon, Max, my orchard is about to burst and if I don't get this tractor fixed now, apples will be droppin' like bombs and won't be any good to me. The apples are perfect now and God knows what I could lose if the tractor is down."

Matthew was putting a new chain on his bike and he listened as Grandpa Max swung into action.

"Cleet, I don't know why you think I have nothing better to do than fix your old tractor. If you weren't so cheap, you'd go and buy yourself a new one. We all know you got enough money to buy a whole fleet. But I'll tell you what I'll do. I'm happy to fix it for you, and I'll even give you a discount, if you let Paulina set up a stand at the cider mill and sell her cranberry apple pies. I guarantee you, those will sell like hotcakes, and she'll even throw in a few for you and the family as well. You agree to that, your tractor will be repaired by 8:00 pm tonight."

Grandpa Max extended his hand and flashed one of his prize-winning smiles. Cleet accepted his hand and became putty in it.

"I know you're busy, Max and I really appreciate your help. You tell Paulina to come see me tomorrow morning and I'm happy to give her a table at the mill. As long as she throws in the pies, the deal is sealed."

"I think she's baking up a few right now, Cleet. Come by around eight and your tractor will be ready to go. Along with a pie."

Matthew watched as Cleet explained what the problem was with the tractor. Grandpa Max reassuringly patted Cleet on the shoulder, and Cleet hopped into the pickup truck driven by one of his farm hands. Max waved them down the road and turned back to the barn where Matthew was wiping the chain grease from his hands on an old rag.

"That Cleet," Grandpa laughed. "His tractor will take me no more than ten minutes to fix, but see, I was able to get your grandma what she's wanted for a long time—to sell her pies at the mill. I was just waiting for the right opportunity to approach him, as your grandmother is too shy, and he took the bait; hook, line, and sinker. He's a good guy, if a little stingy, but your grandma's pies will make a killing and he'll think it was all his idea." Grandpa Max pointed his index finger to his temple. " When you see an opportunity come a knockin', you have to answer it, but always make the other person think it's their idea. Once the opportunity is yours, then you sell yourself and how it was really YOUR idea, but you do it discreetly. It's what I call 'charm on the farm.' It might not make you millions, but you can usually get what you want or need, and sometimes, that's even better. Now, I'm going to run in and let your grandmother know I just granted her wish and she needs to start peeling more apples!" Grandpa Max started toward the house and then turned back and walked toward Matthew and his bike. He bent down and examined the new chain on the bike. He gave Matthew a very serious look and then engulfed him in a hug.

"I could not have done a better job on this myself, Matthew. Well done. You go test it out and after supper you and I will fix Cleet's tractor together. As a matter of fact, I'm going to let you give it a go. How's that?"

Matthew furrowed his brow and dusted his hands on the back of his jeans.

"Well, Grandpa Max, what makes you think I don't have other things to do, but I might consider it if I get that first slice of Grandma's pie."

Grandpa Max burst out laughing.

"Charm on the farm! Matthew, you can have the first slice of all your grandmother's pies! Go take the bike for a spin, and I'll make sure that first slice is on the table waiting for you when you get back."

And now Matthew wasn't going to let this opportunity with Savannah that came a knockin' get by him.

Matthew finished his coffee. "I think it's a good policy that Mrs. Claus not only knows how to cookie decorate and personally deliver letters to Santa, she should also know how to fix a wayward snowman, in the event Sheriff Sugar Plum is trying to put out another fire in *The Enchanted Land of Claus.*"

"Really?" Savannah's green eyes lit right up, and Matthew heard the eagerness in her voice.

"I'd love to. Those things are amazing, and I have been curious as to exactly how they work, but you always seem so busy, I hated to ask, but since you're asking now, I accept!"

"Let's go," said Matthew, extending his arm, which Savannah enthusiastically accepted.

"Oh! Just one thing. Let me put my coat with Sylvene's letter in my locker. I just want to keep it safe and sound until I see Santa later today."

Matthew was again touched by Savannah's thoughtfulness. He fully knew the letter would be safe even if she left it on the kitchen counter, but if it made her feel better, he'd wait all day.

"There!" Savannah announced, joining Matthew. "Now I'm ready," and together they made their way to repair yet another snowball throwing snowman gone wild.

CHAPTER 17

Two hours later Savannah stepped into her warm apartment and immediately put on a pot of coffee.

"Can't have enough caffeine, especially today," she mused, inhaling the fresh dark brown scoopfuls of coffee. She had a few hours before her shift but was too wound up to relax, so a pot of fresh brewed coffee was the obvious answer. Besides, her adrenaline always ran high when she was Mrs. Claus, never feeling tired until the very end of the day when the dress was hung upon its silk hanger. It was an exhaustion of physically and mentally doing something that truly mattered to her—not sitting behind a desk for eight hours, trying to get through mind-numbing computer tasks.

Savannah longed for work that didn't require walking into an office building on a daily basis, but anytime she got close to her nine-to-five escape, waves of apprehension of leaving her comfort zone put a stranglehold on her, and the thought of losing an excellent weekly paycheck and medical benefits always won. Office work was all Savannah truly had known and as she had been doing it since she was eighteen. The summer she graduated from high school, she signed up with a temp agency that kept her busy with a multitude of assignments in different areas—banking, hospitals, law firms, and insurance companies. It was scut work, filling in for vacationing secretaries, making copies, filing, and typing the occasional letter. She hadn't yet declared a major at Calloway Junior College, once known as The Calloway School for Young Ladies. The school was housed in a row of old brownstones in the Back Bay Area of Boston, and when Savannah toured the college in her senior year of high school, she knew she wanted to be a Calloway girl. It was a two-year college program for women only, and upon graduating, she would have an Associate's degree in business administration. All of her coursework credits would be transferable if she decided to continue for a Bachelor's degree, but a four-year program was out of the question for two reasons: Savannah knew she did not want to continue, and two additional years meant extra hefty school loans. Those were the last things Savannah wanted as a college graduate starting out in the working world. Her plan was to work full time and pay her loan off as soon as humanly possible, as she had dreams of working internationally, especially in London. After graduation she became employed by one of Boston's top law firms that had an office in London. She had been with the firm for one year, and an opening for a secretary became available in the London branch, and she applied, but much to her disappointment, Savannah did not get the position. Enid Stetch, one of those older lady types who made the secretarial profession her life's mission was going to London. Enid did everything perfectly—took shorthand at one hundred words per minute although Savannah could do one hundred twenty, typed eighty-five words a minute with no mistakes, and even made coffee and baked cookies for all the attorneys.

Unbeknownst to Savannah, the heartbreaking news of her being rejected for the London position changed the course of her life.

It was a Friday afternoon in January and a devastated

Savannah was on the phone with her best friend Debbi Mallard, crying about how she lost out to Enid.

"Savvy, c'mon. What would you have done in London without me anyway? Listen, go to the ladies' room, wash your face, put on some lipstick and meet me in front of my building at 5:30. We are going to eat like queens and drown your sorrows at The Galway Rose. And no is not an option. See you in an hour."

Debbi didn't give Savannah a chance to respond, so she did what Debbi demanded, and on a freezing cold night they made their way to their favorite pub. It was crowded when they arrived, but Debbi and Savannah found their favorite spot—the last two stools at the end of the long, wraparound dark oak bar.

"I cannot believe these weren't taken!" Debbi exclaimed, as she climbed onto the high-backed stool. They hung their coats on the stools, securing their bags on the bar pedestal, snugly tucked between their feet.

"See it was meant to be, Savvy," Debbi said, picking up the menu.

"You know that menu by heart," Savannah said, already picturing her own order of the double pub burger with cheddar cheese, pickles and mushrooms.

"I know, but I always like to see if anything new has been added. Unlike you, I don't plan on getting a cheeseburger smothered in onions."

Savannah laughed as Debbi perused the overly large, laminated menu.

"Debbi, it's mushrooms, not onions. And portobello mushrooms to be exact, thank you very much."

Debbi shrugged her shoulders, still looking at the menu.

"Ladies, a cocktail before dinner?" Ian Maloney, the owner of The Galway Rose, appeared on the other side of the bar. He was the quintessential Irish pub owner—probably in his forties or fifties, a little hefty, with a head of thick black hair laced with white and a black mustache to boot. His cheeks were always red, most likely from running from one end of the long bar to the other, and mixing a plethora of cocktails in record time. Ian was the reason the bar was so popular especially the young professional crowd. He always made you feel like you were at home at the family dinner table. Savannah didn't know how he kept track of the names of his patrons, but he did, always recalling a name after he was told just once. Names were something Savannah always had a hard time remembering, and she admired Ian for his quick Irish wit and his quick name-remembering mind as well.

"Two Long Island Iced Teas," Debbi answered for both of them. "And a little stronger than usual, especially for Savannah, please." Debbi quickly buried her head back into the menu.

"Savannah, girl, rough day at the office?" Ian's brogue was so delightful and caring, but Savannah wasn't in the mood to pour her heart out to the kindly bartender. Losing out on the job was still raw, and she wanted to drown her sorrows in her cheeseburger.

"Just one of those days, Ian," she said, handing him the menu.

"I truly understand, love." Ian leaned over the bar and whispered, "I'll put some extra cheddar and portobello mushrooms on that burger of yours. That should cheer you a wee bit."

"It will cheer me up a lot bit," Savannah smiled.

"I've got myself a new barkeep, ladies, and I'll put your Long Island Iced Teas, extra strong, in with him, and he will bring them right over."

Debbi was still ensconced in the menu as Savannah watched Ian tap a young man on the shoulder. He turned as Ian pointed toward Savannah and Debbi, and Savannah smiled and waved.

"He's cute," Savannah said to Debbi, finally putting the menu down.

"Who's cute?" she asked, scanning the bar for any young men, even though Debbi was officially off the market. Her boyfriend recently graduated from the Merchant Marine Academy and was on some kind of top-secret submarine mission where he would be at sea until the spring. Debbi was as loyal as an old dog and had absolutely no interest in other men, but she liked to be on the lookout for Savannah, setting up Savannah with blind dates that resulted in abject failures. As much as Savannah loved Debbi like a sister, matchmaking was not one of her fortes. Debbi found herself a wonderful guy, but she just didn't have the knack for finding them for her friends. Savannah didn't have the heart to tell Debbi she needed to stop matchmaking, as Debbi only wanted to see her best friend happy, so Savannah went on the dates, hoping one would work out, but they never did. This was one mission that Savannah would have to accomplish on her own.

"The guy Ian's talking to, the new bartender. He's making our drinks for us."

"Hmm," Debbi murmured as she narrowed her eyes and watched this 'cute guy' as Savannah referred to him, mixing the drinks.

"I don't think he's doing it right," Debbi said, shaking her head. She was very particular about her mixed drinks, especially her coveted Long Island Iced Teas. She could probably jump behind the bar herself and mix the perfect iced tea, along with Cape Codders, Cosmos, and a perennial favorite, a Kamikaze.

"It's a mixed drink," said Savannah, "which means there's a recipe. How can it not be right?"

"Well, I guess we'll find out," Debbi said, doubt creeping into her voice.

Savannah sat, enthralled, watching him expertly measure and pour the vodka, rum, gin, tequila and whatever else went into their favorite drink. He opened the fridge and grabbed a bright red can of Coke, popped the top and poured a splash into each glass. He then grabbed two lemon wedges from a stainless steel bowl, sliced them, and inserted them onto the rim of each hurricane glass. He picked up the glasses and walked toward their end of the bar.

"Good evening, Ladies. Two Long Island Iced teas. Oh," he ran to the back of the bar, "and two straws. Enjoy."

"Have you ever made these before?" questioned Debbi carefully eying her drink. Although she had drunk more than her fair share of Long Island Iced Teas, Debbi, as far as Savannah knew, had actually never made one, but her taste buds were so honed to good and bad drinks, she'd be able to tell with the first sip whether or not 'cute guy' had made one before.

He flicked the towel from his shoulder and flipped it on the counter leaning in toward both of them, and squarely looked Debbi in the eye. She didn't back down, giving him the stink eye right back.

"Are you serious?" he asked.

Savannah detected a hint of a smile forming at the corner of his lips. Cute Guy leaned over the bar and stared at Debbi as if he was ready for a war of words.

"Yeah, I'm serious. Have you ever made one of these before? You looked a little shaky back there." Debbi enjoyed picking a good-natured fight, especially with a cute young guy, and as she unwrapped her straw, Savannah felt the sharp kick of Debbi's boot, indicating that this guy was definitely a cute one.

"Have you ever made one?" He stared intently at Debbi, waiting for her response.

Debbi pursed her lips and furrowed her brow, pulling out all the stops of her expert flirting.

"I cannot say that I have, BUT I will let you know I have drunk plenty of them, and I am going to tell you whether this is a good one or a bad one, and believe you me, I've had more bad ones than good."

"Have at it," he responded confidently, backing away from the bar.

Debbi ceremoniously swirled the straw in her drink, ice cubes clinking against the glass. She bent the straw and took a small sip. She looked him straight in the eye and pronounced "not bad."

"Not bad?" He laughed and shook his head. A shock of black hair fell over his eyes as he smiled. The dark bar was suddenly illuminated by the brilliance of his cocksure smile.

"What about you?" he asked, nodding toward Savannah. "Your friend, the self-proclaimed connoisseur of Long Island Iced Teas says her drink is not bad. What's your verdict?"

Savannah's hands shook as she peeled the wrapper from her straw, praying he wouldn't notice. Her heart raced, feeling his eyes on her, and she felt her blood course with a combination of nervousness and excitement. She took a long sip and let the alcohol run down her throat and into her stomach, warming her instantly and giving her a boost of confidence.

"I have to say it's quite excellent."

He nodded his head affirmatively.

"Quite excellent. Yes. Quite excellent." His blue eyes were fixed straight onto Savannah's and she got the distinct feeling that he was no longer referring to the drink, feeling a hot blush rise into her cheeks.

"Well, Not Bad and Quite Excellent," he laughed,"may I take your dinner order?"

"Oh, honey, order my usual," Debbi said, hopping down from the bar stool. "I have to call home to see if Greg called. I'll bet you anything that he did. Every time I stay home he never calls, but when I'm out, the phone rings. I'll be back in a few."

"What's Not Bad's usual? Couldn't she find it on the menu? She was looking at it long enough."

The brilliance of his smile made Savannah's hands shake harder. She thought he was flirting with her, but unlike Debbi, Savannah never mastered the fine art of flirtation. She was the quiet one and Debbi was the hellion.

Savannah took a huge gulp of her Long Island Iced Tea. Her empty stomach flooded with alcohol was not a good combination, but tonight, with her disastrous day and now meeting this adorable and flirtatious guy, the cocktail would only do her good, giving her the courage to stay on her toes. She'd have to with this one.

"Not Bad doesn't like to miss out on anything so she likes to check the menu to make sure nothing new has been added. You know. In case she'd want to order it."

Savannah scolded herself silently, and thought she sounded more silly than sensuous.

"I guess I can't blame her," he said matter-of-factly.

"What's Not Bad's usual?" he asked, taking a pad and pencil from the pocket of his apron.

"Not Bad would like the tuna melt, Swiss cheese, on whole wheat bread, with an order of steak fries and coleslaw." She watched as he quickly wrote the order. His bright blue eyes then deeply looked into Savannah's green ones.

"And more importantly, what would Quite Excellent like?" he whispered, his voice husky and quiet. If Savannah's heart didn't beat out of her now then it never would. She could feel the pulse in her chest and in her neck. What was he doing to her?

She took another sip and leaned in over the bar.

"Quite Excellent would like a double pub burger, cheddar cheese medium rare with portobello mushrooms and coleslaw. And your name."

Did I really just ask him that? Savannah thought, knowing it was more likely the alcohol asking than she herself.

He placed his elbows on the bar and put his face in his right hand. He shook his head, his eyes never leaving hers, and Savannah felt he was as taken with her as she was with him. She knew at that very moment, that whoever this was, it was the beginning of something special.

He stepped back and extended his hand and that cocksure smile of his almost sent Savannah falling off her bar stool. She

THE PERFECT MRS. CLAUS

reached for his hand and he grasped it firmly; not too hard, not too softly, but absolutely perfectly.

"Brad. Brad the Bartender. Pleased to meet you."

"Pleased to meet you, too, Brad the Bartender. And don't listen to my friend. I'll bet you ten dollars on our way home later, she will tell me that this was the best Long Island Iced Tea she's ever had. She just likes to give everyone a hard time. Especially cute bartenders."

The quite excellent Long Island Iced Tea was certainly working its magic on Savannah and she let it, allowing her to say things she never would have said with just a plain old ginger ale.

"Cute, huh? Like puppy dog cute or Rob Lowe cute?"

"Well, not as cute as puppies, you're not one, and I never really thought Rob Lowe to be that cute. You're Brad the Bartender cute. From now on, that will be my standard comparison: is he as cute as Brad the Bartender?"

"Oh, now I'm a measuring stick? For other guys?" He took the linen towel from the bar and threw it over his shoulder, his cocky confidence flashing, which Savannah found intensely attractive.

"It's a compliment," said Savannah, pushing her empty glass toward him.

"Of course, I missed him," Debbi announced, hopping back onto her bar stool. "I have told him not to call before eight, but I guess his sense of time is off being stuck in a submarine." She took a sip of her drink and nodded her head, and looked directly at Brad.

"I think this needed to sit for a few, you know, so the flavors could meld. Tastes good now."

"Let me put your orders in for you," Brad said, walking backward toward the grill window, his eyes lingering on Savannah, goosebumps rising on every inch of her skin.

"What the heck is this all about?" Debbi asked. "I am gone for ten minutes, and this guy's ready to propose to you!"

Savannah looked at her friend and scrunched her face in

149

annoyance. Debbi always jumped to the wrong conclusions, especially when it came to the opposite sex.

"No. He's just a cute bartender flirting with the customers. See," Savannah said, nodding toward the other end of the bar. " He's flashing that million-dollar smile at that girl. I'm just another customer he wants a big tip from, that's all."

"Yeah, he's flashing that million-dollar smile, as you put it, but those big blue eyes are looking right at you. Who are you kidding, Savannah? Don't act like you're so ordinary. You're pretty and nice and he sees that. Besides, that girl at the end of the bar is nothing compared to you. Her makeup is practically caking off her face, and if I can tell that from this angle, I can imagine what she looks like up close. Give yourself some credit. He's definitely interested in you."

"No, he was just a diversion after the bad day I've had. He is definitely cute and he took my mind off things, but that's all there is to it. Someone like him probably has a girlfriend anyway. So that's the end of it, okay?" Savannah wanted to change the subject. "Did you miss Greg's call?"

Debbi shrugged her shoulders, but before she could answer Ian came waltzing out from the kitchen with two plates bearing a ton of food.

"Mademoiselle Debbi, your tuna melt with Swiss and steak fries and coleslaw." With great flourish Ian presented Debbi her dinner.

"Oh, Ian, this looks divine. I'm starving. Thanks so much," she said, reaching for the bottle of ketchup. pouring what seemed like half the bottle onto her fries.

"And you for you, Mademoiselle Savannah, your medium-rare cheddar pub burger, with extra portobello mushrooms and coleslaw."

The aroma of the bubbling cheese on her burger made Savannah's mouth water, and she realized how hungry she was and couldn't wait to take that first bite.

"Thanks so much, Ian. It looks amazing. As always."

She was just about to pick up her burger when Ian slipped her a piece of paper from the order pad.

"From Brad, my bartender." He winked at Savannah. "He's also my nephew, so be nice to him."

Savannah smiled up at Ian, totally taken aback by what he just handed her.

"Oh my God, Savannah, see I told you!" Debbi seemed more excited than Savannah at this surprise from Brad the Bartender.

"Read it!" Debbi said, stuffing a triangle of tuna melt into her mouth.

SAVANNAH UNFOLDED THE SLIP AND READ IT TO HERSELF FIRST.

Dear Quite Excellent,

I'm late for a class or else I would find some excuse to come back out and talk to you. I'm leaving my phone number so you can give me a call and thank me for dessert.

Maybe we can have a cheeseburger smothered in mushrooms together sometime soon.

Brad the Bartender

"If it's too personal, I understand, but you just met the guy so I'm not sure how personal..."

"Here," smiled Savannah, handing Debbi the note. They were always open and honest with each other when it came to dates and boyfriends, and Savannah thought the note was adorable and actually couldn't wait to show Debbi.

"Dessert?" Debbi asked, stuffing more ketchup covered fries in her mouth. Ian then returned, placing before each of them a pretty little box.

"Oh, Ian, is this what I think it is?" asked Savannah. Ian's wife, Bridget, was a chocolatier and created artisan candies and sold them in the chocolate shop adjacent to The Galway Rose. Bridget's chocolates were the recipients of many local and national awards, and Savannah would only buy them for extra special occasions, such as a birthday or anniversary. And at that, she could only afford one or two pieces at the most, as the box they were presented in was part of the gift as well.

Bridget's aunt hand painted and decorated the boxes and sent them from Ireland from the centuries old family homestead. The boxes were decoupaged from old postcards, decorated with bits of glitter and ribbon. You knew you were special if you received a gift from Bridget's Irish Chocolate Box.

"Oh my God, Ian, I love this box!" Debbi couldn't contain her excitement as she picked up the small square box. A hand-painted scene of the Boston Common was decoupaged on the lid. She opened the box and discovered a most exquisite piece of chocolate in the shape of a beehive. It was caramel colored with dark chocolate swirls and a tiny milk chocolate bee perched on the top, its wings shimmered with gold dust. Debbi read the description on the parchment in the box:

"Sweet Honeycomb Crunch. Sweet cream honey ganache melded with roasted cocoa nibs within a dark chocolate shell. Yum. It's so pretty I don't want to eat it. But I will. Eventually!"

Savannah's box was the same size and had a picture of a swan boat in the pond at the Public Garden. She opened it to find a small folded piece of paper on top of the parchment that covered the description of the chocolate. She tucked this into her pocket, as she wanted to read it alone. Debbi, so enthralled with her box of chocolate, took no notice of Savannah discretely slipping the second piece of paper into her pocket. She then removed the piece of parchment and found a perfectly formed red heart. She flipped over the parchment and read the description:

"Summer Strawberry Always Heart. A bite of sweet strawberries and vanilla cream covered in dark chocolate inside a hand-painted heart shaped shell."

Savannah stared at the piece of chocolate in disbelief. It was absolutely beautiful, and as much as she would have loved to savor the strawberries and cream, she knew she would not be able to bring herself to eat it. It was too beautiful. And it was red. The color of passion. Did Brad the Bartender put a bit of thought into her piece of chocolate or did he just grab what was available? Whatever the case, it was a beautiful piece of candy craftsmanship, and Savannah planned on putting this away just to look at later. Whatever its meaning, it was thoughtful and kind.

Suddenly Savannah felt a hot breath upon her neck.

"Oh my God, Savannah, he gave you a red heart. I told you he liked you!" exclaimed Debbi, ogling the chocolate in Savannah's box.

"Debbi, it's just a piece of candy. I could read something into your beehive, too."

"Yeah, that I have a personality that stings," she laughed.

"Or you are bee-utiful, and that you are as sweet as honey."

"Give me a break," she laughed. "I told the guy that his drink was not bad, when it was actually the best Long Island Iced Tea I ever had, but I wasn't going to give him the satisfaction of telling him that."

"I knew it!" Savannah exclaimed. "I knew you would think it was a great drink."

"Yeah, of course it was, but like I said, I wasn't going to say so. I had to make him sweat it out, you know?"

"I know." Savannah glanced at her watch. "Ready to go?"

"That I am. Greg is supposed to call again at five in the morning, so I want to get in bed so I can be up and ready."

"Sounds good. Let's get a cab. Drop you off first?"

"See you next week, Ian," Debbi called as they were leaving.

Ian came from behind the bar and affectionately hugged both of his favorite customers.

"You two have a great week. Savannah, can I have a minute?"

"I'll get the cab," Debbi offered.

"Thanks, Darlin' it won't be but a minute."

Debbi went over toward the cab stand as Ian took Savannah in a corner near the front door.

"Bradley's a good kid, God knows I love him to death, but he's just out of a bad relationship, so go easy with him, okay?"

"No worries, Ian," Savannah assured him."I'm not in the market for a boyfriend right now anyway. I'm so busy at work. I didn't get that London transfer because they didn't think I was with the firm for long enough, but that office is expanding next year, so I have my eyes on that prize. You know how badly I want to live in London. Right now it's just me and London, England."

"Good for you, sweetheart." He kindly patted her on the shoulder. "But, if anything ever did come of you and Bradley, he would be one of the luckiest men in the world."

Savannah smiled at her friend. "Thanks so much, Ian. That means the world coming from you."

Debbi frantically waved for Savannah as the taxi she was signaling pulled up to the curb.

"Oh, gotta go. Thanks for everything, Ian. See you next week!"

"Bye, love," Ian said, opening the door as Savannah dashed into the cold January night.

Later that evening after Savannah had gotten ready for bed, she set the candy box on her bureau. She heard her mother pad by the door on her way to her own room, and gently tapped and slowly opened Savannah's bedroom door.

"Good night honey," she said, gently kissing her forehead. "I hope you're not too disappointed. I'm sure another opportunity for London will come up soon."

Savannah hugged her mother. "Thanks, Mom. I'm better now. Going out with Debbi always helps as does a cheeseburger from The Galway Rose. I'll be fine."

"I know you will. Goodnight sweetheart. Love you."

"Love you, too, Mom."

Her mother quietly closed her door. Savannah hopped from her bed and walked to her closet and reached into her coat pocket. She pulled out Brad's note on the meal order pad as well as the tiny piece of paper that was tucked inside of the chocolate box. It was a picture of the piece of chocolate but it had two tiny black eyes and a black line drawn in the form of a smile.

Savannah smiled. Thanking him was the perfect excuse to call Brad, but not right away. Debbi was right—it was like the Long Island Iced Tea—don't let him know immediately that you're interested, let him think about it for a while, and then act. As much as she would have liked to pick up the phone at this moment to call him, she decided to give it some time. Like the old saying, good things come to those who wait, and if Brad the Bartender saw Ian anytime soon, Ian would definitely let him know Savannah was a good thing worth the wait.

And here she was, some thirty odd years later. Savannah had that undeniable feeling of the passing of time. It was beyond all comprehension that her little boy was now a grown man and making a life for himself. Even more unfathomable was that she was a widow. Fifty-three-year-old widows were not supposed to exist, but they did, because she was one of them. There were times even memories of her husband no longer seemed enough to sustain Savannah as they once did. When pangs of sadness and loneliness crept into Savannah, she could simply close her eyes and imagine Bradley's arms tightly wrapped around her, feeling the strength of those arms flow into her body, giving her the comfort she needed. Now the simple act of wishing him near wasn't enough, and Bradley's reassuring presence seemed to be floating further away, and it was becoming harder for Savannah to supplicate his celestial existence, as if his angel's wings were flying higher and deeper into Heaven, leaving her Earthbound and alone.

And now there was Matthew Buck. He was a man so unlike her husband but Savannah could no longer deny her developing feelings for this man.

"No," Savannah cried, looking at their wedding picture. "I

could never love another man, Bradley. Why are you doing this to me? Please, don't leave me."

But Bradley made his divine departure and Savannah felt herself in peril—still in love with her deceased husband, but also wondering if it would be possible for a new start with someone else. Is that what she wanted? A relationship with another man?

Savannah let her mind wander back to that fateful day the week before Halloween, and how her life had taken such unexpected twists—becoming Mrs. Claus opened up a novel world for her with new people, and an excitement for life she hadn't felt for years. She loved the peppermint tea-time chats with Fern, and being able to help Sylvene and her mother at Thanksgiving, not to mention all the eccentric and wonderful people who ensured that *The Enchanted Land of Claus* ran like the efficient production company it was. And then there was the elephant in the room—Matthew Buck—so shy, but yet so brilliant and more importantly, humble and kind. Savannah found it hard to believe he didn't have a significant other, since as shy as he was, he was just as handsome, with those mischievous crinkly sea-glass eyes and dimples deeply embedded in each cheek. While she definitely found him to be quirky, Savannah also thought he was sweet and unassuming, and had brilliantly managed *The Enchanted Land of Claus*, never taking direct credit for its success.

"Oh, I couldn't have done it without Fern and Brock and everyone else," he would say when Savannah or anyone else complimented him on the magnificence of *The Enchanted Land of Claus*.

Once added up, that was the sum total of Matthew Buck— unknowingly handsome, sweetly bashful, but brilliant and confident enough to pull off a showstopper like this one, and at such a stalwart enterprise. But most important was Matthew's dedication to his daughter. His eyes glowed with pride when Athena's name was mentioned, and his clumsy manner of pulling his phone from his pocket to show off her latest picture was just as sweet. Although Athena was on the other side of the Atlantic Ocean, no father and daughter could be closer, and Savannah knew theirs was a bond that would never be broken, no matter how many miles or oceans separated them.

Savannah shared a similar bond with her own son. It was just the two of them now, and although Patrick was an ocean away himself, his texts and updates were daily. The distance between Savannah and Patrick was closed with texts, photos, and FaceTime, and it was almost as if Patrick was around the block.

Savannah poured the freshly brewed coffee into her cup, savoring the heady aroma. To Savannah, there were few things better than a fresh-brewed cup of coffee in the morning, but as she sipped it, her mind strayed to Matthew. She hadn't known him for long, but spending time with him on Thanksgiving gave her a better insight about his psyche, sensing that he never grew out of his teenage 'ears', and was still shy and awkward around the opposite sex. She had definitely noticed his magnetism on the floor making his rounds as Sheriff Sugar Plum. Females of all ages, seemed to gravitate toward him, asking how the snowman tipped his black top hat in greeting to exactly how many lights were strung on the ceiling-high Christmas trees. He was in his element as Sheriff Sugar Plum, and it could very well be that like Savannah, putting on that Stetson and cowboy costume made him extroverted, gregarious, and confident, as Savannah was when she donned the Mrs. Claus dress. He was no longer behind-the-scenes Matthew Buck, but a respected sheriff of *The Enchanted Land of Claus*, adored by all.

Savannah knew this was true for her. She was no longer Savannah Brady, quiet and subdued insurance administrator. When she slipped into that magical blue dress, she became transformed into the whimsical Mrs. Claus, doyenne of *The Enchanted Land of Claus*. It was as if a magical Christmas spell had been cast, and she was able to chat up a storm with, as the song goes, folks from one to ninety-two. She could decorate cookies with the ease of a polished baker, whip up hot chocolate better than the most experienced barista, and was more than happy to pose for loads of customer selfies. The dress brought out the Mrs. Claus that was buried deep within her, and Savannah realized for the first time in years, it brought out the old Savannah, the Savannah who loved anything that life brought her way and which she confidently conquered. She was the Savannah when she was wife to her husband Bradley; adventurous and fearless, and ready to tackle anything that life threw in their path. That Savannah retreated into a den of darkness when her life with Bradley ended, and for the past two years Savannah had become nothing more than a shell of her former self. She was like an old tortoise who could easily retreat into her hard shell of armor but able to continue to forge through the motions of life but not truly live it. And now thanks to an accidental "mugging," Savannah, like the old and cautious tortoise, ever so slowly poked her head from the dark and lonely inside of her shell into the bright and colorful world outside and very much liked what she saw: a gentle and shy soul who created a stupendous world of Christmas fantasy. Matthew invited Savannah to join him on his sleigh ride through *The Enchanted Land of Claus*, and now, Savannah wanted to stay on the sleigh forever.

She sat on the stool at her kitchen counter sipping her coffee and looked at Sylvene's letter. Savannah gently touched the envelope, her fingertips feeling the rise of the candy cane, Christmas tree, and reindeer stickers adorned on the front of the envelope. 'Mr. and Mrs. Claus' was written in big block letters in red and green crayon on the front of the envelope. She flipped the envelope over and was overwhelmed by what was drawn on the back flap: a woman in a blue dress, a blue hat and snow-white pompom perched atop of a head of long silver hair.

Savannah was touched by Sylvene's drawing. A few short weeks ago she would never have imagined she would have such an impact on a child who only wanted her mother to be happy. Sylvene was too young to have such a weight on her shoulders, worrying about her mother. Jolene worked so hard to make the best out of a tough situation, and Sylvene was so sensitive to her mother's needs. Jolene's happiness was all that mattered to the little girl. Savannah knew Jolene had been blessed with a very special daughter because she had seen that same sensitivity in Patrick, years ago.

BRADLEY LOST HIS JOB. HIS COMFORTABLE THREE-YEAR contractual position had come to an end.

"Are you sure?" Savannah asked incredulously as Bradley handed her the email he printed.

"It just doesn't seem possible," Savannah said, reading the email and scanning it for the actual dates.

"I know," Bradley said, sitting by Savannah on their well worn leather couch. Savannah inhaled the comforting scent of his aftershave and felt the softness of his old gray flannel plaid shirt brushing up against her arm as he sat beside her.

"Between the job and all the running around for Patrick's activities, time just slipped away. And now I'm at the four-week mark. I was hoping it would be extended, but as you can see, or read, I had been so efficient that I completed the job right on time."

Bradley reached over and took Savannah's hand, gripping it tightly. His large, calloused hand encased her smaller one and his grip felt reassuring, and she knew he did not want her to worry.

"I'll put in for the unemployment, and that will definitely tide us over until my next gig comes along, and it will, but we won't have the health insurance."

Savannah knew what was coming next. She worked on a very part-time basis for an insurance company for pocket money—Patrick's sports teams fees, the once-a-week pizza at Mamma

Gini's Pizzeria. But that's all it was—pocket money, no paid time off, no insurance benefits, unless...

"We have a young child, and I'm not playing Russian roulette with his health, or yours or mine, and if anything ever happened..." Savannah let out a resigned sigh. She did not want to do what she was about to suggest but she had no other choice.

"I'll go back full time. We need one full time salary with benefits, and we don't know when the next job for you will come around. Besides, I want one of us to be home for Patrick. That's more important than anything. We can make it work." She forced a smile and patted Bradley on his knee—reassuring him that this was her decision.

"Savannah, I know how much you love being home with Patrick. I'm not going to take that away from you. I still have four weeks..."

"No," Savannah said firmly. "You work very long hours and next month, collect the unemployment for as long as you need, and I'll work full time. Like I said, Patrick is our first concern, and as long as one of us is here for him, I'm fine. Besides, Mr. DeYoung is constantly asking me when I can be available for full time, so he'll be happy to hear that I am. We're lucky I can do this, so let's take advantage of it. It won't be forever."

"I promise you, Savannah," Bradley whispered as he pulled her into his arms, "as soon as I'm back to work, you are going right back to part time." Savannah rested her cheek on his shoulder. His favorite shirt was well worn and just washed and she could smell the scent of the laundry soap coupled with the fragrance of the dryer sheets. It was as comforting as his embrace and caresses. She felt him kiss her hair, his lips moving down to her cheeks, and then onto her lips. She returned his kiss with fervor and he pulled away from her.

"C'mon," he said, standing in front of her with his hand outstretched. "I think it's time we hit the hay." He smiled that beguiling smile that always sent chills through her blood, just like the night she first met him at The Galway Rose. They checked in on Patrick, who was fast asleep, and Bradley led his wife into the sanctity of their bedroom and quietly closed the door.

Bradley received no job offers, and he was three months into his unemployment. Savannah had been working full time for almost that, and she was exhausted. Although Bradley was a huge help around the house, and she never worried about Patrick, she was still the one who made dinner and lunches and caught up on laundry on the weekends. Bradley supervised all of Patrick's homework and made sure he was at all basketball and baseball games, no matter where the team schedule sent them.

At least I don't have to worry about that, she thought one Saturday morning, after Bradley and Patrick had left at six for a basketball game in a town over an hour away. As much as she loved taking him to his games and cheering her son on, she did not relish driving all over the Eastern part of the state to get him to these games. Savannah would always do a triple check of the directions, making sure she wouldn't miss an exit when she got on the highway, something she had done on more than one occasion. She could never understand why a peewee team had to play fifty miles away and not just locally.

Later that day at Mamma Gini's Pizzeria, they celebrated not only the team's win but Patrick's MVP. As she watched her husband and son relive the day's events, laughing at silly calls and how the referee almost burst a blood vessel over an argument with a parent, a sense of melancholy seized Savannah hitting her with the realization of how much she missed Patrick and experiencing the antics of her son's coming of age in the world of pre-teen sports.

"Mom, you okay?" Patrick asked when Bradley excused himself to pay the bill.

Savannah smiled at her handsome son and marveled at the changes in his face from just a few months ago. Some of the soft baby chubbiness had evolved into thickened muscle and her baby was turning into a young athletic man. She wanted to drink in every essence of this moment and always remember what her son looked like when he was ten: jet black hair that hung into his deep blue eyes that were identical to Bradley's. In fact, he looked so much like his father, people commented constantly, especially when he was a baby. Savannah saw it more when Patrick was younger, but now, as he was getting a little older, although he still greatly resembled Bradley, she could also see that Patrick was developing into his own person. He most definitely had her wider nose, but everything else was Bradley. Savannah used to wonder what her little boy would look like one day when he became a man, and now she was getting a glimpse of the future.

Patrick took one last gulp of his root beer, and Savannah wished time would slow down. He was ten and in a blink of an eye he would be eighteen and off to college.

"Mom," he said, solemnly, chewing on the last piece of ice. Normally she would have told him to be careful, Savannah being fearful he would break a tooth or choke, but as he was getting older, she tried hard to restrain herself. She didn't want to be that mother who was always nagging at every little thing she thought dangerous or foolhardy. But she still watched carefully. Just in case. She could hear his teeth grind the ice and smiled at her son.

"Yes," she said, smiling at his seriousness. "You okay?"

"Oh, I'm fine. But I worry about you. I know you loved staying home and taking care of me, and I know you're sad you're working. I am too, but I don't want you to worry too much. Dad's a real good dad, and well, you know, I am growing up. I still need you, but I just don't want you to be sad."

Patrick thoughtfully examined the two remaining slices of pizza and chose the slice that appeared to have more pepperoni. Just like his dad would.

"You're right, Patrick. I did love staying home and taking care of you. But you are growing up and I know you're in good hands with Dad, so don't worry about me, okay? The only thing I want you to worry about is doing well in school and always doing your best. Deal?"

"Deal!" Patrick enthusiastically said, shooting his mother a big gap-tooth smile, which of course made Savannah think of the braces her son will need in the next few years and how she already started saving for the orthodontist bill.

The contract jobs had dried up, and Bradley had started bartending again. A friend of his former manager owned an upscale restaurant and when his bartender suddenly left with about $1,000 in cash and some very expensive bottles of gin, he asked Bradley if he could fill in for the dinner crowd. Bradley enthusiastically accepted and what turned into a temporary gig lasted the rest of his life.

Savannah wasn't thrilled about it but she had resigned herself to working full time. She was in deep with a decent weekly paycheck, great medical and dental benefits, and a generous time-off policy, there was no way she could leave, especially with Patrick involved with everything from violin recitals to baseball and basketball playoffs, not to mention the braces. Those extracurriculars cost a lot of money, money that Savannah's family didn't have when she was growing up, and she vowed to give her child what she didn't have, and the only way she could do that was by working full time. And when Bradley laid all the cards on the table about the hours being perfect for Patrick, not to mention huge tips, Savannah couldn't argue with him.

"Besides if it were not for my extraordinary bartending skills, I never would have met you, now would I?" he asked, embracing her in his muscular arms, immediately making her feel like the most loved woman in the world.

She kissed him on the neck and looked up into his smiling blue eyes.

"Well, your Long Island Iced Teas certainly attract the ladies, so keep that off your drinks repertoire, if you don't mind."

Bradley threw his head back in laughter, remembering the moment they met.

"Savannah, you and Patrick are my world," he said, holding her close, whispering into her hair. "I love you both so much. Besides," he said, holding her face in his strong and calloused hands, "the moment I met you, I knew that there would be no one else. No one compares to you or to the life that we have built together."

He kissed her deeply and, as with all their kisses, it was as thrilling as their first.

Every now and then Patrick would check on his mother, nonchalantly asking "Mom, are you happy? Mom, are you okay with this?" and although Savannah may not truly have been happy with her work situation, she was happy that her son was growing into a caring and sensitive young man.

"Yes, I am happy," she would tell him, kissing him on the cheek. If Patrick was secure and thriving, that's all Savannah needed to make her happy, and when she answered him, she was not lying.

"HMM. MR. AND MRS. CLAUS," SAVANNAH MURMURED, READING Sylvene's decorated envelope. She took a long sip of her coffee, immediately comforted by its strong aroma and bold taste. *To open or not to open*, Savannah mused as she played with the envelope, thinking that technically her name, well Mrs. Claus', was on it. Savannah had grown extremely fond of Sylvene and Jolene, and if there was something in that letter that Savannah could help with, she certainly would want to try. She carefully opened the envelope and removed the letter.

Dear Mr. and Mrs. Claus,

First I want to thank Mrs. Claus for making my mom and me the most delicious Thanksgiving dinner we ever ate. My mom loved it and I did too!

My mom hurt herself at work. My mom is a nurse and she loves to help people. She is always helping me with my homework and taught me how to bake chocolate chip cookies. But I know my mom is sad because sometimes at night when she thinks I'm asleep, I can hear her cry and that makes me sad, too.

All I want for Christmas is for my mom to be happy again. I want her to feel better and not cry at night. I'm not sure if you make this kind of Christmas wish come true or not, but my mom always says, it doesn't hurt to ask.

Thank you Mr. and Mrs. Claus! Merry Christmas!

Love,

Sylvene Siddons

PS: My mom's name is Jolene Siddons

Savannah sipped her coffee and felt the tears stream from her eyes. Never had a letter touched her heart so deeply. So short, but yet so sweet and endearing, that the depth of Sylvene's love for her mother moved Savannah, and she knew Mrs. Claus had to strike again to make Sylvene's Christmas wish come true. But how? That little girl did not ask for one tangible thing—a pretty necklace for her mom, or a new pair of gloves—Sylvene asked for her mom's happiness. If only Savannah could wave an enchanted Christmas wand and heal Jolene with a magical fairy tale snowfall. Savannah could cook an amazing Thanksgiving dinner, but she could not work miracles.

"I could ask Molly for some advice," she said, wiping the tears from her eyes with her sleeve. She gulped the last of her coffee and saw she had a couple of hours before heading to Howardson's.

A thunderous bolt of lightning struck not only the inside of Savannah's brain but in her heart, and she no longer needed Molly's advice on how to make the Siddons girls happy this Christmas. If a child like Sylvene could forfeit her own Christmas dreams for her mother's happiness, then Savannah could do something similar, and she began to formulate her plan.

Tis the season. It is better to give than to receive. Joy to the world! Those old idioms never rang truer than they did now, and as Savannah readied herself into her Mrs. Claus persona, she realized she could make this Christmas an unforgettable one for Sylvene and Jolene, and because of Savannah's generosity and empathy, this Christmas would be nothing short of extraordinary.

CHAPTER 18

SAVANNAH ADJUSTED THE LARGE WREATHS ON THE WOODEN DOORS of *The Enchanted Land of Claus*. They looked slightly askew, and in this Christmas wonderland, she wanted everything perfect. Within the wreaths she had placed a small chalkboard, with a countdown to Christmas, starting at the two-week mark. Savannah erased the number six and wrote the number five in bright green chalk. She drew a little spruce tree above the 5. A blue spruce in honor of The Blue Spruce Inn.

"Five more days until Christmas. It's unbelievable, isn't it, Fern?" The two women were the only ones in the employee lounge. All other elves and sheriffs reported to duty, ensuring everything was in working order within *The Enchanted Land of Claus*.

"All good things must come to an end," Fern replied matter-of-factly, draining her cup. "Like this cup of tea! Showtime in ten minutes, girlfriend!" Fern rinsed her cup and her fleet feet danced her out the door.

"Showtime," Savannah said solemnly. She was giving herself the once over in the full-length mirror, adjusting her blue stocking hat so the snowball of a pompom was right above her left shoulder. All too soon the beautiful dress will go in storage for the next year, she solemnly thought, flouncing the skirt and turning halfway around to make sure it billowed when she moved. There were five days until Christmas, but that meant only three days for *The Enchanted Land of Claus*, as it officially closed the day before Christmas Eve, and December 23rd loomed like a threatening snowstorm. But Mrs. Claus still had one last gift to deliver, and a few minutes was all she needed to put her plan into action.

"The Blue Spruce Inn. This is Ginny. How may I help you?"

Savannah's Blue Spruce Inn Christmas reservation now belonged to Jolene and Sylvene.

"I will send you an email confirmation immediately, with the details. I will make arrangements for my son to pick them up at the train station as well."

"Yes, an email confirmation would be appreciated. Thank you so much for accommodating me."

"The pleasure is all mine, Ms. Brady. Merry Christmas, my dear. And I can assure you your friends will have a wonderful holiday."

"I have no doubt they will," Savannah said."Merry Christmas."

Savannah put her phone into her bag. She had it on excellent authority from Molly that Jolene and Sylvene would not be venturing out for Christmas, nor would anyone be visiting. Jolene's mother was scheduled to come but Jolene's sister gave birth prematurely, and her mother was going to help. Sylvene's grandmother postponed her visit with her older daughter and granddaughter until Sylvene's February vacation.

"Those two need this more than I do," Savannah whispered, glancing once more into the mirror. A sudden lightness of mood lifted her spirits which were down moments before she phoned the inn to change the reservation. Granting a little girl's Christmas wish was the consummate Mrs. Claus finale. Savannah had not felt this happy in a long time. She was thoroughly delighted by the children who visited *The Enchanted Land of Claus*, as she was with the parents and the older folks who simply wanted to stroll down a happy Christmas memory lane. She felt privileged to be a part of this magical Christmas world that brought not only Christmas back into her life, but some very special people as well, elves and sheriffs she would never have met had it not been for being Mrs. Claus.

Savannah and Fern's friendship wouldn't go into storage like the Christmas decorations. People come and go in life, and they certainly did for Savannah, but she knew Fern Rhodes would be a part of hers forever. The bond they created over endless cups of peppermint tea, soothing crying children, having frosting squirted in the eye, and simply being a part of something so special was cemented in cookie icing for decades to come.

Yes, she thought before hitting the floor in her penultimate appearance as Mrs. Claus, *I have one more Christmas wish left to grant and it is probably the most important one of all.* Savannah then heard the jingle of the opening bell and like Fern, she danced onto the floor of *The Enchanted Land of Claus* with Christmas magic in each step.

CHAPTER 19

Later that afternoon Savannah deftly tied the bright green velvet bow on the gift box. Daisy Torres, the lead gift wrap consultant had given her a lesson once when Savannah filled in for a sick elf and learned the fine artistry of gift wrapping and bow tying. By her own admission, she wrapped gifts horribly, never cutting the paper straight enough or leaving enough for the ends to match up perfectly. And tying bows? When she was a kid she was lucky if her shoelaces were tied as they were always coming loose, leading to the inevitable tripping over her own feet. She secretly envied Patrick's childhood velcro shoes and she would have had a lot less tripping over untied shoelaces if such a thing existed in her own youth.

But Mrs. Claus needed the skills that made a gift look as if it was just pulled from Santa's sack, and thank goodness for Daisy. Savannah marveled at Daisy's nimble hands as expertly she cut thick swatches of wrapping paper, with the most perfectly even edges Savannah had seen.

"Thicker paper is not only prettier," Daisy explained, "but it is easier to manipulate and much more forgiving. Thin wrapping paper tears very easily, and you can't hide it. Well, I can't and then I have to start all over again. With thick paper!"

Daisy attached an almost invisible piece of tape to the edge and turned the beautifully wrapped game of Monopoly over for the piece de resistance—the bow. Daisy explained in origami terms how to tie the perfect bow, but Savannah shook her head.

"Daisy, this is like a geometry lesson. I could barely tie my shoes when I was a kid, never mind a Christmas present bow!"

Daisy smiled. "Well," she said, reaching under the work table, " when all else fails, use these!" She handed Savannah a big bag of Christmas-colored stick-on bows.

Savannah laughed, accepting the bag. "Now that is definitely my speed, but at least I can understand the wrapping part. See?" She took a shirt box and mimicked what Daisy did moments ago for the Monopoly game. She handed it to Daisy who gave it her Christmas glove test, and after carefully examining it handed it back to Savannah.

"A+!"

"But I will practice my bow tying skills. I promise."

"I think I should be worried about my job!" Daisy laughed.

"Not a chance," said Savannah, secretly pleased that Daisy deemed her gift wrapping lesson a success.

Savannah's bad gift wrapping was a family legend, and she and Bradley laughed about competitions over who could do the worst wrapping job. No matter how hard Bradley tried to outdo her, Savannah always won, with the tape never lying flat, always having a ridge within it and sometimes a bit of visible dust or dog hair. She always had extra paper hanging from the corners of a perfect square box. At Yankee Swaps and gift exchanges, everyone knew which gift was Savannah's, due to her wrapping inability. Her gifts, however, were always chosen first, because even though her gift wrapping skills were less than zero, her gift giving skills were beyond stellar. Savannah had a knack for choosing gifts that were beyond the ordinary, but still practical and pretty. From exquisite boxes of European candy to French silk scarves to tiny jars of Moroccan spices, Savannah's gifts were the ones people clamored for and the ones most cherished. Savannah stared at the box containing the train tickets and reservation at The Blue Spruce Inn, very proud of her handiwork. The box was wrapped exquisitely in frosty silver foil with the green bow tied expertly, the loops and ends exactly the same size. A tag with a drawing of Mrs. Claus and labeled *The Siddons Girls* hung daintily from the box. Savannah then summoned the courage to ask permission to leave early."I'd never ask, Matthew, as I know we are down to the wire, but this is for the Siddons girls, so I didn't think you'd mind?" It came out more as a question than a statement, and she shrugged her shoulders in anticipation of his hopefully affirmative answer. "And I'll come straight back to help clean up for the night. I promise."

"Well," Matthew said, "how can we refuse the Siddons?" He shot her that smile which sent her heart racing as fast as a sled dog in the Iditarod.

Impulsively, Savannah ran to him and kissed Matthew on his cheek, something that had totally taken her by surprise, feeling the warm blush rise to her cheeks.

"Oh, I'm sorry," she said, stepping back, straightening his tie. " Sylvene and Jolene mean so much to me." Her blushing went from warm to hot in seconds and there was no way Matthew could not have noticed, his piney aftershave lingering in her nostrils, making the goosebumps rise even higher on her skin.

It's those eyes, she scolded herself, watching his eyes dance with merriment upon her kiss. His smiling face sent her heart fluttering. She wanted to remain loyal to Bradley, but as hard as she tried to fight it, Matthew's awkwardness and humility was just as attractive a feature as any physical one, and kissing him felt natural. Savannah made a difficult promise to keep the day her husband died—the promise to never love another man. As much as she tried to hold on to Bradley, he was no longer here, but Matthew was. It was just all too much, this collision of the past and the present, the love for her husband, and now her emerging feelings for another man. Her head pounded with guilt, and her throat constricted.

"I'll be back in an hour or so." She turned to leave as fast as she could and then felt his gentle touch on her shoulder.

"Savannah, is everything alright?" Matthew asked, coming closer, and she heard the concern in his voice.

"Yes," she replied, slowly pulling away from him, trying to keep her distance. She had gone too far and would not make the same mistake again.

"It's just a little later than I thought, and I'd like to get this to them."

She forced a smile, and she could tell by the hurt look in his eyes that Matthew knew it was not genuine. "You'd better get going," he said, heading to the floor. "Don't worry about coming back tonight. Go ahead on home. Tomorrow's the last day and we'll see you then," he said, dashing through the doors as if he now needed to get away from her.

Now I've done it, Savannah thought, knowing her sudden abruptness hurt him. She then realized something else: Bradley's presence. She noticed these last few weeks that he wasn't occupying her thoughts as much as he always had, and she chalked it up to her exhausting holiday schedule. But for the last day or two especially, he was in her mind constantly. Everywhere she looked she saw Bradley, especially now closer to Christmas. *Are you trying to tell me something, darling?* Savannah half expected an answer from him, but, of course, none came.

She shook her head, trying to clear the cobwebs that left her in tangles these past few days. Savannah would have plenty of time to think about it after tomorrow, when *The Enchanted Land of Claus* closed for the holidays, but right now, Mrs. Claus had one last Christmas wish to grant.

CHAPTER 20

"Cat got that tongue of yours, Mr. Buck?" Matthew was in the employee lounge, feet propped on a chair, swigging the last of the brutally strong and ice cold coffee fermenting in the pot.

"Arg, this stuff must be at least twelve hours old," he said to Fern, who was brewing a cup of tea.

"If you're that desperate for a cup of coffee, I'm happy to make you one. But you could always do that yourself." He could hear the jab in Fern's voice as she sat down with her steaming mug of peppermint tea.

"Not desperate. Just lazy. And exhausted." He winced and tossed the crumpled paper cup into the trash.

"Three points!" he laughed. "Seriously, I will be glad when this is over. It's been fun, and just as important, very financially successful, but I think I'm ready to hop on the sleigh and fly outta *The Enchanted Land of Claus* until next year. I'm not so sure about you and Savannah, but I know that I am."

"What makes you think that?" Fern asked, inhaling the calming scent of the peppermint tea. "You think it's easy being head elf in this joint? I'm with you. I've decorated my last cookie and constructed my last gingerbread house until next year. I hope there's room on your sleigh for me." She sipped her tea and winked at her old friend.

"Savannah has been a wonderful Mrs. Claus. The customers rave about her as do the elves. And this elf is particularly fond of her, so heed your head elf's warnings if you have any disparaging remarks about her. She is a huge part of *The Enchanted Land of Claus'* success. Huge." Fern said with great emphasis on her last word.

"Don't you think I know that?" Matthew got up and spooned ground coffee into the coffeemaker.

"I just think she may have gone a little overboard with the Siddons family. I have no idea what she has up her sleeve, but I hope it doesn't backfire on her." He wasn't going to mention their last exchange to Fern, as he didn't want to admit it, but he was tremendously hurt when she suddenly turned as cold as a North Pole iceberg, even as her kiss still lingered warm on his cheek.

"Matthew Buck. What kind of talk is that?" Fern slammed her cup down on the table in frustration at her beloved friend.

"I've known you for years and have been like a second mother to you. It's been me you always come to with a problem in your romantic life. I know your own mother well, and if she heard you speak like that about someone as special as Savannah, she'd box your ears. And I just might do that, too."

Matthew exaggeratedly put his hands over his chest, as if Fern mortally wounded him.

"Ouch! Fern, come on, Savannah's great, but…"

"But nothing," Fern commanded. "It's been very obvious to me, and everyone else, that you've had a crush on her from the moment you met, and now because she wanted to rush off and make sure Sylvene and Jolene got their gift on time, and you're put off? Listen, pal, there's travel involved with this gift and she needed to be sure they had plenty of time to get ready. It had to be tonight or not at all."

"Travel? What do you mean?"

"I'll tell you what I mean. Savannah planned a Christmas getaway for herself. In case you hadn't noticed, she's alone, but she felt those two needed it more than she did, so she switched the reservations from her name to theirs. She booked them on the 9:00 am train tomorrow, so time is of the essence, buddy."

"Getaway?" Matthew asked. "To where?"

"The Blue Spruce Inn. Ever hear of it?"

Matthew then recalled Savannah mentioning her Christmas vacation, but with all the hecticness of the season, it slipped his mind. Matthew felt the bore of Fern's hard stare, and had the distinct feeling she could see straight into his soul. Matthew was the recipient of Fern's penetrating looks numerous times when Matthew had misstepped and needed to be pointed in the right direction. Just like a mother would. He leaned into Fern's face and stared right back at her, and then broke into his huge affable grin.

"I could kiss you. And I will," he said, enveloping her in a bear hug with a peck on the cheek to boot.

"That's better," Fern laughed. "I will never lose my faith in you, Matthew."

"I'll see you tomorrow. Last day!" He grabbed his coat from the closet, and Fern gently grabbed his arm.

"It's the last day of *The Enchanted Land of Claus*, but it could also be the first day of something bigger. Go get her, Matthew, or you'll forever wish you did."

Matthew leaned in and gave Fern another kiss on the cheek.

"I don't know what I'd do without you." he said, dashing through the frosty December night.

CHAPTER 21

The twinkling bright lights of the Christmas tree lot beckoned Savannah on her way home from the Siddons. The huge handmade sign declaring 75% off all trees helped, too, and Savannah found herself wandering through the tiny lot. Pickings were slim, but there were still some very pretty trees left for latecomers.

Savannah's family never bought a real tree—she and Bradley didn't want to break their own family traditions when they had Patrick and always had an artificial tree. They bought a spectacular eight-foot-tall tree, in Howardson's, at a pre-Christmas sale. Two weeks before Christmas when Patrick was four, she and Bradley spent the entire night assembling and decorating it. When Patrick awoke the next morning, he couldn't believe his eyes at this spectacular tree now standing in his living room. "Santa must think I'm real good this year!" he exclaimed as he gently touched the ornaments on the tree—a combination of those Savannah had saved from her childhood, as did Bradley whose mother had sent a box of old ornaments the year they were married, to the ones made by Patrick's tiny hands—paper chains and styrofoam snowmen with photos of Patrick in place of two coal eyes and a carrot nose. Savannah and Bradley carried on this tradition until Patrick was eight and announced that he wanted to help decorate the tree, and a new Christmas tradition was born: the annual day-after Thanksgiving event of foraging in the basement and hauling out the tree and ornaments, not to mention the lights, which no matter how careful Savannah was the year before, always ended up in a tangled mess. It became Patrick's job to untangle all the lights, which he proved very good at, and help place them on the tree. He became so adept at his light placement, that the following year it was solely left to him, and the effect was nothing short of spectacular.

As Savannah walked through the lot of trees, she found herself smiling at her Christmas memories. Not long ago, these memories brought tears of sadness to her eyes, but now, she could feel a smile stretch across her lips. She was a woman with a family who created beautiful moments in her life, moments that she got to live and to feel. She knew many had not experienced the look of joy on a child's face on Christmas morning or the comfort of the loving arms of a spouse. Savannah's memories were no longer sorrowful losses—they were the fabric of a person well-loved in life, and in death. She felt Bradley's love every day and it would always be with her, and she knew that love truly did not die when a person did, for it lived on. Savannah also realized, as she gravitated toward a small table-top tree perched on a wooden bench in a green planter, that love could be reborn as well, and that this could possibly be happening with Matthew. It was too early to know if it was true love, but her gut feeling told Savannah she might be able to open herself up to another man. Might.

"I'll take this one, please," Savannah said to the older gentleman standing near the back of the lot. She looked at him and smiled.

"You've probably heard this a million times, but has anyone ever told you look like Santa?" Savannah smiled.

"I know, I know," the man laughed as he took Savannah's twenty-dollar bill.

"I wish I had a castle, even if it was at the North Pole. But I do have a red pickup truck." He nodded toward the parking lot where a beat up old truck was parked. It was decorated to the hilt, with a wreath on the front bumper, fuzzy antlers on each side of the front windows, and large decals of Christmas trees, Santa heads, and snowmen adorned the truck. In bold white cursive on the driver's door was written *Sandy Claws. I'll do the work while you Christmas pause.*

"Sandy Claws?" Savannah laughed, picking up her little tree.

"Named the business after my old faithful companion, Sandy, a little yellow mutt I found wandering the streets one Christmas. I took her home and we were inseparable until she passed on last year. She was my faithful companion for nineteen years. Anyway, when I retired, I started my little Christmas decorating business, and she sat right in the driver's seat of the truck while I climbed ladders, stringing lights and hanging wreaths. That little girl is still with me every day, right on my lap when I get in the truck. Still looking after her old man."

"I have no doubt she is," Savannah said, gripping her tree.

"You have a Merry Christmas, sir," she said, smiling at the old gentleman, turning to make her way home.

"And you as well, Mrs. Claus."

Savannah turned, but the man was no longer there. The lot suddenly became very crowded, and he must have gone off to help a customer. She then heard the rattle and sputter of an old engine as lights as bright as a full winter moon shone in her eyes. She spied him in his truck, waving, Savannah could have sworn she also saw a little yellow dog sitting in the man's lap.

"Oh, don't be silly, Savannah," she said, as she and her little tree walked onto the street and toward their home.

"There you go, my little Charlie Brown tree," Savannah said lovingly, looking at bright red, green, yellow and blue lights she had strung. It looked pretty and festive perched on the kitchen counter, and it certainly gave the apartment the dash of Christmas cheer it sorely needed. She shut off all the lights and basked in the cheerful glow of her pretty little tree.

Savannah was exhausted and knew she should climb straight into bed since tomorrow would be busy, but the lights of the tree were so comforting. She reclined on her couch and pulled one of Patrick's Christmas fleece blankets around her—his favorite, decorated with Santa Claus and Rudolph. She marveled at the comfort and happiness the little tree brought into her life—how something so small, but so meaningful, could change the entire atmosphere in her apartment. A few hours ago it was just an average, run-of-the-mill apartment, but this little tree, simply bedecked with a few strings of colorful lights, instantly transformed her lonely apartment into one of comfort and joy. As the Christmas tree lights hypnotized Savannah, and her eyelids grew heavy, visions from Christmases past—of Patrick running down the stairs at two o'clock am, with delighted screams of "He came! He came!" upon seeing the mounds of presents under the tree, and of Bradley making that first pot of holiday coffee and whipping up his legendary Christmas French toast with homemade whipped cream sprinkled with cinnamon.

And again, as in the tree lot, there was no sadness in these memories, as Savannah closed her eyes feeling nothing but contentment and gratefulness for the wonderful life she had with her two men and would cherish for all the days of her life.

"Merry Christmas, little tree," she murmured. "Thank you for helping to bring Christmas back to me."

Wanting to spend more time with her tree, Savannah settled in with a cup of peppermint tea in front of the roaring electric fireplace. Fern had sent what seemed like a whole case of tea to Savannah's apartment with a hand-drawn card of a figure that resembled Savannah in her Mrs. Claus dress, and inside had written *An Early Merry Christmas present to our own Mrs. Claus. Lots of Love this Christmas. Fern.*

And now the end was here. One more day to spend in that captivating dress. This had been such a special time for Savannah, and she didn't think it could ever be replicated. But did she want it to be?

"Things are rarely better the second time around," she murmured into her tea cup, looking at her tree. She knew that she wasn't just thinking about *The Enchanted Land of Claus* either. She was thinking about Matthew and how different he was from Bradley. Where Bradley was shorter in stature, Matthew was that much taller and thinner, with Bradley more muscular, working out every day with his beloved weights. Where Matthew was professionally driven, Bradley was content with his contracting positions, leaving him time for his family, and was especially happy when his last contract job ended and he returned to bartending.

"I told you this would be lucrative," Bradley said one night. It was actually almost four o'clock in the morning. Savannah always had been an early riser, but she was up earlier than usual when she realized Bradley wasn't home.

She was nursing a cup of coffee when he walked in, and he reached into his backpack and threw what seemed like hundreds of dollars on the kitchen table.

"The bachelor party didn't close down until three. At this rate, I get a few more parties under my belt, Patrick will never have to take a loan out for college. That's my goal for him. I want him to have a good start in life, and if this is what it takes, I have no problem working these crazy hours."

So bartending it was, while Savannah worked at the insurance company and their little family life continued on until Bradley's untimely death.

Although the house was quiet, Bradley's absence spoke volumes. His presence permeated the house, and his ghost haunted every room. She swore she could smell the lingering scent of his aftershave, the traditional perfume of Old Spice. A small bottle remained in the bathroom cabinet, and every now and then, Savannah found herself pulling the stopper from the top and holding it under her nose, inhaling what was left of her husband. No matter how many times she washed the sheets, she could still smell it when she went to bed at night. When she opened the door of their bedroom closet, it escaped from there as well, the cologne still lingering on Bradley's clothes. But Bradley's ghost was not the only one haunting her; so was the ghost of the little boy that used to live in the house. From the height markings on the wall of the half bath outside of the kitchen to the dinged-up living room window blinds, victims of Sunday football games, to Patrick's bedroom and the myriad boy stuff he accumulated throughout his life.

Her home, once filled with bliss and contentment now only harbored loneliness and grief. There was no son, no husband, no dog to greet her now at the end of a long day, only the assailant of sadness. She knew the memories would eventually bring comfort, but now they brought only grief, and Savannah made the heartbreaking decision to sell her family home.

It was hard to believe just a year ago this past fall her former life was neatly wrapped into moving boxes and she was starting a new life in her own apartment, the first time she had ever been on her own. She lived frugally and started a vacation fund for a Christmas vacation at The Blue Spruce Inn. Like the currents of the sea, Savannah knew all too well how life changes swiftly and quickly. It would be Sylvene and Jolene, not Savannah, spending Christmas in the White Mountains with the Blue Spruce golden retrievers and enjoying the holiday at the country inn.

The happiness of a single mother and her young daughter would be enough of a Christmas present for Savannah this year, knowing that she was able to help with a little girl's unselfish wish of giving her mother a Merry Christmas.

CHAPTER 22

"MERRY CHRISTMAS, EVERYONE!" MATTHEW GREETED, UNCORKING bottles of champagne and sparkling apple cider. Savannah and Fern passed glasses to all the elves and sheriffs at the store's Christmas party in the employee lounge. The wooden doors of *The Enchanted Land of Claus* closed on a very successful season, and Matthew catered a party from the Yellow Pumpkin.

"Before we dig in, I just wanted to thank you all for your hard work. As fun as it was, we certainly weren't without our challenges."

"You tell 'em, Sheriff Sugar Plum," shouted Brock, still decked out in his Santa costume.

"I will!" exclaimed Matthew, lifting his glass.

"I truly mean it when I say that *The Enchanted Land of Claus* would not have been the success it was without each and every one of you. Customers were happy and kept returning because of all of you."

"Hear!" yelled Fred from the back of the lounge,"C'mon, Matty, we're starving!"

"Okay," Matthew laughed. "Just a few more thank yous and then you shall feast! A special thanks to Fern Rhodes for all of her amazing costume design, not to mention enduring the chaos of cookie decorating. I had no idea how dangerous that could be!"

Loud applause and cheers broke out celebrating the seamstress. Fern graciously curtsied and held her glass out to Matthew.

Matthew winked and lifted his glass again.

"To Brock Harvey, Santa extraordinaire!"

"HO, HO, HO," laughed Brock as he lifted a full glass of champagne to his lips.

"And one more special thanks to Savannah Brady." He looked directly at Savannah, and for a moment, it seemed as if it was only the two of them in the lounge. "Savannah, thank you for making our customers feel extra special this year, as well as this sheriff in particular. Thank you and Merry Christmas."

Matthew wanted to say so much more, but this was not the time or the place. The blushing pink of Savannah's cheeks alerted him to make it short and sweet. For now.

"Let's eat!"

The crowd clapped and cheered, and Matthew raised his glass toward the crowd of hungry elves and sheriffs. Savannah lifted hers, and then turned and bolted out of the lounge.

"What did I do now?" Matthew asked Fern, totally puzzled once again by Savannah's behavior.

"Go after her, dummy," said Fern, pushing him in the direction Savannah had gone.

He handed Fern his drink and headed out into the empty store. Only the Christmas lights were lit, giving *The Enchanted Land of Claus* a cozy, but lonely glow. He turned and spotted Savannah sitting on Santa's throne, her head in her hands, and from the shaking of her shoulders, he knew she was crying.

"Savannah?" His voice was barely a whisper. He was used to crying females with Summer and Athena, but their cries were angry, generally directed at him. Savannah's cries sounded sorrowful. Matthew quietly knelt in front of her and placed his hand on her knee. She clasped it with her own. The softness of her touch jolted him, and his heart broke at her sadness.

"I'm sorry, Matthew," she said between sobs. "I was fine until you thanked me and then all of a sudden this dam of Christmases past I've tried to hold off for so long just broke. I couldn't stop it. I'm sorry for flying out of there like I did, but I couldn't stay."

She looked at him, and Matthew saw those pretty green eyes had lost their constant twinkle. Matthew reached into his jacket pocket and pulled out his handkerchief and began to wipe away her tears.

"You would have a handkerchief," she smiled through her falling tears.

He nodded in agreement.

"That's my mother for you. She made sure my brother and I always had one in our pockets. We were so embarrassed, we never took them out when we were kids, but we did what she asked, and we both still carry them today. It's actually my grandfather's, my father's father. Our mother found tons of them in my grandfather's dresser drawers when he passed away, and she made sure my brother and I always had one. She said carrying one would be like having our grandfather with us always. And she was right."

Matthew handed Savannah the handkerchief. She unfolded it and saw the initials *MB* embroidered in the corner.

"Your grandfather's name was Matthew, too?"

"No, it was Maximillian, or Max. My father was Michael, I'm Matthew, obviously," he chuckled, "and my brother's name is Mitchell. We always joked with our mother that she made sure we had the same initials so that she wouldn't have to order more handkerchieves."

He watched Savannah's shoulders bob with laughter and not tears.

"Smart woman," she said, taking the soft piece of cotton and drying her eyes.

"That she is."

Savannah's eyes met Matthew's and again he felt that familiar feeling of longing tightly grasp inside of him. He wanted to take this wounded soul into his arms and comfort her, but did he dare? Fearing he'd never have this opportunity again, he took the chance, and he wrapped his arms around her and felt her body surrender to his. He could smell the sea breeze scent in her shining silver hair and held her tighter, kissing the top of her head.

"It's alright," Matthew murmured softly, stroking her hair and gently kissing her once again.

He felt her pull away and looked at her tear-stained face. Matthew thought Savannah had never looked more beautiful.

"Everything just hit me suddenly," she said, wiping her eyes with his handkerchief.

"I really thought I was okay. I even bought a little Christmas tree for my apartment on the way home from dropping off my present for the Siddons. I was fine at home, finally feeling the happy spirit of Christmas, but in the lounge with everyone made me realize it's just me this Christmas. My husband is gone, my son's in a different country. At least with Mrs. Claus I had a purpose, and now she's gone, too. These past few weeks have been the happiest for me in a very long time, Matthew." Savannah sat erect in Santa's chair and squared her shoulders."I'm sorry, Matthew. I didn't mean to burden you. It's not like me just to break down like this."

Savannah bowed her head and Matthew watched her slender fingers twist his handkerchief.

"Thanks for this," she said, motioning the handkerchief with her hands toward him.

"You keep it," he smiled. "There's plenty more at my mom's."

"Thank you," she whispered.

"You're welcome," Matthew said as he stood up and extended his hand to Savannah. "You're coming with me."

"I can't go back in there, Matthew," Savannah said, shaking her head."I'm not in a festive mood right now. I think I'll go home."

"Exactly," Matthew said, a huge smile broadening across his face."I'm taking you home so you can pack a bag. I want you to come home with me. For Christmas."

"What?" Savannah asked, rising from Santa's chair. "No, really, Matthew…"

"No," he laughed,"not my apartment, my family home. It's a few hours north, and if my mother ever found out I left a lady, especially Mrs. Claus, in distress, at Christmas, she would disown me. Or worse." He looked into her face and detected a hint of a smile.

"Well, if it were my Patrick, I would do the same. Or worse."

Matthew's heart lightened as he saw that twinkle return to her sparkling green eyes, now dried of tears. He looked into those eyes and knew he wasn't going to leave her alone for Christmas or for any holiday, and if there was even the slimmest chance she felt the same, well, he was willing to jump in and find out. There could be no better Christmas present.

Savannah slipped her hand into his. Her hand was soft and warm, and he gave it the slightest squeeze, which Savannah returned. She stood facing him and Matthew felt the strongest urge to kiss her, to hold her as close to him as he possibly could and not let her go. But not here. No, he would wait until they were away from the city, away from the store, away from life. He wanted it to be special and unforgettable, and he sensed, from what he knew about Savannah Brady, this would be what she would want, too.

Matthew led Savannah out from the darkened *Enchanted Land of Claus*, to what he hoped would be their own enchanted winter wonderland.

"C'mon, Mrs. Claus," he whispered. "Time to get you out of the city and to my own North Pole."

CHAPTER 23

Ginny Buck stood in her kitchen not knowing what to do next. The kitchen looked as if a bomb of flour detonated, with huge white splotches covering the jet black and stainless steel stove and the pale gray tiled floor. Ginny could barely pull herself away from Sylvene, but work waited for no one and there would be no dinner or dessert if she didn't get a move on now, but that little girl reminded her so much of Athena when she was that age —that most wondrous age especially at Christmas time.

Sylvene was fast asleep on the couch in front of the fireplace. The hike and sleigh ride wore her right out, and when Ginny came into the living room bearing mugs of hot chocolate, the little girl was already in dreamland.

"Here," said Ginny to Jolene, who was half asleep herself in the chaise by the front bay window.

"You go up to your room and rest for a while. I'm just in the kitchen, and Moonlight is right by Sylvene's side. You have nothing to worry about."

"I could use a rest on that amazing bed," Jolene said, gratefully eying the mug full of a wonderful smelling chocolate.

"Of course you can and you should," said Ginny. She grabbed

the crutch Jolene had been using and held her arm out for Jolene for balance as she helped her up the few stairs to their room.

"There, get off your feet," Ginny said, placing the crutch by the bed with the steaming mug of chocolate on the bedside table. Jolene could maneuver going downstairs with little difficulty, but going up was another story, and she needed just a little bit of assistance.

"Thank you so much, Ginny," said Jolene, as she hopped onto the feather soft queen-sized bed. "You've been so kind to me and Sylvene, I only wish I could help out in the kitchen."

"Nonsense," Ginny said, tucking the covers under Jolene's legs. "You didn't come here to be kitchen help—you came here for a much-needed vacation, and that's what you're going to get. You rest up and later we can all set the table for dinner. How's that?"

"I'd love nothing more," Jolene answered, giving Ginny the thumbs up.

"And don't worry about Sylvene. She's in good hands. And paws."

"Thank you, Ginny."

Ginny closed the door and went downstairs. She gently patted Moonlight's silky golden head who looked up at his mistress through sleepy eyes. Moonlight's siblings, Mermaid and Meringue, were already sleeping in front of the fire. Meringue was pregnant and rested as much as she could in the days before her delivery which would be around New Year's Day. Meringue hadn't been eating much and was restless until now, which made Ginny wonder if her due date wouldn't be sooner. She made a mental note to call Dr. Ruthmon to make sure she was in town for the holidays, and if not, which of her staff would be available should the time come sooner.

"You watch over her and your siblings, sweetheart. I'm just in the kitchen." Ginny leaned over and kissed Moonlight, who responded with a kiss of his own. She then knelt in front of the fire and patted Mermaid and Meringue's downy heads before returning to her kitchen duty.

She finished mashing the potatoes for the evening's dinner of shepherd's pie which would go into the oven in about an hour. The only guests at the moment were Jolene and Sylvene with one other guest arriving Christmas morning. Ginny decided she wanted a smaller guest list this Christmas at the Inn. Usually, the Inn accommodated ten guests at the holidays, but this year she was just not in the mood to cook and cater to an inn full of Christmas guests. When Wanda Basz, Ginny's long-time friend and devoted employee, decided to open a new chapter in her own life, Ginny knew this Christmas was going to be different.

"You know how much I love you and the Inn, Ginny," Wanda said one June day as they were folding clean towels for guests who would be arriving later that afternoon.

"I just won't get another opportunity like this again. I'm pushing seventy, and well..."

"I've pushed seventy, so I certainly know how you feel." Ginny gently patted Wanda's hands, reassuring her that she understood it was time for Wanda to move on.

"Heck, if I got an opportunity to spend the next year in Poland, I'd leave here too."

Wanda stacked the ivory towels in a neat pile. "I was so happy to receive my cousin's letter. We've been pen pals for decades, but both of us have been so busy with our lives. Now the kids are grown, well, a nice long visit was what we both wanted. We're free to travel, so that's what we are going to do. A year traveling Poland and beyond. Then I'll be back. I promise."

"I want no such promise, Wanda, do you understand me? I hope you meet a handsome Polish count and become countess of some castle I couldn't even begin to pronounce. When do you leave?"

"I'll be here for the Fourth of July barbecue and then I fly out the night of July 5th. There was no way I was leaving before Independence Day."

Ginny rolled out a pie crust thinking that was six months ago, and that was when Ginny closed off the Christmas reservations, with only a reservation for Savannah Brady and one other guest. Athena wasn't coming this year due to a horseback riding competition which started on Boxing Day, so keeping it smaller seemed like the right thing to do.

"But we have Sylvene and Jolene this year," she said, and as if on cue, Mermaid padded into the kitchen. Mermaid in particular stayed close to Ginny, especially when she was in the kitchen, as some kind of scrap always conveniently fell right on the floor before Mermaid's nose.

Sylvene. Jolene. Savannah. Matthew was very brief on the phone about her, but she knew in an instant, she was special to her younger son. Ginny already knew that when Savannah changed her long-held reservation from her own name to the Siddons girls. Savannah had made her reservation right before Wanda broke the news of her departure, and she had been the only guest to request a monthly payment plan. All of her previous guests would just charge it and forget about it, but obviously Savannah had to be careful with her money, and her payments always arrived right on time. Ginny had just received Savannah's final payment when Savannah phoned to change her reservation.

Now, through some strange coincidence, or not, Savannah was coming as Matthew's guest, and she would be staying in the carriage house. Ginny stood at her kitchen window gazing at her beloved carriage house.

It will be nice to have it occupied again, she thought as she turned back to her pie crust. As much as she loved the cooking and the baking and the general running of the inn, this year seemed peculiar to her, and she not only felt Wanda's absence, but her husband Michael's as well. Although Michael had been gone for quite some time, it was at Christmas, especially, that she felt the emptiness without him. It was Michael who was the true heart and soul of The Blue Spruce Inn, his dream turned into a reality with nothing but hard work and sheer determination.

Ginny noticed a restlessness in Michael when Matthew started kindergarten. She sensed his increasing dissatisfaction with his work as a marketing executive for a top Boston investment firm, working long hours, not to mention many weekends, keeping him away from his home and family, and Ginny knew Michael was becoming more wistful for a place like his Brightmore, New Hampshire roots.

"The air is always stale in Boston, Ginny, and nearly impossible to look for constellations in a winter sky. The city streets are littered and crowded. If we lived in the suburbs, the boys would have a big yard to run in, and we could get one of those golden retrievers you are always talking about. We could actually live."

Ginny had put her arms around her husband's neck and nuzzled into his chin. She had noticed the first wisps of gray in his hair, and she knew Michael felt the passage of time faster than she did. He was two years older and always laughed that she was two years behind him in his thinking. She felt his arms lovingly embrace her, as she harbored a secret, one she would never tell anyone: that she was in love. In love with the city and most of all in love with the Beacon Hill townhouse they scraped every penny to buy eight years before, right after Matthew was born. To say it needed work was an understatement, but Ginny was adamant. They had rented it from an elderly, retired attorney who lived in Maine and really wanted nothing to do with the place. When he died, he left no heirs, and his will simply stated to sell the brownstone. Ginny and Michael were offered the right of first refusal.

"Michael, this is a goldmine," Ginny said one evening, after the estate attorney had been in touch with them. "There's plenty of room for the boys, maybe a golden retriever..."

"Ginny," Michael said, sipping his evening brandy from his favorite crystal glass, one Ginny found at a tag sale, "my salary is good but it's not great. I just don't think we could afford it. Especially with two growing boys."

"Well, I have some money saved from baking for the Atlantic Diner. And I promise to paint, wallpaper, whatever it takes, all on my own."

She watched him pour himself another glass and as he did she could see the wheels turning in his brain, and she knew exactly how he would respond, so she beat him to it.

"Michael," she said, getting up and sitting on the arm of his old leather chair. She began to massage the knots from his neck, and like a seasoned attorney, she began to plead her case.

"Look, I know you want to move to the suburbs, but if you think this house will cost money, that will cost even more. Your commute into the city alone would be over an hour, and you hate traffic. Here, you hop on a bus or subway, or when the weather is nice, you can even walk to the office. The boys love the Museum of Science and the Boston Common is their playground. They have friends and they're happy at St. Hedwig's school and oh, well, Michael, the suburbs are just so bland. All the houses look the same, there are no—"

"You can rest your case, Ginny." Michael pulled his wife into his lap and kissed her passionately on her soft pink lips. He pulled her in close to him, and Ginny never wanted the moment to end. She loved this man with all of her heart and soul, and if she couldn't convince him to stay, well, she would follow him anywhere.

"We'll stay. We'll figure it out financially. But I'm warning you," he said with that musical laugh that always melted Ginny, "when retirement rolls around, we're heading to New Hampshire."

It took Ginny a few years to gloriously restore the brownstone, with the occasional help from contractors who were fathers of her boys' friends. It was the first brownstone in a line of ten and the smallest, as the rest of the row belonged to Calloway Junior College, with its elegant classrooms and dormitories. Ginny's renovations included a kitchen and mudroom on the first level, while the second floor had two bedrooms, as did the third, one of them consigned as Michael's study. Their home had good bones, but needed new plumbing and electrical, leaving the rest strictly cosmetic. In between caring for her family and her baking job, Ginny painted, wallpapered and shellacked the woodwork to its original glowing beauty. It was cozy and warm. It was their home, and Ginny never saw, after all her intensive labor and getting it to be exactly how she wanted, what was thundering in the very near future.

"IT'S NOT AN OPTION, GINNY. WE HAVE NO CHOICE."

Ginny remained as stoic as possible when her husband told her that his firm went bankrupt through bad investments and would be closing at the end of the year. In two months.

Michael drained his glass of brandy and immediately refilled it.

"Dad just bought himself a smaller place five miles from the house, and he'll sell the farmhouse to us for a song. Calloway's been hounding us for months now to buy this place, so we can make them an offer they can't refuse, pay Dad, and we'll be mortgage free. I know it's not what you want Ginny, but right now I don't have a job, which means we don't have a lot of options."

No, it's not what I want. Ginny held her tongue. If she didn't, a huge fight would erupt and words would be said that could never be forgotten. Michael never drank more than two glasses of brandy, but right now he was starting on his third, and Ginny had to tread carefully. Her husband lost his job. All the long hours, weekends, missing the boys' school events, and for what? No. She wasn't going there. She could feel her heart cracking into a million pieces—for losing her home, for her husband losing his job, for her losing the contented family life she worked so hard to create.

Lying in bed later that night, and unable to sleep, Ginny remembered something her mother once said.

"Remember, honey, a house is just a dwelling, but a home is love."

Home. She could be home anywhere as long as she had her boys with her. Michael, of course, had convinced Mitchell and Matthew that moving to Brightmore would be their greatest adventure of their young lives. It was nonstop "when are we leaving? Can we play hockey, ski, and snowmobile?" Her sons were beyond excited and happy to leave their cozy little brownstone.

Matthew and Mitchell had just come home from school, throwing their shoes and books all over the mudroom floor. Christmas break was a week away, and Ginny had been packing as the plan was to move up north during the Christmas vacation and have the boys start at Brightmore Elementary in January.

"I can't wait to get to Brightmore," said Mitchell, stuffing his second chocolate chip cookie into his mouth and swishing it down with a glass of chocolate milk.

"I thought you loved it here," Ginny asked, wiping up drops of spilled milk.

"We do, but we love it there, too, Mom. Remember how Matthew couldn't stop bawling when we had to leave last summer? How Grandpa Max taught me to fish and taught Matthew how to fix the tractor motor? We love that stuff."

"Yeah, we love that stuff," his little brother parroted, carefully watching his older brother, mimicking him in every way possible from stuffing cookies into his tiny mouth to wiping his milk-stained lips with his shirt sleeve.

Ginny continued to wipe the counter listening to her sons marvel about the wonders of rural New Hampshire.

"Yeah. Dad said when he turns the farmhouse into an inn, we can all help out. He wants to get a horse and a carriage and give rides around the farm and he has all these different ideas for different times of the year. You know, apple picking in the fall, sleigh rides in the winter, and fishing in the spring. There'll be tons to do, Mom."

"Yeah, tons to do," Matthew said, following Mitchell to the kitchen counter and dropping his cookie-crumbed plate into the sink.

"You've obviously discussed this extensively with your father," Ginny said, quite amazed at the wealth of information Mitchell was excitedly spewing.

"He says it's going to be the family business, and we're the family. Oh, and he said, the kitchen is so big there, you'll have plenty of room to bake tons of pies and cakes and cookies."

"Yeah, tons of room," Matthew said, wiping his hands on the back of his pants.

"Matthew, don't do that; you need those pants for school tomorrow."

"Oh, sorry, Mom. I'm going to change anyway." He started to head upstairs, but turned back into the kitchen.

"You know, I will miss everyone at St. Hedwig's but Sister Lucilla said that when God closes a door, he opens a window, although I'm not sure what that means."

Ginny walked toward Matthew and took her younger son into her arms and kissed his tousled light brown hair.

"Sister Lucilla is a very wise woman. It means that when one chapter ends, another begins."

"Yeah, Dad's job ended but he can begin again in Brightmore," said Mitchell in his older brother-wisdom voice, dashing up the stairs in the daily race to beat his brother.

Matthew remained for a moment, still wrapped in his mother's arms.

"You're happy about the move, aren't you, Mom?"

Ginny looked into her little boy's sea-glass eyes, and saw them cloud with doubt. He was still a young boy at eight, and his mother knew he needed her comforting reassurance.

Ginny pulled Matthew closer. The top of his head reached her nose, and pretty soon he'd be taller than she. Matthew was smart and sensitive, and she knew she had to be honest with him.

"I am happy now. At first I wasn't because I love this house. But then I remembered it was just a house and home is wherever my boys are. And that includes your father."

"I'm glad, Mom. It's like what Dad always tells us, happy wife, happy life."

"Oh does he now?" Ginny couldn't help but laugh as her son broke from her arms and thumped upstairs to join his brother.

And now, several decades later, Ginny was living a life quite unexpected. She became so wrapped up in helping Michael turn the farmhouse into an inn, there were times when she completely forgot about the Boston brownstone, the Common, and the museums she thought had fulfilled her life, as well as that of her sons, and she pleasantly discovered that she had been completely wrong. The boys loved their new school and made friends easily, always going off to someone's house after school, or having their new-found friends congregate at Grandpa Max's barn. Maximillian Buck and his wife, Paulina, raised Michael and his sister, Irene, or Reeni as everyone called her, in the house that was now the inn, making Michael's family the third generation to grow up in the Brightmore farmhouse. Reeni lived in Atlanta, moving there after marrying her husband, a Georgia native. She and her husband had their own house outside of the city, and she made it very clear that she loved living in Atlanta and had no intentions of returning north to New Hampshire.

"You know I'm settled here, Michael," she told him one night over the phone. Her brother phoned to let her know he wanted to buy his father out of the house. "I know how much you love that old house, Mikey, and truly, there's nothing for me there. My life is in Atlanta, and besides, Ben and I have been talking about traveling cross-country the next few summers while the kids are still young enough to enjoy it. It's all yours, big brother. But thanks for thinking of me."

So, with only sheer will and determination to succeed, Michael Buck put every penny from the sale of the brownstone into modernizing the farmhouse, and he had created a masterpiece.

"The first room on the remodeling agenda is the kitchen. You tell me what you want, and it's all yours."

"Is that your way of saying I'll be chief cook and bottle washer of this little inn, my dear?" she laughed one night as they were going over blueprints.

"Well," he said, leaning closer, whispering into her ear, "only the best for the best."

Ginny still shivered after all these years of marriage when he whispered into her ear. His powers of seduction were still very strong, and she was helpless and always succumbed to his flirtatious winks and whispers.

Ginny gazed into his gray eyes, the color of the sea on a cloudy winter day. She always lost herself in that ocean of his soul and sank into his chest. His arms, more muscular, and stronger, after moving to the farmhouse and from long days of hammering and lifting, engulfed her in a tight embrace.

"I'll never say no to you, Michael." She gently kissed him on his lips and his embrace tightened.

"How about putting the blueprints away for tonight and going to bed. You won't say no to that, will you?"

"No, I will not." She rose from the old wooden kitchen table and put out her hand for his. He lifted her up from the floor and carried her to their bedroom for a fiery night of passion that Ginny still remembered to this day. She now laid a cool hand to her burning cheek, thrilled at the memory, yet slightly embarrassed by her thoughts while baking pies, and with a little girl asleep in the next room.

"You old fool," she laughed to herself, glancing at the clock. She still had two more hours before Matthew and Savannah arrived, and she wanted to make one last check on the carriage house.

"Need some help?" Jolene's sleepy voice asked as she entered the kitchen.

"That was a short nap," Ginny said, removing her apron and hanging it on the peg near the back door.

"I don't want to sleep the day away. It's too beautiful here." She gently rubbed her knee and put her crutch near Ginny's apron.

"I swear my knee feels so much better since we've been here. I know it's only been a day but there absolutely is a difference."

Jolene stretched her leg back and then grabbed her foot with her hand, giving her thigh muscle a good stretch.

"Well, I do believe that fresh air, especially cold fresh air, has healing powers, so I'm not surprised. But don't overdo it." Ginny winked at the pretty young mother.

"Hard not to," she said. "Can I help with anything?"

"I was just going to head over to the carriage house for a last look around before Matthew comes with his guest. I just put some pie crust in the fridge and it won't be ready to roll out for an hour. Why don't you sit by the fire with Sylvene. Something tells me she won't be waking up from dreamland for quite some time."

Jolene laughed. "She hasn't had a nap since she was two. Playing with the dogs wore her out."

"Dog-tired, you might say," Ginny laughed as she grabbed her fleece.

"Go join your daughter. I'll be back in a bit. Oh, here, take this with you."

Ginny grabbed a mug from the cupboard and poured Jolene

her famous rich and thick hot chocolate. She bent under the sink, pulled out a bottle of brandy and poured a shot into the chocolate.

"Will do your knee even better," Ginny said, handing the mug to Jolene who immediately took a sip.

"Mmmm. Nothing like a warming shot of cocoa brandy. Thanks, Ginny. You think of everything."

"Enjoy the quiet."

Jolene padded into the living room to join her sleeping daughter as Ginny opened the backdoor. Tiny flurries danced from the gray sky, sprinkling the ground like heaven-sent confectioner's sugar. Nothing more than afternoon-evening flurries were predicted, and Ginny was thankful as Matthew would be on the road. Even though they grew up driving snow plows and snowmobiles, Ginny always worried about her children driving on slick roads. Hitting one minuscule patch of slush could hurtle a car right into a ravine.

"Stop that," Ginny scolded herself, stepping into the cold. She could see a faint break of lavender light in the gray sky and knew the sun was trying to poke through, but a gray cloud quickly scudded across the sky, and hid the sun behind it, with the streak of lavender vanishing with it. She grasped the collar of her coat, pulling it tightly across her neck, as she hated nothing more than getting a draft on her neck, which always felt like it settled right in her insides and left her chilled to the bone. Ginny quickly walked the few yards to the carriage house, being careful not to slip on the newly fallen snow.

"Carriage house," she laughed as she put the key in the front door lock. It was actually nowhere near the size of a true carriage house, certainly not big enough for a horse carriage.

"Who said it had to be a horse carriage?" Michael asked, as he put the finishing touches on the house so many years ago. "A baby carriage or two would fit fine in here," he laughed, hugging his wife as Ginny's face lit up with pure happiness.

"Call it whatever you want, Ginny. It's yours. You're the one woman in a house full of boys, and well, I thought you might like your own place, of course, not too far from us."

The carriage house was a replica of their own home, albeit, of course smaller. It was painted white with black shutters, but, unlike the main house's front door of pristine white, the carriage house's door was painted an ocean blue.

Ginny found herself embraced in the essence of tranquility inside her carriage house, and she hoped Savannah would feel the same. Calming dove-gray painted walls illuminated the large main room. There was a bay window next to the blue door and one on the back wall as well. There was a daybed, as well as a chaise lounge, and a rocking chair. Framed pictures painted by Ginny's cousin, Marylou, who had passed away the previous year, adorned the walls. There was a bath at the rear of the house with an extra-large walk-in shower. In short, it was absolute perfection. Ginny changed very little over the years. The daybed still stood and was now winterized with cozy flannel sheets, pillowcases, and a handmade quilt with a large blue spruce in its center. She added a wing chair, with a matching pillow. She repainted the walls last spring, a shade called Falling Snowflake, which had a hint of gray, making the house feel warmer than the original bright white. Light blue curtains hung on the windows, giving the carriage house a homey and cozy feel.

"Oh," Ginny said, snapping her fingers in annoyance. She headed back outside around the carriage house to the wood pile and gathered a few logs and hurried back inside and started a fire. She looked up at her grandmother's antique cuckoo clock perched above the fireplace.

"Cuckoo!" The clock chimed at the one o'clock hour, and the happy little bird poked from the inside out just once, the doors shutting until the next hour. Ginny smiled at the clock that had been keeping time for her entire life, starting at her grandmother's home, then to her own home on Beacon Hill, and now in New Hampshire, in its sacred spot above the fireplace in her precious carriage house. The clock was more than a possession; it was a friend, signaling at every hour that it was working hard, still counting the hours of all of Ginny's seventy-three years. She could even hear it when she was in the kitchen of the main house, and she lovingly referred to it as her own version of Old Faithful.

"I just hope you don't bother our guest," she said looking up at the clock, suddenly aware that Savannah may not like a little wooden bird reminding her of the time every hour.

Although Matthew didn't directly tell Ginny this woman was special, she could tell from the tone of his voice when he phoned.

"I can have the carriage house made up for her, do you think she'll like that?"

"I was hoping you'd suggest that." Ginny could hear a smile in Matthew's voice and she could picture her son, his mischievous sea-glass eyes crinkling with happiness.

"Or I do have rooms available inside the inn. I think I told you that I didn't want to fill it to capacity this year, so…"

"ARE YOU OKAY, MOM?" GINNY DETECTED CONCERN IN HER SON'S voice and answered him as benignly as possibly.

"Of course I am. I just wanted a quieter Christmas this year. And besides, when you moved back East and told me you'd be coming home, I didn't want an inn full of guests to wait on—I just want to wait on you." *There. That should satisfy him,* Ginny thought. She could always pull off a good white lie.

"That's the last thing I want you to do. I'm just really looking forward to coming home, Mom."

Now, Ginny knew for sure her younger son was looking forward to not only coming home, but coming home with Savannah. Her mother's intuition was always spot on with her boys.

THE PERFECT MRS. CLAUS

"Well, you tell Savannah not to worry about a thing, and if she forgets anything, I'm likely to have it."

"Thanks, Mom. See you soon. Love you."

"I love you too, Matthew. See you soon, and drive carefully."

Truth be told, as much as Ginny loved having the inn full for Christmas, it was getting to be too much. She knew when Wanda left it would be near impossible for her to cook and bake, and as much help as Mitchell and his sons Davey and Jake were, well, they had their own teenage lives, and she did not want the inn to consume them. Davey was sixteen and Jake almost fourteen. They were both involved with every sports team imaginable, and with all their schoolwork, Ginny did not want them feeling obligated to help her.

"Gramz, you know we don't mind at all," Davey told her. It was Labor Day weekend, and Ginny was gearing up for leaf peeping season. Wanda was gone and for the first time since opening the inn, Ginny was solely responsible for the comfort of her guests, making her particularly anxious.

She looked at her older grandson. Davey was at that point in life where his boyish features were meshing with that of a young man's. She could see the hair thickening over his upper lip and he had lost much of the chubbiness in his face, now leaner and more that of a young man. His sandy brown hair was combed neatly and slicked back over his head, while his wide hazel eyes sparkled in the morning light.

"Yeah, Gramz, we love to help you," Jake echoed. He and his older brother were almost identical except where Davey's eyes were hazel, Jake's eyes were dark blue; the color of blueberries in summer.

"I know you do," Ginny said, kissing them each on the top of their heads. She pulled out a peach cobbler she made the night before, just for them, and spooned some on a plate for each of them.

"But, you're young men now, and I don't want you to ever feel

203

you have to help out here. I know you're both busy with sports and school and that comes first."

"Family comes first, Gramz," Davey said, shoveling the cobbler into his always hungry mouth.

"We're always here for you, Gramz. Especially when you have peach cobbler," echoed Jake.

Ginny engulfed her grandsons into a huge bear hug, knowing that their father did a wonderful job with his boys, and all by himself. The boys' mother, Mitchell's wife, Penny, up and left just after Jake's first birthday, declaring she did not want to be a mother any longer nor live in some hick farm town where she had spent her whole life.

Mitchell had woken up at his usual 3:30 am to start work on his up-and-coming horse farm, when he had found the note on the kitchen table;

Mitchell,

You know that I have been unhappy for a long time. Believe it or not, I do love my sons, and that is why I am leaving. I do not want them to grow up with a mother who resents her life, and I would never want to take this resentment out on my sons. I am leaving now while they are young enough <u>not</u> to remember me. This may sound cruel to the average person, but they will be better off without me, and so will you.

You may not believe that either, but I love you as well, but I do not love this life. I have loved you since I was a girl and I loved you so much that I wanted whatever you wanted—the farm, children. I thought that if it was enough for you, then it would be for me too, but, as I have discovered over the years, it is not. I was able to give you what YOU wanted, but I had forgotten myself along the way, and when I came to that realization, there simply is no way I can give myself to our sons, to you, to our marriage.

I don't expect you to forgive me, Mitchell, nor would I ask. I also do not expect you to understand my choice now, but hopefully someday you will. When I land where I need to be, I will let you know.

I am doing this for love. For my love for you, for my sons, and for myself.

Penny

Mitchell never revealed to his sons their mother's goodbye note and Mitchell swore Ginny to secrecy.

"They don't need to know this, Mom," he said after the Hawaii State police department contacted him about Penny's death a month after her departure. She was on board a puddle jumper, island hopping in Hawaii, when the weather took a bad turn making the pilot unable to see the runway, and crashing into a mountain, killing all on board the small plane. All the boys knew was that their mother was helping a sick friend in Hawaii when her plane crashed. Penny was rarely mentioned in their lives and that was how Mitchell wanted it, and Ginny respected her older son's wishes. It was enough for them to know their mother loved them, and Ginny was grateful neither one of her precious grandsons actually remembered their mother.

Sadly, the boys rarely asked about their mother, never really knowing her. Ginny always made sure Penny was remembered on her birthday, serving each boy a red velvet cupcake with pink buttercream frosting, Penny's favorite. But as the boys got older, absence did not make their hearts grow fonder. In fact, they asked less and less about her, which suited Mitchell just fine.

"I guess it's true," Mitchell said to Ginny one day grooming Beachtree, his newest horse. It was Penny's birthday, and the boys did not ask for the annual cupcake.

"What's that, Mitchell?" Ginny was admiring the horse's gorgeous blonde mane.

"You don't miss what you don't have. I know they're getting older, but they didn't ask for a cupcake this year. Matter of fact last year, I had to remind them. I guess I will this year too. After all, they wouldn't be here if it wasn't for her."

Ginny laughed. "No, they wouldn't. And she is, was, their

mother. She should be remembered on her birthday. I'll stop at Nutmeg Nancy's today and pick up cupcakes for dessert."

"Thanks, Mom." Mitchell put the brush on the hook and hugged his mother.

"You're the only mother they've ever known."

"Oh, you're going to make me cry. You know I love those boys more than anything. Just as much as you and your brother," she laughed, wiping away a stray tear.

"Sometimes I do wish Matty was around more," Mitchell said, as he locked up Beachtree's paddock.

"Well, you know your brother. As much as he loves it here, he cannot resist the call of the city. I understand. I used to be like that too. I loved living in Boston when you and your brother were babies. But I wouldn't go back for anything, now."

"Why weren't we as lucky as you and dad? I married a woman who had to find herself, left her family and was killed, and Matty's wife was so career focused, it ruined their marriage."

"Well, Matty and Summer were never perfectly matched, in my humble opinion," said Ginny.

"As for you and Penny, well no one was more surprised than me when she up and left. She pined for you when you were at college, never dating anyone, just hanging around here all the time trying to glean any kind of news about you I was willing to give. I told her as gently as I could for her to move on with her life, but it did no good. She said to me one day, 'Mrs. Buck, Mitchell is worth the wait'. So she waited and I thought, well, nothing can stop true love."

Mitchell shrugged his shoulders and gave a sarcastic laugh.

"I probably should have told her that myself. But having the most beautiful girl in town follow you like a devoted puppy, well, I guess it strokes your ego. That's not to say I didn't love her. I think I loved her devotion to me more than anything, and my head swelled. And the rest is history."

"We can't beat ourselves up about the past, Mitchell. We have to see the gifts that it has given us—my grandsons and my granddaughter—and be thankful. Pray for those departed and for those with us, and hope for happiness and live our lives as best we can. And I think we're doing a pretty good job with that."

"I don't know what I'd do without Davey and Jake," Mitchell said.

"And like you said, they wouldn't be here if it weren't for Penny. Now, lunch is ready in the kitchen, so sit yourself down and eat. I'm off to Nutmeg Nancy's."

Now, back in the carriage house, Ginny felt a chill run through her blood. She and Michael worked hard to raise two wonderful, caring men, and she could not for the life of her understand why both of their marriages failed. Could she be blamed for this? Ginny tried not to be too overbearing with her opinions on her sons' choices of girlfriends and eventual wives. She knew she had to look the other way when Mitchell announced he was marrying Penny and then Matthew announcing he was marrying Summer. They were grown men who had to make their own way in life with the women they chose for their wives, good or bad. Work and Davey and Jake consumed Mitchell, but now his own sons were getting older and would be ready to leave the farm at some point. Then what? And Matthew, her workaholic son, as creatively brilliant as he was, she knew a lonely soul lived within him. Their lives were full, but there was truly something to be said for a rock-solid relationship, and she continued to pray that each of her sons would find it one day.

The chill still lingered as she looked at the thermostat. It read sixty-three degrees.

"The fire should warm up the place soon," she said. She threw another log on and watched the bright flames jump and dance, and Ginny felt the fire warming up the carriage house.

"I think Savannah will love this," she said, as she felt the vibration of her phone in her back pocket. She pulled it out hoping to see a text from Matthew.

Hi, Ginny. Sincerest apologies but I won't be able to get to the Inn for Christmas. Haley surprised me with a trip to New York City! Let's call it a postponement and not a cancellation as you know how much I love Christmas at Blue Spruce. I'll be in touch after the New Year. Merry Christmas! Love, HM

Honey Malone and her daughter Haley had been coming to the Inn for the last ten Christmases. They were friends in Boston and lost touch when Ginny moved North, but after Honey's divorce, she found her way to the Inn with her daughter, Haley. Two lost souls who needed a home for Christmas. Jolene and Sylvene reminded Ginny of Honey and Haley but only in the simple fact that they were mother and daughter on their own. Where it took Honey years to become confident and independent, Ginny knew that Jolene had well passed that point, as working full time and raising a child alone will do that to a woman. Ginny hoped for a chance to get to know her guests better, and now, with just her three guests, Ginny was glad she would get the chance. She quickly texted Honey that she would see her in the New Year.

"A small Christmas miracle," Ginny said, checking one more time on the carriage house. It was ready and waiting for Savannah.

Ginny stepped out into the dusting of flurries still falling from the winter sky and walked briskly back to the main house. As much as Honey was like family and she loved her dearly, Honey proved to be on the demanding side, which never really bothered Ginny, as she enjoyed indulging her ego-fragile friend. But with Matthew coming home, she longed for a less busy Christmas, and she had just gotten her wish. She'd still be plenty busy, but Jolene and Sylvene were easy—that precious little girl was so content playing with the dogs, and Jolene seemed to be recuperating nicely, now able to walk a little further than she did even a day ago.

Walking back into her toasty kitchen she checked on the dough for the pie crust. She pulled her calendar from the wall and looked at the block of days in December. It was pretty hard to see anything as there were so many notations on it regarding certain guests and dinner menus.

"You don't need that old thing anymore," Wanda had said shortly before her departure. "Everything is updated in the computer. If you'd take a minute just to sit and take a look, I'll explain everything. Easy peasy."

"Easy peasy for you," Ginny retorted. She never cared for the administrative side of the business—Michael took care of that until Wanda came along. Ginny much preferred to make her guests feel like family with her wonderful meals and desserts.

"Well, Mitchell and the boys know how to use it in case your paper calendar goes up in flames someday. Maybe you should move it closer to the door than near the stove, in case you need to make a mad dash out of here. You can grab the calendar on your way out."

"Wanda, that's enough. Just because you're smarter than me when it comes to that thing you call a laptop, doesn't mean I don't know what I'm doing. I've lived by my calendar for decades and I'm not stopping now. But the computer is a good back up, I must admit." Ginny laughed and shrugged her shoulders.

"Besides, what would the boys get me for Christmas? They always do find the prettiest calendars." Ginny leafed through this year's calendar, a seaside theme, with gorgeous pictures of the ocean, lighthouses, sea creatures, and sunsets. December's photo was particularly beautiful—a lighthouse on the coast of Maine, sitting on a craggy rock, the sky a dusky hue of sunset purple and snowflakes capping the black top of the lighthouse's lantern room.

Ginny loved her calendars. It was the one gift that Mitchell and Matthew gave her jointly when they were children, and now the tradition continued with her grandsons. Athena was in on it as well, and Ginny always received a smaller purse-sized version from her granddaughter, which was just as invaluable as her precious wall calendars.

Athena. Ginny thought of her granddaughter as she sat down at the table with her calendar and pen and crossed Honey's name from the December 25 block. Athena was the only missing piece of this year's Christmas puzzle. Ginny was much more up on technology than she let Wanda believe. Every day she checked the laptop for an email from Athena, who was a wonderful granddaughter, emailing her grandmother every day. Yesterday, her email was a short one.

Hi, Gramz! Today Gemini and I had a great practice. He's looking amazing, and I think we shall do well. Gotta go—stable mucking is calling, but I'll email more tomorrow.

All my love, your granddaughter, Athena—how lucky am I to be your ONLY granddaughter!!

Smiley faces with their lips puckered into kisses and red hearts followed her name.

Ginny laughed at the only granddaughter reference as if Athena had just Ginny for a grandmother, but she may as well have. Although Summer's mother was very much alive and kicking, she never had much to do with her granddaughter, always jetting about with her boyfriend of the month. Marlena Graystone was only a year older than Ginny, but Marlena had an uncanny talent of only meeting and dating top-notch dermatologists and plastic surgeons. She most certainly did look 'plastic-y' but she wasn't a bad person. As soon as Summer left home for college, Marlena moved on to what she referred to as the 'second chapter' of her life, by having a face lift, tummy tuck, and God knows what else. Her first serious boyfriend after her divorce was the surgeon who performed her eye lift and when he passed away, it was the dermatologist who botoxed her on a regular basis.

So while Marlena was living the life of Riley, with little contact with Athena, other than monetary birthday and Christmas gifts, it was Ginny who gave Athena true gifts—the gift diving off the old wooden dock into the pristine cold blue water of Lake Brightmore. The gift of raking jeweled colored leaves surrounded by the autumnal muted tones of the White Mountains. The gift of truly dashing through the snow in a horse-driven sleigh. The gift of purple and yellow crocuses poking their hearty heads from the melting snow, with pink and green buds blossoming under a warming spring sun. The time she spent at the Blue Spruce with Ginny during Athena's young life was priceless, and she knew that it helped shape her granddaughter into the person she was today. A confident teenage girl who would take on the world—as long as it was on horseback, of course. As much as Ginny was happy for Athena, she missed her terribly, but Ginny also knew that moving to England was an opportunity that might never come again, and there could be no better place than the English countryside for Athena to master the art of equestrianism.

Most of all Ginny was thankful for Athena's relationship with her father. Matthew and his daughter were so much alike. Not only did they have the same colored eyes of blue-green sea-glass, they also had a distinct way of crinkling every time they smiled or laughed. Although Athena possessed the high cheekbones, fair complexion and gorgeous coal black hair of her mother, the rest was all Matthew—the thin athletic build that was perfect for speed —Matthew's running his hardest and sliding into home and Athena's prowess as an equestrienne, were all from the Buck genes. But the similarities didn't stop at their physical appearances. Deep down they were both painfully shy people. Where Mitchell was gregarious and outgoing, Matthew was quiet, preferring to tinker with broken down gadgets in the quiet of his grandfather's barn. Matthew tried to emulate his older brother, but he was much more comfortable hanging out with his Grandpa Max fixing broken motors and building birdhouses. Matthew could fix anything and loved his time with his grandfather, but Ginny also knew that he should be out with friends his own age, so she asked her father-in-law to have a talk with her younger son.

"Matthew, as much as I love your help around here, there is one thing that I want you to do for me."

"What's that, Grandpa Max?" Matthew was barely listening to his grandfather, as he just located the broken spring in the motor of an old lawnmower and was eager to replace it to make sure it worked.

"You know, I loved tinkering with motors when I was your age, but I loved something else, too."

"What?" asked Matthew, incredulous that anything existed besides grease, broken springs, and anything with a motor.

"Baseball. I just loved listening to the Red Sox on the radio, and I imagined that one day I would play in Fenway Park. I even built a pitch back outta an old frame and some sailboat ropes I found lying around the barn. Wasn't the best thing of course, but it did the trick. But when I made the Little League team when I was about your age, well, I thought that was even better than fixin' a motor. I got to hit and pitch and run and slide. Well, I thought I had died and gone to heaven."

"LIKE MITCHELL. HE LIKES IT TOO. BUT I THINK HE'S BETTER AT basketball. Just sayin'."

"Well, we all have our talents, Matty. And yours is being able to fix just about anything. But it's good to learn something else, too. I like to take a break from fixing things from time to time. Hey, I have an idea. Why don't we throw the old ball around? I think you'll like it. I got my glove, and I know I can scrounge up an old ball somewhere. What do you say we take a break from fixin' things and try something new?"

Matthew gave his grandfather a stern and quizzical look. He shrugged his thin shoulders and simply answered. "Okay."

Ginny was eternally grateful to her father-in-law, as it set Matthew in motion on a course that would forever change his life. He also discovered, like his grandfather, a love for baseball that would carry him through little league, even making it to the finals in the Little League World Series, to high school, to a partial college scholarship at Stony Oak College. Being on their baseball team enabled him to travel, and his business courses opened up a new world for him, where he especially found his niche in marketing and advertising, all roads leading to his successful stint in Chicago and now at Howardson's. Ginny thought him brilliant in the boardroom, and Matthew could come up with slogans for almost everything, from dog food to cell phones, but he gave all the credit to his grandfather, Maximillian.

Matthew was getting ready to leave for a summer internship in Boston his senior year in college, and Ginny was making sure everything was packed. "I'm the one who spent the most time with Grandpa Max. He was always coming with up rhymes, like his *charm on the farm* or *I sigh at one of Grammy's pies.* But I think my favorite was *don't put off until tomorrow; that will be time you'll have to borrow.*"

Ginny laughed as she tucked some extra monogramed handkerchiefs under Matthew's socks, listening to her son reminisce about his beloved grandfather.

"You may not have realized this, but I used to be one of the biggest procrastinators in the world," he laughed,"until I finally understood what Grandpa Max meant. Remember how I hated math homework and you bugged me constantly to get it done the first thing when I got home from school, and I said I'd do it later?"

Ginny laughed. "Later rarely came and you were always scrambling at breakfast to get it done. I wanted so much to scold you but your grandfather told me that you would figure it out, and when you did, there'd be no stopping you. And he was right."

"I tried to be like Mitchell and his straight As and National Honor Society, Mom, but it just wasn't me. But I did eventually learn to get my homework done on time."

Ginny sat on the bed, gently stroking the embroidered MB on the of handkerchieves she was packing.

"There's no comparison between you and your brother. I knew that and your father and grandfather did, too. I can honestly say I never compared the two of you. Never. You and your brother are two separate individuals, with traits that are unique to each of you. You're both doers, very obviously, but in such different ways. Where Mitchell sees a direct path to his goal, you prefer to take the circuitous way to yours. Mitchell knew he wanted a horse farm, so as soon as he graduated college, he bought his first horse. You'll fit in somewhere in the world, and I think this internship will make you realize that."

Ginny also knew that women found Matthew's shyness extremely attractive, and there was never a shortage of Brightmore girls riding their bikes by Max's workshop, knowing Matthew was always there to help with a broken bike chain or a flat tire.

No matter how confident Matthew was in his professional sphere, he was still shy and unconfident in matters of the heart, and unbeknownst to him, this was his fatal flaw, for it attracted beautiful women who wanted to take care of this man who had no idea how to deal with their amorous attentions. Summer Graystone came along in his junior year of college, and she thought she could change him, to make him more outgoing and less shy, to propel him to professional and staggering heights.

As aggressive as Summer was with Matthew's future success, she was even more aggressive for her own, and when they broke up before graduation, Ginny was greatly relieved. Summer was offered a position in an up-and-coming hotel chain relocating her to Minneapolis, and then a fateful encounter at that hotel brought them back together. Ginny felt they were two familiar souls who mistook loneliness for love. So when Matthew announced they were marrying after reuniting, Ginny had hoped that the years had tempered Summer, but they did not, and in Ginny's opinion, Summer was more hungry for success and the trappings that went with it—a husband as successful as she was.

But this was not her life—it was Matthew's, and if he wanted to marry Summer, she would give them her blessing, no matter how much she felt her younger son was making the biggest mistake of his life.

Ginny recalled their wedding day, now seeming so long ago. She and Matthew were standing in the very spot Ginny was now as she remembered her son's furious pacing in the kitchen. There was a worn area on the floorboards that Ginny attributed to Matthew's shoe soles from that day.

"Matthew, it's never too late, you know."

All of her son's nervous habits came to fruition that day—the pacing, the handkerchief wringing, the rubbing at the back of his neck. Whenever he was anxious about something, whether it be an exam or a job interview, usually one of these symptoms appeared, but on his wedding day, all three were in full force.

"Never too late for what, Mom?" Ginny had to hold herself back from grabbing Matthew's hand, which was rubbing furiously at the back of his neck, but she restrained herself.

"To call off the wedding," she replied matter-of-factly.

Matthew looked directly at his mother and she saw sheer panic in his sea-glass eyes.

"You're kidding, right?" Ginny heard a slight tremble in his voice.

"No, I'm dead serious. If you think this is wrong for you, Matthew, don't do it. It's that simple."

"No, Mom, it's not that simple," he snorted in disbelief.

He sat down at the kitchen table, running his hands through his thick wavy hair.

"I do love Summer, and I believe there's a reason why she and I reconnected. We're both of a certain age and there are things we want in life—marriage, a family. I see Mitchell's boys and I know that's what I want, and Summer is the woman who will give that to me. She's changed, Mom. You'll see."

Ginny put her hands on her son's shoulders and spoke the reassuring words she knew Matthew needed to hear.

"All I want is for you to be happy, Matthew, and if Summer is the woman who can make you happy, then that's all I need to know."

"She is, Mom."

Ginny felt the arms of her younger son embrace her in a hug as tears stung her eyes. Although she knew deep down in her mother's heart that Summer Graystone was absolutely not the right woman for Matthew, she stopped her tears, hugged her son tightly, and smiled up at him.

"I don't usually do this, but I think you and I could both use it." Ginny pulled her step stool from under the sink and stood on it to reach the highest cabinet. She pulled down a sapphire and gold box that contained her special liquid gold. It was a bottle of Courvoisier that a guest had given to her and Michael after the inn's inaugural opening. She carefully set the box on the counter and pulled the oval cut glass bottle from the box. The color was of pure amber—warm and inviting. She only opened the bottle once —after Michael's funeral in which a sadness as no other engulfed her like an ocean riptide, and she felt she would never be released from its grievous clutches. The pull into grief and despair was so strong and she had indulged after Michael's funeral.

Have your drink and your cry, Ginny and then no more. Life goes on. Live it. She could have sworn she heard her husband's voice, and his gentle touch on her shoulder as she sipped the cognac in the home they built together, the tears ceasing and her grief gently subsiding. Ginny had her drink, her cry, and felt the grief subside as she realized as long as there was The Blue Spruce Inn, Michael would live on.

She took two Irish crystal glasses from the cabinet and poured an equal amount of the brandy in each.

"Mom? Courvoisier? I knew the inn did well, but..."

"Laugh all you want. You know I'd never splurge on something like this. It was a gift." Ginny lifted her glass.

"There is nothing more precious or sacred in this world than a happy marriage, Matthew. To you and Summer. May you always be blessed with happiness." They clinked glasses and sipped the soothing and calming cognac.

Matthew drained the rest of his drink and Ginny saw the tension behind his sea-glass eyes ease.

"C'mon. I have a son to marry off." She put her arms around her younger son and stood on her tip-toes and kissed his forehead, as the top of his head hadn't been reachable for years. And just for one brief moment, Matthew was her little boy again in need of the comfort of his loving mother's arms and reassurance. She felt his strong hands grasp her arms and she was suddenly back in the present with her adult son.

"I love you, Mom," Matthew whispered and Ginny grasped him tighter, gently kissing her on the cheek. "We have a wedding to get to," he said, extending his arm, which Ginny happily accepted. Matthew opened the kitchen door and they walked to the front of the house where the limo was waiting. Just as they were about to get inside, a shower of orange and yellow leaves fell upon their shoulders.

"When autumn leaves fall on a wedding day, peace and calm prevail, they say."

Matthew laughed as he helped his mother into the car.

"Another one of Grandpa Max's positive proverbs?" He laughed as he got in beside her.

"No, just made it up myself," she said, as they rode off to meet Matthew's future.

And now that future was part of the past.

Ginny stood in her kitchen and listened as the winter birds tweeted outside in the falling snow. She heard the soft breathing of her sleeping dogs nestled closely by Sylvene. It was peaceful, and it was Christmas, and Matthew was coming home with a friend, and even though Ginny had never met her, she had the feeling Savannah Brady was going to make a great impact on her younger son's life.

"Time to get a move on," she said, pulling the chilled dough from the fridge, and rolling it out for her famous apple pie for Christmas Eve dessert.

CHAPTER 24

"About fifty miles to go," Matthew announced as they passed a sign indicating they were now in the White Mountains of New Hampshire.

The last hour and a half passed quickly, with chat about work and the challenge of raising children. It was easy and comfortable, but Savannah noticed Matthew didn't say much about his own family life. He could go on forever about Athena but kept pretty closemouthed about his family of origin. Savannah had to admit to herself that she did find this a bit disconcerting as that's where they were heading, but something told her to hold back on asking. She trusted him, and there must be a reason for his evasiveness.

"When was the last time you were home," she asked. She turned toward him and watched his face soften and a smile form.

"Too long," he said, turning to look at her, smiling that crinkly-eyed smile. Savannah swore she felt her heart skip a beat as the butterflies quickly fluttered in her stomach. She knew she could no longer deny her feelings for Matthew.

The heart fluttering, the butterflies, the trembling of promise when she would see Matthew come through the door. He seemed so unaware of when Savannah was stealing looks of admiration whether he was on duty as Sheriff Sugar Plum or just adjusting the bright red bulb of Rudolph's nose. She also noticed her sadness when he wasn't at the store when she was, or when he didn't text her just to say hello. That combination of feelings meant one thing: she was falling for Matthew Buck, something she thought she would never experience again. Matthew was most certainly a charming man, but more importantly was the simple fact that he was kind, and he was gentle, and greatly loved his daughter, and she wanted to know more.

"I drove up when I first got back to the East Coast, and that's been it. The job was brand new, so I lived and breathed it from the moment I started it, and with a couple of quick flights to London to see Athena, well, I haven't had the chance to visit much. My mom and I FaceTime a lot. She still works and she's busier than ever, especially around this time of the year, and my brother's busy with his work, too. But come hell or high water, there was no way I wasn't getting back here for this Christmas."

"What does your mother do for work?"

Matthew stared straight ahead at the road.

Did he hear me? she asked herself.

"She's a baker," he finally responded. "So, you can imagine, she's quite busy."

"I see," said Savannah. There was something about his tone that told her he didn't want to elaborate further, so she decided not to pepper him with more questions. She would find out soon enough.

He turned and smiled at her, those crinkles even deeper and more attractive than they were yesterday. "I don't want to say too much and spoil the surprise for you."

Savannah laughed, understanding the reason for the brevity of his answer.

"So you have something up your sleeve, do you?" she teased.

"It wouldn't be a Christmas surprise without a little mystery, now would it."

"Oh!" Savannah exclaimed as a huge sign came into view.

The Blue Spruce Inn. The sign was in the shape of a huge blue spruce tree, the top of the tree indicating to continue straight.

"Fern overheard you on the phone, and told me what you did for Sylvene and Jolene," Matthew said. "That was unbelievably thoughtful of you, Savannah."

The gentleness of his voice touched Savannah so that she felt the sting of tears stab at the back of her eyes. "Tis better to give than to receive, right?" She felt the prickling of the tears subside, and silently gave a prayer of thanks. The last thing she wanted was to start the waterworks again, as she was still embarrassed about the night at the Christmas party.

She saw Matthew shrug his shoulders behind the wheel.

"It is, I believe that, but I also believe it's okay to be kind and generous to yourself, too, Savannah. Look, I know it's been rough for you, and I certainly understand what it's like not to have your child with you at the holidays. It's the worst."

"I know you understand, Matthew," Savannah whispered. "I was feeling so lost in my life. And little did I know that the day you almost knocked me down would put my life on a different course. Being Mrs. Claus made me feel like a mom again. I miss so much having a child and watching that child discover and rediscover the magic of Christmas. Whenever I put on that dress, I was transformed. I think I was starting to get a bit reclusive, but being Mrs. Claus brought me back to the world, where I needed to be. And I thank you for that." Savannah heaved a sigh of relief.

As if on cue from the heavens above, tiny flakes of snow blanketed the windshield.

"Snow!" exclaimed Savannah. She pushed the button on the car door rolling the window down and instantly her lap was covered in perfect tiny snowflakes.

"Hey, roll that up!" laughed Matthew. "It's dropped about twenty degrees."

"I thought you were a winter kind of guy," she laughed, as the window locked back into place, excited as a child about newly fallen snow.

"That I am, but I like my winter outside, not in my car."

"Forgive me." She turned and saw him smile that crinkly eye smile at her, and she felt her heart skip a beat, but she could also hear the laughter in his voice that she had become so fond of.

Another sign for The Blue Spruce Inn came into view. "Oh, Matthew, would you mind if we stopped by the Inn? Jolene texted me when they checked in and said it was absolutely beautiful. Sylvene spent the afternoon playing with the dogs, and I'd love to surprise them to wish them a Merry Christmas in person. But only if it's not too much trouble."

"No trouble at all, Mrs. Claus," he laughed, slowing the car as the road suddenly turned rocky and unpaved. Although the snow had stopped, the dusting was just enough to make the driving a bit slippery and Matthew took his time on the rocky road.

"Oh my goodness." Savannah's voice was barely a whisper as the tallest tree she had ever seen suddenly came into view. The blue spruce of The Blue Spruce Inn was taller than the large farmhouse it stood in front of, as it sparkled with hundreds of multicolored lights, the effect made even more splendid by the fresh snowfall.

"It was beautiful on the website, but this is just breathtaking!"

"It sure is something," she heard Matthew say as he put the car in park and unlocked the doors.

Savannah gravitated toward the tree. The silvery-blue toned tree shimmered with the snowflakes and lights. It stood at least twenty feet tall, lights glimmering on every branch. It was like a dream from a North Pole fairy tale.

Savannah was mesmerized by the Christmas-red cardinals, downy gray titmice, and black-capped chickadees as they flickered in and out of the tree's branches. The birds were Mother Nature's perfect ornaments dancing through the branches of the tree. She then noticed some of the decorations were made of birdseed on which the birds sat and eagerly pecked at their meal.

A large white farmhouse next drew Savannah's attention. It was surrounded by a post and beam fence bedecked with boughs of greenery, adorned with bright red bows securing the boughs on the post. Tiny frosty white lights expertly studded throughout the boughs twinkled like starlight on this gray afternoon. The large wrap-around front porch was decorated similarly, with cheerful evergreen wreaths hung on every window. The warm glow of candles flickered in the large windows, and at each end of the porch smaller potted pine trees stood as holiday sentinels decorated with tiny sparkling lights. There was no doubt in Savannah's mind that The Blue Spruce Inn was the quintessential Christmas inn, and she couldn't be happier that Jolene and Sylvene were spending Christmas in this charming picture-perfect place.

"Pretty, isn't it?" asked Matthew as he joined Savannah in front of the tree. Savannah inhaled the cold clean air tinged with the scent of pine, still mesmerized by the winter wonderland that stood before her.

A jangle of bells cut through the snowy silence as Savannah turned to see a horse and carriage ambling from a path from the woods behind the house. The driver enthusiastically waved at Savannah and Matthew.

"Do you know him?" she asked, returning the wave.

"I've known him all my life," Matthew said, looking like the cat who ate the cream."He's my brother."

"Brother?" Savannah turned to Matthew. *What was going on?*

"I'll introduce you," Matthew said, extending his hand to Savannah who accepted it, walking toward the horse and carriage. A huge bright red barn sat directly behind the farmhouse, and Matthew's brother steered the horse and carriage to the barn's open door. The man jumped down from the carriage and embraced Matthew in a huge bear hug.

"It's about time you got here. Mom's been jumping out of her skin every time she thinks she hears a car. I'm surprised she's not out here now."

"Well, I am now! I've been up to my elbows in pie crusts!"

Savannah turned at hearing the woman's familiar voice. "I'm so glad you're here!" she said, reaching up to embrace her son. She was Savannah's height and dressed in flour-spotted jeans and a pink sweater with blue reindeer embroidered on the collar. Her hair was the same salt and pepper as Matthew's and was cut into a very flattering layered bob that bounced with her every step. Three golden retrievers appeared, encircling Matthew as their thick yellow tails wildly wagged, and Matthew bent to greet each of them with hugs and kisses.

This is his mother? Savannah thought, watching the woman move with the grace of someone half her age. She did not have one line on her face, save for the same crinkles around her eyes like Matthew's. "Oh, forgive me! You must be Savannah!" the woman said, wrapping her arms around Savannah in a friendly greeting. Savannah wasn't sure what was happening, but the woman's friendliness made her feel perfectly at ease.

"I'm Ginny Buck. I spoke with you on the phone about your reservation. Your friends are wonderful. They just returned from a carriage ride with Mitchell and they'll be so happy to see you. These are our dogs, Meringue, Moonlight, and Mermaid. That's Mitchell, my older son, in front of the barn. Welcome to The Blue Spruce Inn! I was so happy Matthew told me he was bringing you for Christmas."

Ginny turned toward Matthew and to Mitchell, who was coming from the barn, and then like a giant snowball, it hit Savannah: Matthew's family ran The Blue Spruce Inn.

"Matty, you can play with the dogs later. Bring Savannah's

bags to the carriage house—that's where you'll be staying. I think you'll like it. Dinner will be ready in a couple of hours so that should give you time to settle in. Matthew has told me how wonderful you've been as Mrs. Claus, and you're all that little girl talks about—she's such a darling, as is her mother. Anyway, I won't keep you. Matty will see you in." Ginny started toward the house, and the three dogs followed her back inside.

"Let me get that for you." Mitchell Buck walked up to Savannah who warmly shook her hand introducing himself. "If you wait for my little brother to do it, your bag will be sitting here until New Year's Eve." He resembled Matthew, and there was no mistake they were brothers, but where Matthew had blue eyes, Mitchell's were amber. He was taller than Matthew and a bit stockier, but he still had the same handsome features as his younger brother. Where Matthew had his irresistible crinkly eyes, Mitchell had a deep dimple in the middle of his chin.

"Very funny, big brother," Matthew laughed as he and his brother threw their arms around each other again.

"I see you have old Stanley still working. I thought you were going to retire him?"

"No one ever retires around here, Matty," said Mitchell, giving the horse a rub on his nose. Mitchell reached into his pocket and pulled out some cut up carrots, which he fed to the horse, who hungrily nuzzled his hand, munching happily.

"I'll take Savannah's bags to the carriage house. You can unhitch Stanley and walk him to his stall. That is if you can remember how to lead a horse, city boy."

Matthew gently punched Mitchell in the arm.

"I may have *become* a city boy," he said, emphasizing become, " but I was brought up in the country, and that will never change. Believe it or not, big brother, I can not only lead Stanley to his stall, but I can hitch him up to the sleigh, and I can even ride him. You'll be amazed."

"Oh, no doubt," said Mitchell, as he picked up Savannah's bags.

Savannah felt a nudge and turned to find Stanley's pewter gray face resting on her shoulder.

"You'd better go with them, Savannah," Mitchell said, heading toward the carriage house. "Stanley obviously wants to show you where he lives. You better watch out, little bro. Stanley's a handsome older gentleman and will give you some competition." Mitchell winked at Savannah. "Stanley always gets the girl. We have a few of his offspring we can show you later up at my farm."

"I would love nothing more than that, Mitchell. Thank you." said Savannah, still bewildered at her arrival at The Blue Spruce Inn.

They watched as Mitchell made his way toward the carriage house.

"So my perfect Christmas destination belongs to your family. And you never said a word."

Matthew stepped toward Savannah and took her hands into his. She liked the way they felt clasped around her own—a bit rough, but strong and solid.

"What's Christmas without a surprise or two?"

Matthew's strong hands gently caressed Savannah's face. He looked into those twinkling green eyes and he tenderly kissed her blushing lips.

"I KNEW THERE WAS SOMETHING SPECIAL ABOUT YOU THE MINUTE I saw you. I almost didn't chase you down that day, but something I can't explain pushed me to, and I'm glad I did. You are a huge part of Howardson's success this Christmas. When Fern told me she overheard you on the phone changing your reservations and giving up your Christmas vacation so Jolene and Sylvene could have one I knew it was my turn to be Santa and grant a wish for you. You do so much for others, others that you hardly know,

Savannah, and that is something beyond rare, especially these days."

Savannah's body trembled at Matthew's heartfelt words. She looked into his eyes, unable to speak as she was overwhelmed by his kindness and thoughtfulness. She then felt the gentle brush of his lips upon hers again, making her blood rush with feelings she thought would never return. This was no coincidence, her meeting Matthew, being Mrs. Claus, and now at The Blue Spruce Inn with this very special man. It was time to move on in life. Savannah would never forget Bradley, and she knew in her heart he was part of the magical forces of Christmas that brought her to this moment. And for that, she would be forever grateful.

Savannah felt Matthew's embrace tighten. "Merry Christmas, my perfect Mrs. Claus," he whispered, and together they made their way to their own *Enchanted Land of Claus*.

PLEASE RATE AND REVIEW

We hope you enjoyed *The Perfect Mrs. Claus* by Barbara Matteson. If you did, we would ask that you please rate and review this title. Every review helps our authors.

Rate and Review: The Perfect Mrs. Claus

5 Prince Publishing
Arvada, Colorado, USA

PUBLISHER ACKNOWLEDGMENTS

The team at 5 Prince Publishing would like to give special thanks to the following people for helping make The Perfect Mrs. Claus the best that it can be:

Bernadette Soehner, Cate Byers, Marianne Nowicki, Sophie Jefferson, Cayla Rusielewicz, Lindsey Haggerty, and Daisy Salgado Pham. We would also like to thank our Brand Ambassadors, touring companies, bloggers, and influencers that help to promote the work of Barbara Matteson.

MEET THE AUTHOR

Barbara Matteson is a life-long New Englander, currently residing outside of Boston with her husband, son, black lab, and leopard gecko. She recently became a published writer when her essay, The Birds of Winter, was published in the January/February 2022 edition of Victoria Magazine. She also enjoys writing movie reviews, hiking, baking, reading, and traveling.

OTHER TITLES FROM 5 PRINCE PUBLISHING

WWW.5PRINCEBOOKS.COM

The Happily Ever After Bookstore *Bernadette Marie*
The Princess of Prias *Courtney Davis*
Paige and the Reluctant Artist *Darci Garcia*
A Spider in the Garden *Courtney Davis*
Megan's Choice *Darci Garcia*
Something New *Bernadette Marie*
Something Forbidden *Bernadette Marie*
Something Found *Bernadette Marie*
Something Discovered *Bernadette Marie*
Something Lost Bernadette Marie
Ashes of Aldyr *Russell Archey*
Telephone Road *Ann Swann*
Paige Devereaux *Bernadette Marie*
Max Devereaux *Bernadette Marie*
Christmas Cookies on a Cruise Ship *Parker Fairchild*
Chase Devereaux *Bernadette Marie*
Kennedy Devereaux *Bernadette Marie*
The Seven Spires *Russell Archey*
At Last *Bernadette Marie*
Masterpiece *Bernadette Marie*

235

OTHER TITLES FROM 5 PRINCE PUBLISHING

A Tropical Christmas *Bernadette Marie*
Corporate Christmas *Bernadette Marie*
Faith Through Falling Snow *Sandy Sinnett*
Walker Defense *Bernadette Marie*
Clash of the Cheerleaders *April Marcom*
Stevie-Girl and the Phantom of Forever *Ann Swann*
The Last Goodbye *Bernadette Marie*
The Gingerbread Curse *April Marcom*

www.ingramcontent.com/pod-product-compliance
Lightning Source LLC
Chambersburg PA
CBHW020552020726
47494CB00006B/2034

* 9 7 8 1 6 3 1 1 2 2 9 2 7 *